# FIGHTING FOR BRIELLE (SPECIAL FORCES: OPERATION ALPHA)

DEE STEWART

*This is dedicated to everyone serving in the Armed Forces,
especially my father who served in the Air Force for twenty-one
years, and then went on to serve his unit as a civilian for another
twenty before he could no longer work due to Parkinson's disease,
which he developed because of his exposure to Agent Orange. Sadly,
he passed in 2010. He loved his country and he loved the military.*

*This is also dedicated to the brave men and women in law
enforcement agencies across the United States.*

Editing: Grace Augustine, A Touch of Grace

Cover Design © Drew Hoffman Buonoamicipress

Dear Readers,

*Welcome to the Special Forces: Operation Alpha Fan-Fiction world!*

If you are new to this amazing world, in a nutshell the author wrote a story using one or more of my characters in it. Sometimes that character has a major role in the story, and other times they are only mentioned briefly. This is perfectly legal and allowable because they are going through Aces Press to publish the story.

This book is entirely the work of the author who wrote it. While I might have assisted with brainstorming and other ideas about which of my characters to use, I didn't have any part in the process or writing or editing the story.

I'm proud and excited that so many authors loved my characters enough that they wanted to write them into their own story. Thank you for supporting them, and me!

READ ON!
Xoxo
Susan Stoker

# CHAPTER 1

Justice McQuaid stared at the 3D image of his brain, unable to make sense of it. Before the ambush, before his SEAL teammates perished, his brain functioned like a microprocessor: absorbing data, analyzing it, and spitting it out at lightning speed in order to solve problems and plan rescue missions. Now, he could barely follow the conversation with his neurosurgeon. Or maybe he didn't want to. Honestly, the brain injury was only one of his problems. Another was the embedded shrapnel in his spine, making it impossible for him to walk.

He recalled feeling as if he'd been stung by a hundred deadly desert scorpions. That pain, however, paled in comparison to losing his team, guys he'd known for the past seven years. He jerked his attention back to his neurosurgeon, swallowing the hot bile rising in his throat.

"When the swelling decreases, some of the symptoms you're experiencing, such as memory loss and the inability to verbally express complex thoughts, should become less severe and hopefully dissipate altogether. In the meantime..." Dr. Nolan broke off as Justice interrupted him.

"In the meantime, I'm brain-fu…"

"Justice," his father, Rear Admiral Franklin McQuaid, cut in smoothly.

"Yeah, well, at least I haven't forgotten how to curse," he muttered. "Sorry, Doc. You were saying?"

"We'll map your progress and see how it goes."

Justice nodded at the doctors sitting at the conference table. "Next up?"

Another doctor rose to his feet and pulled up Justice's spinal images. "The surgery to remove the shrapnel was a success. You're not going to have any permanent damage."

*Unlike my brain.*

"Wonderful. Does that mean I'll be able to walk again?"

"Yes. With time and intense physical therapy."

"Hot damn." He slapped the arm of the wheelchair.

*That* earned him a stern warning look from his father.

"I'll put in an order for physical therapy to begin immediately."

The doctor directed his remark toward Rear Admiral McQuaid which annoyed the hell out of Justice. It was just like his father to make his recovery another one of his missions.

"Hey, shouldn't you be talking to me?" Justice demanded. "After all, I *am* a ranking officer in the SEALs. Lieutenant Commander, if my memory serves me correctly."

"*That* rolled off your tongue without any difficulty at all," Franklin noted with a wry tone.

Fed up with this counseling session his father assembled, Justice unlocked his wheelchair. "I'm done here," he declared.

"But Lieutenant Commander," the surgeon who'd operated on his back protested. "We…"

"I said I'm done!"

As he wheeled himself toward the door, he heard his father say quietly, "Let him go."

Alone in his private room at Walter Reed Hospital, a scream rose in Justice's throat. He couldn't believe he and his team had been ambushed as they conducted a peace mission in Afghanistan. More to the point, he couldn't believe he'd survived. He should have died along with his men. But, somehow, he'd been thrown free of the Humvee as it exploded. He supposed this was God's way of playing a joke on him. To deprive him of his team and his skills. The two things that mattered most to him. *Now what?*

Several hours later two rear admirals flanking his father entered his room. He saluted them and waited. Waited for his world to explode again.

Rear Admiral Simpson gazed with sorrow at him as he officially intoned, "The Navy thanks you for your faithful service, Lieutenant Commander McQuaid." He handed him an envelope. "As of today, the twenty-third of March, you're retired with full pension and benefits."

No! This couldn't be happening! He tossed the envelope aside as hot tears stung his eyes. Rear Admiral Simpson left with his companion, his duty done, and Justice glared at his father.

"Just don't stand there! Do *something* to stop this. Please. The Navy is all I have…"

And then his speech became garbled as the pressure in his brain increased with his anger and frustration. Furious and helpless, he cried unabashedly in his father's arms.

The terrible moment went from bad to worse when Justice started seizing. Franklin yelled for help and stood by, impotent, as well-trained nurses rushed to his son's aid. He stayed with Justice through the night, sleeping on the hard couch in the hospital room and offering soothing words of comfort during his nightmares.

\* \* \*

After he'd been summarily retired from the Navy with letters of commendation and the promise of a medal, Justice lost all interest in his recovery. He refused to eat or participate in physical therapy. No amount of pleading or arguing with him could change his mind. He wished he'd died along with his buddies. Losing his commission in the Navy was a fate worse than death. Without a wife and family, he didn't even have a girlfriend, for Christ's sake, Justice envisioned a long and empty future. What was the point of walking again when his brain had turned to mush, and he'd lost the only career he'd ever dreamed about?

A week later, after another fruitless argument with his pigheaded son, Franklin rushed out of Justice's hospital room and ran into Matthew Steele and John Keegan, who happened to be visiting amputees that day at Walter Reed.

As they exchanged greetings, an idea struck him. "I know you're busy, but if you could spend some time with my son, Justice, I would appreciate it." Briefly, he explained what happened in Afghanistan.

Both men expressed their sympathy and nodded.

"No problem," Steele assured him. "We'll be glad to talk to him."

Franklin shook their hands. "Maybe you can reach him. I certainly can't."

Steele and Keegan entered the dark room. The blinds were drawn, and Justice lay staring straight ahead at nothing in particular.

When the men moved in front of his line of vision, he muttered, "You've got to be fucking kidding me. I don't need a pep talk by a pair of old legends like you two."

The friends grinned at each other.

"Did you hear that?" Steele asked. "We're legends."

"No, man." Keegan punched him playfully on the arm. "We're just fucking *old*."

Justice rolled his eyes. "Great. A couple of damn comedians."

Steele moved toward the bed and held out his hand. "I'm Matt Steele. This is John Keegan. Our friends call us Wolf and Tex."

Politeness and ingrained respect for fellow SEALs prompted Justice to shake their hands.

"Look, I don't want to seem rude or ungrateful, but there isn't anything you can possibly say to me that will make me feel better about my situation. I lost my team and my career in one fell swoop. The Navy was my life, don't you get it? My life! I've got nothing to live for now."

Tex inclined his head toward the door. "Let me speak to him alone."

He pulled up a chair and told Justice his story. It was one Justice had heard a dozen times, but something in the tenor of Tex's tone kept him focused and listening. Tex spoke for over an hour, discussing what happened to him, his recovery, and how he found meaning and purpose in his life. When he talked about his love for Wolf and the rest of their special team, and especially about his all-consuming passion for his wife and children, his eyes gleamed with a fierce, protective light.

"Believe me, Justice, I understand what you're going through. You feel guilty because you're alive. But that's the point. You're *alive*. And once a SEAL, always a SEAL. No one can take that away from you. You *will* walk again. And as far as your brain injury is concerned, you'll recover from that, too. You may not be able to think as quickly as you used to, and you may not feel like yourself for a long while, but you'll find a way to cope. Because you're a SEAL. And we don't quit. Or give up."

By the time he finished speaking, tears were running down Justice's face. Once the dam broke, he couldn't stop, and through his sobs he told Tex his story, including details he couldn't share with his father. His sobs turned to dry wracks as the last conversation he and his team had before their Humvee exploded poured out of him.

"We were laughing, you know? Just shooting the breeze, not thinking we wouldn't make it back to base. Bear, I mean, Joe, had just decided to propose to his girlfriend. We were giving him shit about it, about waiting too long... And then..." Justice closed his eyes and shook his head. "And then...the last sound...the final sound I heard...screams. *Their screams.*" He rubbed his forehead, and let the tears flow unheeded down his cheeks.

Several moments later, Justice opened his eyes. "Is that even possible, Tex? That I heard my men screaming? I don't remember anything about what happened."

He could see the doubt on Tex's face. "Man, I don't know. But you need to move on, Justice. It's what your team would want you to do."

"Yeah, I know. It's hard. Surviving. I don't know who I am without the Navy."

They spoke about that for a few minutes, with Tex offering comfort and support, until Justice ran out of tears and things to say.

As Tex rose to leave, he said, "If you need a job, you can join any number of security companies I could recommend. They'd be happy to have a retired SEAL on their team." He wrote his cell phone number on a napkin. "Keep in touch, McQuaid. I want to hear from you."

"I will. Thanks, man. For taking the time to talk to me, and most of all, for listening."

They shook hands, and Tex patted his shoulder. "No

thanks are necessary. Ever. Take care, Lieutenant Commander."

Justice dragged his hands down his face and took deep breaths. He hadn't realized how much he'd needed to bare his soul with someone who understood what he had gone through, surviving an attack on his team and facing life-changing injuries. Sharing that with Tex was somehow easier than speaking to his father about it.

Moments after Tex left, Franklin entered Justice's hospital room. Their eyes met. Mutual love flowed between them. Justice finally understood what his father wanted from him.

Perseverance.

Justice's eyes shone with determination. "I'm ready." No need to elucidate.

Franklin nodded. "I'll have your shift nurse send someone from physical therapy to start working with you immediately." Reaching down, he gripped his son's shoulder a moment before he moved toward the doorway.

"Dad. Wait," Justice urged. "Thank you. For not giving up on me."

He offered a smile. "We're McQuaids. We're SEALs. We never give up."

* * *

Justice made his father's three short declarative statements his mantra during the days and weeks of his rehabilitation. His physical therapist was an Amazon woman with a body of steel and an attitude to match. Sergeant Donna Belden put him through her special version of hell, barking orders at him like his former drill sergeant, yelling at him to conquer his pain and get his ass moving.

She was an incredibly strong woman who lifted him as if

he weighed no more than a five-pound bag of potatoes. It was humiliating. She laughed at him, slapped his rear, and shouted, "Who's your daddy, SEAL?" If he didn't answer that she was, she'd increase his reps. She did, anyway, because she was just that sadistic. But by then she was indeed his daddy, completely in control.

During the hours they spent together working on his recovery, they'd forged a genuine friendship. He trusted her. Hell, he probably loved her a little, too. She was by no means a pretty or beautiful woman, but handsome, he thought, and cherished by her equally imposing giant of a fiancé.

The first time Justice walked the length of the physical therapy center, Donna and her fiancé sneaked a bottle of scotch into his room, and they celebrated in style. He almost got drunk and complained when Donna snatched the bottle away from him.

"When you get released, we'll get rip-roaring drunk together," she promised.

Justice pouted. "I hate you."

"Yeah, I hate you too, Navy Boy."

The tests of mental acuity, though, were tougher than his physical therapy. When he couldn't compute even the simplest algebraic equation in his head or on paper, when he couldn't comprehend complex text or read a map, Justice took his rage and frustration out on Donna.

She let him and used it to her advantage, pushing him harder toward his ultimate goal: to regain his former physical condition. Donna's regimen included helping him walk again, but she also knew that building up his body strength affected his mental and emotional well-being, which she drilled into his head.

For the most part it worked. By the time Justice was discharged from Walter Reed a month later, he could walk without any aid, and neurological imaging and testing showed marked improvement. A career that required him to think quickly on his feet or problem solve might be out of the question at the moment, but he felt hopeful about the future regardless of his current situation.

Much to Franklin's disapproval, Donna and her fiancé kept their promise. As soon as he stepped out of the hospital, they whisked him away to their favorite bar and got him rip-roaring drunk. Franklin allowed his son to sleep off the effects of his wild night of drinking at their hotel, and late afternoon of the following day they flew home to New Haven, Connecticut. Staring at each other over dinner, father and son thought exactly the same thing: Now what?

\* \* \*

At the beginning of May, the Navy presented Justice with the Distinguished Service medal. The ceremony took place on the South Lawn of the White House. For the occasion he'd cut his hair and shaved weeks' worth of growth from his face. He and his father wore their sharp white dress uniforms and gazed with solemnity at one another. Justice doubted he'd ever wear it again.

The South Lawn crawled with dignitaries, most of whom Justice didn't know and could care less about. He cared, though, about the families of his fallen team members and what they thought about him. Shivering in spite of the heat, he waited for them to condemn him, waited for them to ask why he was still alive and the others weren't.

He should have had more faith in the bond he shared with them. He was ashamed of his doubt, especially when they hugged him, said they were glad he'd made it out alive, and exonerated him from any blame. When the President presented him with his medal, they applauded as loudly as anyone else, truly happy for him.

As the crowd dispersed, a dark-haired man with unique amber eyes approached him and offered his hand. "Secretary of State Washburn sends her congratulations, Lieutenant Commander McQuaid, and regrets she couldn't be here today. I'm Brendan McAdams, her senior staff member."

Justice shook his hand. "Thank you, Mr. McAdams. I appreciate that."

Brendan leaned toward him and lowered his voice. "She wanted you to know she's personally investigating the attack on your team. Such unprovoked aggression is intolerable, especially since you were delivering medical supplies to one of the villages in the area."

"Again, appreciated."

"In exchange..."

Justice snorted in derision. "Go on. This ought to be good."

He and Franklin flew home to New Haven later that night. Justice changed out of his dress uniform and hung it in the closet. Wearing Levi's and an old T-shirt, he joined his father on the patio where Franklin sipped a cup of coffee. He threw himself into a comfortable low-backed chair with a neutral-colored cushion and stretched his long legs. They ached a little tonight, but he'd take the pain over not being ambulatory.

Franklin indicated a mug on the frosted-glass patio table. "For you." As Justice took a sip of the dark brew, he continued, "Are you ready to share the conversation you had with Brendan McAdams?"

"It was bizarre, to say the least. Something is going on, something domestic. Secretary Washburn needs my help. My eyes and ears, specifically in Laguna Beach. Arrangements are being made to retire the current chief of police, and I'll take her place."

Franklin frowned. "That doesn't make an ounce of sense. She's got several elite military teams in California to be her eyes and ears. Why you, of all people?"

Justice shrugged. "Beats me. I'm not even up to par. How do you think the cops on the force are going to react when I show up? I still can't read a fucking map," he complained.

"Are you taking the job?" Franklin asked in disbelief.

Justice blew out his breath. "Yeah. I'm curious about what's going on, and I want to help, if I can. I need this opportunity, Dad, and I was wondering if you'd come with me. To help me get settled." He gazed at his father. It cost Justice his pride to ask for assistance in light of his limitations.

"Call McAdams. Tell him you're in. And so am I."

"Even if I'm nothing more than a glorified beach cop?" Justice asked. Bitterness burned in him.

"Yes, even if. Deep down, though, you're a SEAL. And don't you forget it."

* * *

Secretary of State Barbara Washburn gazed at Brendan as he pressed the END button on his cell phone. Tall in stature, she used her height and penetrating stare to intimidate others into doing things her way. Fifty years old and a mother of five, she had her eye on the presidency in the near future.

Knowing Lieutenant Commander McQuaid had been given bad intel which caused him to lead his team to their deaths, she needed him focused on another issue closer to home. Something was brewing in the U.S., something ugly. She felt it in every fiber of her being, and she planned to stop it before it got out of control. And then she'd have to come clean with McQuaid about what really happened in Afghanistan. It was the reason why she'd pushed for his retirement.

"Well?" she asked, impatient.

"The lieutenant commander said he'd do it. He's just waiting for the green light."

Barbara brushed a stray lock of hair out of her eyes. "Fantastic. Everything will be in place by tomorrow morning." She met her senior staff member's direct amber stare, which always disconcerted her. "You don't approve."

"No, I don't. Using McQuaid like this is just plain wrong. My God, Barbara, you robbed him of his career. He may have a brain injury, but he's not stupid. His IQ is off the charts."

"Would it make you feel better if I told you that I prefer to use your sister Brielle?"

Brendan's eyes grew hard. "And I told you that my sister is off limits. My family has suffered enough. Almost losing my brothers Trey and Ben ten years ago hit us hard. It's the reason why Brielle changed her major from pre-law to criminal justice and went to the police academy. Now she's training to be a SWAT officer, and I'm not going to allow anything to get in her way."

Barbara lifted an eyebrow, heavily penciled. "Not even a little thing like national security?"

He scowled. "Please don't throw that in my face. You're going to have a huge problem on your hands when McQuaid finds out the truth about Afghanistan."

She waved her hand in a dismissive gesture. "He won't. I gave him a new mission to occupy his time, and trust me, he'll do his best not to let me down. And we may just prevent something catastrophic from happening in our own country."

\* \* \*

Brendan left the State Department and headed toward Alexandria where his eldest brother Trey and his wife Kerry lived. As the youngest brother of four, he always felt invisible. His older brothers had successful careers. Trey had rejoined the BAU in the FBI after teaching high school science. Ben, a former DA, now ran his own lucrative law firm and Legal Aid office in Rutherford, Maine. Bryant was a former Denver Bronco who'd led the team to a Super Bowl win and was now a high school principal in Colorado.

But he'd never fit in, mostly due to the fact that his parents, Cameron and Brianna, named him after a man who loved his mother, was engaged to marry her, and died in a plane crash. Brendan Stewart left her the Triple B Ranch in Boulder where they resided, and he always believed his mother never stopped blaming herself for her fiancé's death. Sometimes he thought he was just a ghost, though he knew his parents loved their children equally.

Letting out his breath, he knocked on his brother's door and waited. Several seconds later it swung open, and he stared into a face similar to his own. "Hi, Trey."

# CHAPTER 2

The call came at ten-thirty the morning following the ceremony, straight from Madam Secretary herself. Justice's gut curled with suspicion. Seriously, what did she want with him?

"Good morning, Lieutenant Commander McQuaid. First, let me begin by expressing my condolences on the loss of your team. They were good men. This tragedy is not going unnoticed, believe me. I'm sorry I missed the ceremony yesterday."

A strange feeling crawled across Justice's scalp. Something was definitely off. Was it just his imagination or was Madam Secretary trying too hard to reassure him?

"Mr. Stewart conveyed your regret," he replied, his tone clipped.

"He told me that you accepted the job in Laguna Beach. I'm really…"

"Not so fast," Justice interrupted her. "You need to tell me what this is all about, starting with why you're involved and why you chose me."

"I can't go into too many details, but I've received intel

that there's suspicious activity occurring on the beach. Homeland Security is aware of it, of course, but I want someone no one would suspect..."

"You mean someone like me who can't think worth shit."

She laughed softly. "Precisely. Chief Ferguson is an excellent cop, but she lacks your skills. The simple truth is I need you out there keeping an eye on things for me. I wish I could give you more information, but we just don't have a handle on the magnitude of the situation yet. Chief Ferguson is expecting you tomorrow at four o'clock. Can I count on you to make it?"

Justice rubbed the rough stubble on his chin. "I'll be there. But I'm not making any promises. If I don't like the vibe I'm getting, I'm not staying. Is that clear?"

"Of course, Lieutenant Commander," she placated him.

He felt his blood pressure rise at her condescending tone. His father must have noticed his face turning red because he laid a comforting hand on his shoulder.

"If there's nothing else, Madam Secretary, I'll say goodbye. I've got plans to make." He pressed the END button on his cell phone. "Total bullshit!"

"Calm down," Franklin urged. "Please."

Justice grabbed a bottle of water from the fridge and gulped half of it. Dragging his arm across his mouth, he muttered, "She wants me out of the way."

The older man nodded. "I agree."

When Justice had been told that the Navy was retiring him, he'd been surprised. He still had five years left until he could retire with twenty years of service. Even if he couldn't lead missions anymore, he could still be useful behind the scenes.

Justice gazed at his father. "Afghanistan. Do you know something I don't?"

"No. But I could pull strings to find out."

To his shame Justice felt tears sting his eyes. "Dad, what-ever happened…I don't remember too many of the details. Was it my fault?"

Franklin shook his head. "No. Let's not worry about it right now. We have to pack and book a flight to California."

As they tended to their individual tasks, Justice's mind whirled with the possibility that someone had screwed up and he and his men had paid the price. And the last thing Madam Secretary wanted was for Justice to find out the truth.

* * *

The McQuaids landed at John Wayne Airport, about fifteen miles away from Laguna Beach, close to midnight. They rented a car and thirty minutes later checked into their hotel on the beach. After stripping down to their boxers, father and son wished each other good night and fell exhausted into their separate beds.

Bad dreams plagued Justice, as they had every night since losing his team. He tossed and turned, and drenched in sweat, he awoke shortly after dawn.

His father, noticing the messy bed, remarked, "You had another restless night."

"Yeah. I'm taking my shower first, if you don't mind."

"No. Go ahead."

After both men had showered and dressed, they discussed where to have breakfast.

"A local diner," Franklin suggested. "There's bound to be gossip, and if we're lucky, maybe we'll run into a couple of cops."

Justice agreed, and they grabbed their wallets, cell phones, and car keys. In the lobby of their hotel, he asked the desk clerk to recommend the most popular diner for breakfast.

The young woman offered a flirty smile that suggested she was single and available before she replied, "Everyone loves Pop's Diner. It's only a couple of miles east of here. Do you need directions?"

Justice deliberately flashed one of his brilliant, sexy smiles which caused his father to roll his eyes. Holding up his cell phone, he shook his head. "The wonders of modern technology."

As they ambled toward their car, Franklin admonished him, "Get your mind out of the gutter."

Justice chuckled. "Aw, Dad, come on! She's probably ten years younger than I am. Just a kid."

"Well, don't encourage her. You've got work to do."

Ah, Rear Admiral Franklin McQuaid, the workaholic. He never took a vacation. And never encouraged it in his son, either. Justice let out his breath. He'd like to settle down, get married, and raise a family with a woman who made his heart race, a woman he couldn't live without. He longed for the kind of relationship his parents had. Maybe now that he was retired from the Navy, he could fill the empty place in his soul with the love of a good woman.

He'd given some thought to what she'd be like. He didn't particularly care if she was beautiful or not, as long as he was attracted to her. She'd be intelligent, kind, loyal, compassionate, and most of all, loving. And, he grinned to himself, her sexual appetite would definitely have to match his. He wanted a wife who lit their bed on fire with her passion.

Did the woman of his dreams even exist? Probably not.

Justice clasped his father's shoulder. "Whatever, Dad. Let's go."

When Franklin pulled up Pop's Diner on Google Maps, he laughed. "That poor girl doesn't know directions! The diner is two miles *north* of here, just across the street from the beach."

Justice glanced sideways at his father. "Give her a break. At the moment I'm lousy with directions, too."

"I meant no offense."

"I know. I just need time to adjust to my new normal."

Ten minutes later Justice pulled into the crowded parking lot of the diner.

"Popular place," Franklin commented. "I hope the food is good."

Justice inclined his head toward two Laguna Beach patrol cars. "Cops are here."

An overhead bell rang as they entered the diner. A busy waitress carrying a coffee pot instructed them to seat themselves, and as luck would have it, there was an empty booth behind the one where four Laguna Beach cops sat eating breakfast.

Out of habit, Justice's eyes swept the interior of the diner, noting the location of the exits and the customers who were sitting alone, particularly at the counter. He noticed an attractive young woman with her sleek dark hair pulled into a ponytail. She wore black leggings, a light hoodie, and jogging shoes. As she ate breakfast, the cops kept making suggestive remarks about her.

A vein in Justice's temple began to throb, and his eyes darkened in anger. He wanted to toss them on their asses and teach them a lesson they wouldn't soon forget.

Apparently, the woman had had enough of their lewd comments, for she slammed money down on the counter and rose from the stool. As she moved past the cops, one grabbed her arm.

"You're nothing special," he said. "What makes you think you're better than us?"

Jerking her arm out of his grasp, she muttered, "Go to hell," which sent the cop's partners into uproarious gales of laughter. Justice and Franklin heard what she said, too, and smiled at each other as the woman left the diner.

Justice slid out of the booth and murmured, "I need to have a few words with those guys."

"Justice, no," Franklin hissed.

He ignored his father and approached the cops. "Good morning, Officers."

They didn't look up from their plates which pissed him off even more.

"Do you think that sexually harassing a citizen and manhandling her is an acceptable standard of behavior for the Laguna Beach Police Department?"

That got their attention. Four heads snapped up and swung in his direction.

The sandy-haired, burly cop who'd spoken so rudely to the young woman waved his fork at Justice. "Buzz off before I haul you down to the station for disturbing my breakfast."

His companions guffawed.

Justice glanced idly at his watch. "Funny you should mention that. I've got an appointment at the station with Chief Ferguson today at sixteen-hundred hours. I'm her replacement. Chief of Police Justice McQuaid." He gazed steadily at the three officers who'd suddenly stopped snickering. "Still think Officer Dooley is hilarious?" he continued, reading the cop's nametag.

Their faces turned bright red, and they chorused, "No, Chief."

"Good. I expect to see all four of you in my office tomorrow morning at eight o'clock sharp. Have a nice day, Officers. And be safe out there." Justice smiled and returned to his booth.

He assumed he'd ruined their appetites because a couple of minutes later the officers laid money on the table for their waitress and hastily left the diner.

After they finished breakfast, Justice said, "Let's go talk to a realtor about a place to rent, preferably on the beach."

Franklin nodded. "Sounds like a good idea." He Googled realtors and added, "Laguna Beach Realty is located three miles east of the diner. Pull onto the highway, turn right, and then turn right again on the first street."

Justice repeated his father's words to himself a couple of times. He still had difficulty processing multi-step directions and worried whether or not he'd be able to perform his duties as police chief. He thought he'd done a fair job of hiding his concern from his father, but Franklin knew him well.

"You're doing great," his dad commented. "Now, continue on this street for a mile, and you'll see Laguna Beach Realty on your left."

When they entered the mid-size business, a lovely woman, probably in her middle fifties Justice guessed, stepped forward to greet them. She wore her brown hair in a French twist and was dressed sharply in a business skirt and coordinating jacket. Her deep brown eyes sparkled as she assessed both men, especially Franklin.

She held out a soft, well-manicured hand. "Good morning. I'm Adrienne Bosco. How can I help you?"

Justice gripped her hand firmly, but Franklin barely held it and then dropped it as if he'd been scalded.

Adrienne's mouth curved in a small smile.

"Good morning. I'm Justice McQuaid, and this is my father, Franklin. I just accepted a job in the community and am looking for a furnished house to rent on the beach."

"I have quite a few rentals up and down the coast," she replied. "Let's look at the listings and then you can decide which ones you'd like to visit."

The McQuaids settled themselves in front of Adrienne's laptop and started looking at the houses she suggested. She hovered behind them, answering their questions with her expertise.

After Justice chose three rentals he liked, Adrienne hung a CLOSED sign in the window, and led them to a white Cadillac. Justice slid into the backseat, deliberately allowing his father to sit in the front with the pretty realtor.

The first house was located ten miles up the coast, and during the drive Adrienne entertained them with stories about Laguna Beach's history. Every so often Justice noticed his father's eyes glance sideways at her.

When she fabricated a story about Laguna Beach pirates, Franklin turned his head, studied her lovely profile and remarked, "Now, you're just telling a tall tale, Mrs. Bosco."

Adrienne risked looking at him. "Yes, I am. And please call me Adrienne."

Franklin thought the first house was practical and suited his son's Spartan lifestyle while Justice found it stifling. His bathroom at home in Connecticut was larger than the total living room space! The second house had more square footage which Justice favored, but his father hated the floor plan and the flashy color scheme.

"Pepto-Bismol pink." Franklin grimaced. "It looks like someone chucked a gallon of Pepto-Bismol at the walls."

Adrienne laughed out loud. The sound stirred Franklin's attention. Justice noticed his father peering closely at the realtor. He recognized the expression on Franklin's slightly pink face and smiled to himself.

"I can paint the walls," Justice asserted, though Franklin hardly heard him.

"Yeah, yeah, I suppose so," he murmured before he tore his gaze away from Adrienne.

"Let's take a look at the last one," Adrienne interjected. "I think both of you will love it."

"Just for the record, Dad, real men *can* wear pink," Justice reminded him, his tone peevish as he climbed into the back-seat of the Cadillac.

"Not on the walls of his home," Franklin argued, "and certainly not that hideous shade of Pepto-Bismol pink."

"You always have to have the last word," Justice muttered.

Franklin heard his son's comment and pressed his lips together, his jaw set.

Adrienne pulled into the driveway of a California split level home built into the cliffs above the beach. The style of the architecture impressed both Franklin and Justice. Stone steps led up to the front door, and when Adrienne let them in, they entered the foyer which opened into the main living area. Only the kitchen, dining room, great room, and a guest bathroom were on this level. A short flight of stairs led to the upper level where three bedrooms and two bathrooms were located. Another flight led down to the lower level which contained a family room and a den. Justice liked the clean lines and *white* walls, starkly complemented with a black leather sofa, loveseat, recliner, and glass-topped accent tables. The kitchen had been remodeled and enlarged and opened onto the re-finished deck and patio overlooking the ocean.

They stepped outside to admire the view, and as he glanced down at the beach below, Justice watched a young woman run down the coast until she reached a set of wooden stairs a few hundred yards away that led to a multi-million-dollar, multi-level modern glass and concrete home that looked like Tony Stark's mansion in the movie *Ironman*.

"Hey, Dad, do you see that woman? Isn't she the same one from the diner?" he asked.

Franklin shielded his eyes from the glare of the sun and squinted. "Yes. Same dark ponytail and jogging clothes."

Justice turned toward Adrienne. "I'll take it."

* * *

Hot and sweaty from a ten-mile run along the coast, Brielle walked into her luxurious bathroom, shed her clothes, and stepped into the shower stall. Cool water rained down on her sore body. She noticed fresh bruises on her torso and on her arms, but she didn't mind, even as she winced in pain. Training to be a SWAT officer was worth it. After passing a written, verbal, physical, and mental exam, she and one other woman in the LAPD were chosen to move forward... meaning she'd landed back at the police academy for further instruction and intense fitness training. The other woman had already been dropped after two weeks because she couldn't handle the physicality.

Brielle was determined to make it all the way. Her rank as a sergeant, her intellectual brilliance, and sharpshooter status weren't worth a damn if she couldn't take the physical bouts with a sparring partner bent on taking her down, and the other challenges tossed at her. So, she worked out with a personal trainer five days a week, a former heavyweight boxer to be exact, in LA's famous Main Street Gym, the same one used as the interior for Mighty Mick's in *Rocky I*.

As she dried her tender body, the physical pain involved with her training wasn't nearly as bad as the emotional pain her ex-boyfriend inflicted upon her heart. Sometimes she couldn't help thinking about their final confrontation.

After a long day in the field where she'd been caught in a gang war, she'd gotten home late, too tired to do anything but take a shower and fall into bed. She'd completely forgotten about Malcolm's art exhibit at The Broad. It was a once in a lifetime opportunity for him, and she'd missed it.

When he stumbled into their bedroom, half drunk and furious with her, he screamed, "What the hell, Bri? Where were you? I can't believe you stood me up on the most important night of my life! For God's sake, wake up!"

She jerked awake, stunned by his tone of voice and the contemptuous expression on his face. Rising to a sitting position, she mumbled, "I'm so sorry. I forgot. I got home and…"

Malcolm's face turned red. He grabbed her arm and pulled her from the bed. "You *forgot?* You're never there for me when I need you. All of our friends, no, *my* friends, told me to dump you months ago even though I love you. Not anymore. Not after tonight. I'm tired of taking a backseat to your career. I'm sick of your emasculating me every time I turn around. I'm not tough enough for you, not able to protect you, not able to offer you anything you need. I'm done."

Brielle watched in horror as he started flinging drawers open and tossing her clothes at her. "Get out. Take what you can carry tonight, and I'll pack the rest of your things. You can pick them up outside in the hallway tomorrow."

She couldn't believe Malcolm was throwing her out of their apartment, actually *his* apartment, in the middle of the night when she didn't have anywhere to go. With as much dignity as she could muster, she dressed and made sure she had at least one clean uniform and her guns.

Standing at the front door, gazing at him with something akin to pity in her eyes, she declared, "I truly am sorry. I never meant to hurt you. But the fact that you feel less of a man because you can't handle my career is not my problem. It's yours."

She lifted her chin, looking exactly like the daughter of Cameron "Hurricane" McAdams should. Her father taught her pride. However, her mother's gentle, loving spirit also ran through her blood, and her tone and expression softened.

"I'm not the woman for you. I can't give you what you need, and you definitely can't give me what I need, either. One day I hope you meet a woman who will love you unconditionally and give you what you both need and want."

She'd spent the night at a hotel, and for the first time in her life she called in sick in order to look for a place to live and pick up her personal possessions. For a girl who grew up on the wild coast of Maine and the wide-open spaces of Boulder, Colorado, Brielle hated living in LA.

She drove south until she reached Laguna Beach and found the house on the cliff. When Mrs. Bosco at Laguna Beach Realty learned she was a sergeant with the LAPD, she slashed the asking price by one fourth. Too good of a deal to pass up, she bought it instead of renting. It also helped that the realtor recognized the McAdams name. A month later she'd been accepted into the SWAT program and the ugliness with Malcolm didn't matter anymore. Oh, she missed the sex, but not his constant whining and complaining about the lack of time she spent with him.

"Screw that," she muttered, reaching for a bottle of water in the fridge. "I don't have time for relationships."

But if she did, she'd want a man so comfortable in his own skin he wouldn't feel as if he had to compete with her career for her time and attention.

Thinking about relationships brought her best friend Faith to mind. It'd been too long since they'd spoken. Just as she reached for her cell phone, it vibrated with an incoming call.

Her face lit up with a smile. "Hey, Faith! What's up? I was just thinking about you."

# CHAPTER 3

"Nothing's up. I just wanted to touch base. It's been awhile since we've talked…" Faith's voice trailed away.

An unexpected shiver ran up Brielle's spine. She'd never heard that shaky and nervous tone in her friend's voice before now. They'd been best friends since sharing a dorm room at Northwestern University their freshman year. The moment they'd started talking about their personal experiences and family history they realized how much they had in common. Their families were actually connected since Brielle's brother Trey was an FBI agent and Faith's uncle Patrick Stoker was a former FBI commander. Back in the day Tex worked for Stoker before he quit and joined the SEALs. When Faith's parents were killed flying over the Alps in a small charter plane, she went to live with Uncle Patrick and Aunt Susan. At the moment her physically active aunt and uncle were hiking in Europe.

"What's wrong?" Brielle asked. "You don't sound like yourself at all."

"Nothing, really. Boyfriend trouble," Faith responded.

Brielle frowned. *"Boyfriend trouble?* You didn't tell me you were dating anyone."

"Well, um, it's a new relationship. We're figuring things out, I guess."

Brielle didn't believe a single word out of her friend's mouth. "Huh." Instead of pursuing the boyfriend track, she changed the subject. "So, what are you working on now? I thought you deserved a Pulitzer for that four-part series you did last year on Latoya, the homeless teenager."

Faith gave a nervous laugh. "So did I. But I guess my story about a homeless girl fighting for her survival every day while earning straight A's in high school and receiving a full ride to Northwestern didn't rate any recognition."

"Your writing was phenomenal."

"Thanks. I've got…a few irons in the fire at the moment."

Again, Brielle thought Faith sounded strange. "Anything you'd like to share?"

"No, nothing dramatic or important," she answered. "Just promise you'll be careful out there on the street."

"I always am. When can you come out for a visit? I know Tex would love to see you. He and Melody are here for a while in their beach house."

"Soon. Maybe within a couple of weeks or so. We'll have to see."

"You know you can trust me, right?" Brielle reminded her.

"Yes, of course."

"Well, then, we'll talk again soon, okay? I've got to run. I have a class starting in an hour and a half."

"Yeah, sure."

* * *

She knew it was a mistake to reach out to Brielle. She never could fool her. Faith gazed at a wall in her office filled with pictures and notes, the emerging story both unbelievable and bone-jarring frightening. Her skin turned icy, and she glanced behind her, as if expecting someone to creep up on her in the apartment. Faith transfixed her eyes on the wall. Her legs buckled beneath her, and she sank hard into her office chair. What she'd accidentally stumbled onto while investigating why a prominent American businessman and his family disappeared off the grid made her physically sick with fear. Leaning over a wastepaper basket, she vomited.

Oh, God! How could something like this, something that threatened the very fabric of America, be happening? Wiping her mouth, she focused on her map. The west coast of the United States. Laguna Beach.

Brielle had no idea what was occurring right beneath her nose. And she couldn't tell her. Not even Uncle Patrick.

* * *

Brielle's badge hung from a chain around her neck. She shoved her Glock into a shoulder harness, strapped her department issued service weapon to her ankle, and grabbed her motorcycle helmet, her keys, and backpack. Her parents hated the fact that she rode a motorcycle, but since Malcolm threw her out of his apartment, she'd had to commute a little more than an hour to get to her precinct every day. The motorcycle came in handy during rush hour traffic as she was able to slip between lanes of bumper to bumper cars or ride on the shoulder, waving her badge for proof of right of way. And, she had to admit, she enjoyed the exhilaration of letting out the throttle and flying down the open highway.

Heading north, she thought about Faith. Her friend didn't sound like herself at all. She didn't even protest when Brielle never asked the name of the man she was supposedly dating but allowed her to change the subject. In the past they used to gush with excitement whenever there was a new man in either of their lives. No, something was definitely wrong, something Faith didn't want to share with her. Well, she'd just have to pry it out of her the next time they spoke.

As soon as she arrived at the LAPD police academy in Elysian Park, Brielle sent her parents a quick text: *safe and sound at PA*. She knew if she didn't keep in touch with them, they would worry about her, and her father wasn't above calling out the entire police force to look after her.

After securing her motorcycle, she took a deep breath and entered the sacred halls of the academy which always filled her with awe. So much history had occurred inside these walls.

She located her classroom and took a seat. Eyes constantly watched her. Half of the men in the SWAT program hated and resented her for daring to apply and make it this far into a male-dominated elite unit. They treated her roughly, physically, and often made crude remarks that their instructors never heard. She knew their behavior was part of the reason Edie Perez gave up. However, as soon as they discovered Brielle's family had deep pockets and connections to other wealthy families and to the White House, they toned down their attitude toward her. The other half welcomed her, albeit reluctantly, and treated her like she was their kid sister or one of the guys. With four older brothers, she was used to both. Sometimes, after their training sessions, she joined them for drinks or dinner when she wasn't working out at the gym.

One of the officers, Howie Macklin, leaned over and whispered, "Any plans tonight?"

"Swimming laps and sparring with my PT."

"Don't you ever take a break?"

"Can't afford to."

"Wanna go out Saturday night?"

She had to give him kudos for persistence. He asked her the same question every day. "Sorry, Mack, I can't."

He grinned, not the least bit put off or disappointed. "Maybe next time."

Brielle smiled. "Yeah, maybe."

Officer Marcus Finnigan, Brielle's biggest detractor, turned in his seat and glared at them. "Shut the hell up, Mack, and stop humiliating yourself. And *you*," he addressed Brielle with a sneer, "I don't want you on my team. You screw with our heads and that makes you a danger to all of us. I don't trust you, and certainly don't want you next to me in a life or death situation."

Mack murmured, "Fuck you."

At that moment their instructor strode into the class-room. He greeted them and got down to business. After two hours of instruction on tactical maneuvers, they spent another two hours running the obstacle course. At one point Finnigan bumped so hard into Brielle that she took a hard fall. Macklin held out his hand to assist her.

"Finn is sabotaging you," he commented as he jogged next to her.

"Don't worry. I'm taking him down," she swore and gritted her teeth.

"I don't think like he does. I would trust you with my life, Sergeant McAdams."

She flashed him a grateful look. "Thanks. Now, let's climb that wall!"

* * *

When the McQuaids and Adrienne returned to Laguna Beach Realty, she pulled up a rental agreement on her laptop and started typing as she spoke.

"I just need to get some basic information. There will be a

background check, of course, but it shouldn't take too long. Now, if you'll…"

Justice interrupted her with a chuckle. "Are you really going to conduct a background check on Laguna Beach's newest chief of police? Not to mention a retired Navy SEAL, Lieutenant Commander, to be exact." He produced his military ID and so did Franklin.

"Oh. My. Goodness. Well, then, this is something. My deceased husband spent thirty years in the Marines, Special Ops."

Justice nodded. "I appreciate his service."

"How long did you serve?"

"Fifteen years," he replied. From the closed expression on his face, he indicated he didn't want to discuss it.

Adrienne rose to her feet. "Excuse me a moment, gentlemen. I need to make a couple of phone calls."

She rejoined them ten minutes later, a bright smile on her face. "So, we're all set. Due to your position in our community and your service to our country, I'm giving you a ten percent discount, waiving first and last month's rent, and paying the deposits for electricity and utilities, which are being turned on as we speak. You don't need to do a thing."

Both men leaped to their feet and protested Adrienne's generosity. "No, absolutely not!" Justice exclaimed. "There's no way I'm allowing you to do that for me. It's a huge financial loss for you. I'll pay whatever I owe."

"Justice is right," Franklin added. "We can't accept such generosity. As goodhearted as it is meant to be, some may misconstrue it and accuse Justice of taking advantage of his position."

Adrienne tucked tendrils of her hair behind her ears. "All right. I see your point. Will you agree to the ten percent discount, first month's rent and security?"

Justice glanced at his father who nodded his head. "Deal." He held out his hand.

After they finished the paperwork, Adrienne handed Justice a set of keys and grinned. "Feel free to move in whenever you'd like, Chief McQuaid."

"Nice doing business with you, Adrienne," Justice replied as she escorted them to the door.

"You, too," she replied, her voice warm. "I don't suppose you and Franklin would like to join me for dinner?"

Franklin tilted his head. "I'll defer to my son."

"I'm so sorry, Adrienne, but tonight isn't good for us. I have a meeting with Chief Ferguson at four, and after that I don't know what's happening. I wouldn't want to accept your invitation and then cancel at the last minute."

"Of course. I understand." Her face reflected her disappointment.

Seeing her reaction, Justice let out his breath. "However, I don't see why we can't join you tomorrow evening. Is seven too late?"

She perked up and smiled. "No, no, not at all. Let me give you my address."

Justice typed the information into his cell phone, and they left.

As they climbed into their car, Franklin commented with a dour expression on his face, "I don't know why you obligated us to have dinner with that woman."

Justice glanced in surprise at his father. He thought he'd noticed Franklin responding to Adrienne. Ah, now he understood. *"That woman* is a sweet, lovely lady who misses her deceased husband as much as you miss Mom. Didn't you notice the abundance of family photos on her desk and on the walls?"

Franklin grunted. "I guess."

"You guess? Well, we're having dinner with Adrienne, and

you're going to treat her with polite deference." At his father's stubborn silence, he continued, "Before she died, Mom told me not to let you live like a recluse. She wanted you to be happy. Being alone for the rest of your life is no way to live."

Franklin stiffened in his seat. "I will *not* be unfaithful to your mother. I pledged my fidelity to her forever."

"Forever didn't last," Justice pointed out. "Mom said you shared an active sex life. She wouldn't want you to be celibate, Dad."

Color shot into Franklin's face. "She said that, huh? Well, your mother was so beautiful I couldn't keep my hands off her. Would you like to know where you were conceived? On top of the…"

"Uh, no, Dad. That's just…*ew*… I don't even want to think about you and Mom doing the deed on top of the…whatever you were about to say."

The subject was dropped as they drove aimlessly around Laguna Beach, noting the sights and getting their bearings. On their way back to the hotel, they stopped to get burgers, fries, and Cokes. After they ate, Franklin took a nap while Justice watched a little TV before showering again and dressing for his meeting with Chief Ferguson. His hands shook so badly that he had difficulty tying the black tie he wore with his white dress shirt.

Franklin heard him swear beneath his breath and approached him, brushing his hands aside. "I'm worried you've taken on too much. Look, I will admit I want you safe behind your desk at home, working cyber security or something like that, not running an entire police department with everything it entails." He paused as he adjusted the tie. "And if I'm being completely honest, I…I just want you home. Period."

When Justice remained silent, he gripped his shoulders. "Talk to me, son. Do you have a migraine?"

"No. Just good old-fashioned nerves."

"Would you tell me otherwise?"

Justice offered a slight smile. "Probably not."

"If you begin to feel overwhelmed, walk away. Tell Madam Secretary to find someone else. Or volunteer to be an ordinary cop."

*Ordinary.* He'd never been an ordinary *anything* in his entire life. Not when it came to his superior intellect, academic achievements, talent on the football field, or career in the Navy. He lifted his chin a little. "I'm good. But if something feels off, I'll reconsider."

"All right." Franklin stepped back and appraised his son's firm jaw and determined eyes. "Ready?" he asked in a quiet voice.

"Yeah. Let's do this."

* * *

The façade of the Laguna Beach Police Department was reminiscent of California's Spanish missions. The McQuaids stepped into the busy lobby where officers came and went, and others were taking statements from citizens and handling phone calls. And then something unexpected happened. Officers snapped to attention. They saluted the McQuaids, and chorused one after the other, "Welcome, Lieutenant Commander. Rear Admiral. Thank you for your service to our country."

Hot emotion swelled in both men as they shook hands with the officers and returned their greetings with heartfelt gratitude and thanks. One female officer, who wore her bright red hair in a tight bun, and whose hazel eyes appraised the McQuaids, detached herself from the others and approached them with her hand outstretched.

"Good afternoon, Lieutenant Commander. I'm Sergeant Tawny Westfall." They shook hands with a firm grip. "Please follow me. Chief Ferguson is waiting for you."

"Nice to meet you, Sergeant." Justice glanced back at his father who nodded his head in the affirmative, a sign he understood to mean that Franklin wasn't going anywhere, that he'd be there for him if he needed him.

Sergeant Westfall led Justice through a maze of corridors, smiling and nodding at officers and chattering a mile a minute. He barely heard what she said because his nerves were skittering in time to her chatter. Finally, they came to a large, glassed-in office and she said, "Here we are."

Justice thanked her and opened the door. Attired in her formal black uniform, the color of the Laguna Beach Police Department, outgoing Chief Ferguson moved from behind her modern glass-topped desk and smiled warmly at him. She presented an imposing and authoritative figure—tall and lean with brown eyes and hair and a plain, honest face.

Gripping his proffered hand in both of hers, Chief Ferguson declared, "Welcome aboard, Lieutenant Commander. When I learned you were my replacement, I couldn't have been happier with the mayor's choice. I knew my men and women would be in good hands."

Heat rose in him. He didn't think Madam Secretary left the mayor with a choice. And Linda Ferguson didn't look like she was ready for retirement. He definitely could relate to that. They'd both been forced out of the positions they loved.

Embarrassed, he began, regretting his decision to wear a tie, for now it felt like a noose around his neck, "Thank you, Chief, but…"

"No buts," she replied, her voice firm. "This isn't about

either one of us. I don't believe you were given any more information than I was. Look, I've had a good run and instituted changes for the betterment of this department and community. I know you will do the same because you're a true leader." She indicated a huge three-ring binder with a glossy cover embossed with the title *Laguna Beach Police Department Policies and Procedures*. "This is your new Bible."

Justice gazed at it as dismay turned his stomach sour. He couldn't do it. There was no way he could absorb the information in that binder. No way. "Um...I don't think I'm the man for this job."

"Nonsense. You're the perfect man for this job. Sergeant Tawny Westfall is your go-to girl. She knows this department inside and out. Right now, she's working on condensing the manual into a smaller, comprehensive version for you. As you make the transition into being chief, she'll be invaluable to you." Linda glanced at her watch. "The mayor is swearing you into office at six o'clock. We need to get you fitted for a uniform to go along with this." She handed him a brand-new badge with his title on it. Chief of Police. Laguna Beach.

He stared at it, feeling more than its weight in his hand. Feeling the weight of his duty to serve and protect and wondering whether or not he would be able to do either.

Linda's stern voice cut into his thoughts. "Come with me, Lieutenant Commander." As he followed her, she continued, "We pride ourselves on our uniform shop. Sally Russo is our resident seamstress who provides the force with the best-looking uniforms in the region."

Too overwhelmed to speak, Justice lost all sense of direction as he walked next to Chief Ferguson through another maze of corridors until they arrived at a double set of glass doors. Inside he could see racks of uniforms and shelves containing Laguna Beach Police Department hats, T-shirts, coffee mugs, water bottles, and other similar items for sale.

A woman, seventy years old, Justice guessed, approached them, smiling. "Oh, you must be our new chief! You *are* a handsome devil, aren't you? Come with me, Chief McQuaid. I need to take your measurements." Sally winked at Linda as she led him into her inner sanctum. "I promise I'll be gentle with him."

\* \* \*

Linda heard her chortle as she turned away and found Officer Nash Carson staring at her. A shiver crawled up her spine. "Is there…something you want to say, Officer?"

He shook his head. "No, ma'am. I'm just here to drop off my uniform. I lost a button. I guess Sally is busy with the new chief."

"She is."

"That's okay. I'll wait."

"Suit yourself." She studied him a moment before she excused herself.

*Remember.*

# CHAPTER 4

Sally cooed as she measured Justice's broad chest, his long muscular arms, and his slim waist.

"Oh, you are a *fine* specimen of a man, Chief. Don't take this the wrong way, but I have to measure your, um, inseam now."

Justice grinned as she knelt in front of him. "Careful, Sally. I may have to arrest you for being inappropriate with an officer."

She laughed in delight. "I'm old enough to be your grandmother."

"You're not a day over twenty-five."

"Handsome *and* charming. That's a lethal combination. Let's find a uniform to wrap all that goodness in."

She wouldn't settle for anything less than the crispest, newest pants and shirts on the rack in Justice's size. First, she fitted him with his dress uniform. Even though he was wearing black dress shoes, Sally brought him a pair that looked like the rest of the officers', and then checked to make sure the length of his pants was perfect. When he slipped on the jacket, he noticed it bore the stripes indicating his rank.

"I haven't earned these stripes," he remarked in a soft voice. "I'm not worthy of them."

Sally tsked. "I'll bet your Navy dress uniform is covered in medals and stripes."

"It is," Justice admitted. He was never one to boast, but he added, "Would you like to see it?"

"Yes, I would."

Justice rummaged through his pants lying on the fitting room bench and pulled out his cell phone. He scrolled through his pictures until he found one taken at the awards ceremony a few days earlier.

He showed it to her and she smiled. "Impressive."

"I just did my duty to my men and to my country."

Sally straightened his jacket. "That's why you're going to make a great chief of police."

"I hope so."

After she placed two everyday uniforms in a garment bag, she said, "You can pick these up after you're sworn in."

"Will you be there?"

"Of course. Wouldn't miss it. When you come to get your uniforms, I'll give you a hat and a T-shirt."

Justice grinned. "Sure."

"It's five-fifteen. You'd better join Chief Ferguson." Sally paused. Her expression grew serious. "Linda is a great cop. We've known each other over twenty years, but...but she's grown complacent. She's allowed things to slip by her, lost control of her men and women to a certain degree. Don't get me wrong. She's had a great run. But it's time for a change. You're going to be good for us."

"I appreciate your confidence in me."

"Go on now. You don't want to keep Chief Ferguson waiting."

"Yes, ma'am."

Justice left the uniform shop and found Sergeant Westfall waiting for him.

"I figured you'd need help getting back to Chief Ferguson's office." She looked him over with a critical eye. "Sally is amazing, isn't she? She makes us look spiffy."

"Yes, she does. I love her already."

"I made a map for you, Lieutenant Commander, but honestly you should just wander around until you get the lay of our facility."

"Appreciate it. And you're right. I'll study the map tonight and find my way around tomorrow."

After Sergeant Westfall delivered Justice back to Chief Ferguson, she excused herself and returned to her desk.

Linda gestured for Justice to take a seat. She handed him a flow chart depicting the department's different divisions. "We're in the process of restructuring the department. The budget is tight right now. You've got some hard decisions to make. Currently, we're a hundred strong, fifty-five sworn and forty-five civilian positions, not to mention the seasonal beach patrol officers, which bring the number to one hundred and thirty."

She pointed at the first column in the flow chart. "There are three divisions. The Field Services division, which boasts thirty officers, is run by Captain Everett Locke. He goes strictly by the book. You'll probably like that about him."

Justice gathered by the scornful tone of her voice that Linda wasn't fond of Captain Locke's style of leadership. He took the opportunity, when she paused, to ask if she'd review the Field Services division with him again, partly to absorb the details and partly to ascertain whether or not he'd judged Linda's attitude toward Captain Locke unfairly.

He hadn't. The longer she spoke about the officers in the field the more she revealed her bias toward the captain and the difficulties she'd experienced with him. Until Justice had the chance to speak to the captain himself, he'd take Linda's comments with a grain of salt.

By the time Linda had answered all of his questions, Sergeant Westfall poked her head into the office to announce the arrival of Mayor Elliot Gage.

"Thank you, Sergeant. Tell Mayor Gage we'll meet him in the press conference room shortly."

"Yes, ma'am."

Linda straightened her uniform and reached for her white gloves and hat. She looked at Justice and offered a sad but reassuring smile. "Time for the changing of the guard, so to speak. Are you ready, Lieutenant Commander?"

"For the announcement? Yes."

She laughed softly. "A very diplomatic reply. Diplomacy and tact will serve you well in this job."

"I've never been diplomatic, Chief Ferguson."

"A straight shooter, huh?"

"Yes."

\* \* \*

The entire Laguna Beach police force and nearly half of the civilian employees attended the swearing-in of their new chief. Inside the press conference room, bodies were packed into the tight space. The local news media were also present en masse to capture the mayor's announcement, and their curiosity was peaking. One clever reporter recognized Franklin and spent a few minutes interviewing him. Franklin carefully spun the story he and his son had rehearsed, preparing for this inevitability. It helped that Franklin possessed charm and a natural authoritative manner that everyone he spoke to hoped he'd passed on to his son.

In the moments preceding the mayor's announcement, Linda introduced Justice to Elliot Gage. The mayor smiled, shook his hand, and welcomed Justice to Laguna Beach, but both his voice and his eyes lacked warmth. Justice intuited that Mayor Gage wasn't likely to be his ally or his friend. But that didn't matter. He'd faced opposition before and over-come it. Running a cohesive unit was more important to him than garnering political support. He didn't need it or want it. Owing favors to the wrong individuals eventually came back to bite you in the ass. It was bad enough he'd allowed Madam Secretary to manipulate him, and he wondered, again, if he'd made a huge mistake.

At precisely six o'clock Mayor Gage stepped in front of a pack of microphones. The consummate politician offered a broad smile, greeted the crowd, and played to it by performing his duty with aplomb. After Justice took his oath of office, he delivered a short, inspirational speech, assuring the officers of his dedication, loyalty, and support. As his gaze swept the room, it landed on Officer Owen Dooley, who smirked at him before he turned his back and left. It didn't matter. He'd deal with Dooley in the morning. Officer Nash Carson's hard stare, though, disturbed Justice more than Dooley's insolence. Justice returned it, his own hard gaze never wavering. He'd deal with him, too, but thought there was something off about Carson that niggled at his core.

Within twenty minutes the press conference room cleared. Mayor Gage approached Justice and said, "A word, please."

They stepped into an interrogation room unlike Justice had ever seen. It was bright with light and glassed in. One side was a two-way mirror. The table in the center had a metal top that, to Justice, seemed out of place given the modern structure of the room.

The mayor closed the door. "I'll get right to the point. I strongly opposed the Secretary of State forcing you on my town and my police department. The federal government has no business poking its nose into local affairs. Chief Ferguson was doing a fine job and didn't deserve to be pushed into retirement. And *you*," he pointed at his head, "you're damaged. How badly, no one knows. If you freak out on the job, you could cost lives. You're a liability, not an asset. Believe me, *Chief*, I'll be keeping a close eye on you. One screw-up, one bad decision, and I'll make sure you're out, and very publicly, too. Do you understand me?"

The only outward sign of Justice's anger was a muscle ticking in his cheek. He thought the mayor's reaction to his being chief of police wasn't commensurate with his complaint. In fact, it was over-the-top and raised suspicion. He wondered if Mayor Gage was involved in whatever dangerous business Madam Secretary wanted him to investigate. Being a SEAL had taught Justice to keep his cards close to his chest. The mayor, though, had just showed his, and Justice smiled to himself. He moved the mayor to the top of his list of people to watch.

Thinking it best to allow Mayor Gage to believe he'd been cowed, he said in a meek tone of voice, "Yes, sir, I understand."

"Good. I'm glad you see things my way. Now, let's join Chief Ferguson and pretend this is the beginning of a great working relationship."

*Arrogant weasel*, Justice thought as they headed back to the press conference room. *I hope I'm right about you. I'd love to throw your ass in jail.*

Linda handed him a large set of keys. "The watch is all yours, Chief McQuaid. Be careful out there." Though she smiled, her eyes passed warily between Justice and the mayor.

Was it a warning? A threat? Or a well-meaning sentiment? Justice's head pounded. Trying to process everything he'd learned tonight was beginning to take its toll on him. He wanted to be cautious, not paranoid.

Returning Linda's smile, he took the keys and gripped her hand. "Thanks. Take care, Chief Ferguson." Justice turned toward the mayor. "Mr. Mayor."

"Chief McQuaid." He shook the proffered hand.

Justice watched Ferguson and Gage leave together.

Next to him Sally commented, "A match made in hell, if you ask me."

He glanced down at her. "You and I need to talk, but not tonight."

"You know where to find me. By the way, I met your father a little while ago, and he took your uniforms out to the car. I gave him a hat and a T-shirt." She grinned. "What a handsome devil."

"You're throwing me over already?" Justice teased.

"Franklin is closer in age." Sally's eyes sparkled. "Good night, Chief. I'll see you tomorrow."

"Good night."

Justice chuckled and shook his head. As he approached his office, without getting lost, he noticed a blond-haired man dressed in plain clothes waiting for him. His badge was attached to his waist along with his gun.

Smiling warmly, the officer held out his hand. "Hi, Chief McQuaid. I'm Sergeant David Hutchinson, your IT guru. Everyone calls me Hutch. I've got your laptop and tablet ready to issue to you. I'll walk you through the system, and we'll set up a login that is unique to you."

"Nice to meet you, Hutch. Let's go into my office."

They'd been working for half an hour when Sergeant Westfall brought them a platter of grilled shrimp tacos and bottles of water.

"I thought you'd be hungry, Chief." She grinned at Justice. "Your father is chowing down at my desk. He's been having a grand time ordering the officers around. If one didn't know better, one might think he was chief."

Justice chuckled. "Yeah, that's my dad. I hope he hasn't frightened my squad too much."

"Nope. By the way, Kalani's food truck on the beach serves the best tacos in the area."

"Good to know. Thanks, Sergeant."

"You're welcome. When you're finished here, I'll take you to the armory. You need your guns, Chief."

"All right. Give us thirty."

"Yes, sir."

* * *

"Dad, I think you'd better drive back to the hotel." Justice handed his father the keys. "I don't feel so well."

In the overhead light Franklin noted his son's pale face and the sweat beading on his forehead. Justice's body trembled as he leaned back in his seat.

"Tonight was overwhelming, but you did it, son. It will be easier tomorrow. Just relax now."

Justice didn't reply. He closed his eyes and willed the heaviness in his head to go away.

When they arrived at the hotel, Justice removed his uniform and took a long, cool shower. The water sluiced down his back as he propped his arms against the tile and hung his head. What had he gotten himself into? He felt as though someone had slammed a meat cleaver into his head, but he needed to figure out a few things before he went to bed.

Justice dressed in a pair of navy sweatpants and joined Franklin in the main area of their suite. He invited him to look over the organizational chart and offer an opinion.

Franklin rubbed his chin, and after a moment of

thoughtful consideration said, "There are a number of civilian positions that either need to be eliminated or main-streamed. Also, I don't think the department needs that many seasonal beach patrol cops. Being new to the area, though, I can't say that's a valid observation."

"Well, the season has just started so I'll keep a close eye on it. As far as the civilian positions are concerned, I agree. I'll do my best to transfer employees because I really don't want to fire anyone."

"So, what do you plan to do, son?"

"Do what I do best. Form an elite team of five men and women I trust implicitly to have my back."

"Good plan."

They discussed their impressions for another half hour before Franklin suggested they hit the sack. Justice popped a couple of Advil liquid-gels and stretched out on his back with his hands clasped beneath his aching head. Anxiety caused his heart to pound, and he began to sweat. If he failed, he wouldn't be able to live with it. Live with himself.

And then in the darkness he heard Franklin's comforting voice.

"You're a McQuaid. A SEAL. And you don't quit. Not even in the face of failure."

Justice relaxed. Closed his eyes. Breathed in and out. And with every breath silently thanked God for his father.

\* \* \*

It felt good to be in uniform again. Justice pinned his badge to his breast pocket, checked and loaded his Glock and shoved it into the holster around his waist. Franklin snapped a picture. Justice frowned at him.

"This isn't the first day of school, Dad."

Franklin snickered. "Isn't it?"

"Very funny. Well, how do I look?"

Franklin cocked his head. "Spiffy. Official."

"I was expecting you to say *intimidating.*"

"That, too."

"Huh."

Franklin grabbed the car keys. "Time to go to school, Chief."

Justice made a face.

A few minutes later they pulled into the spot reserved for the chief of police.

"I'll get the house ready while you're here," Franklin offered. "Call me if you need anything."

Justice read between the lines. God, he loved his father. "No worries. Don't forget we're having dinner tonight with Adrienne."

Franklin rolled his eyes. "How could I forget? You gave me hell about my reticence."

"Pick me up at five-thirty."

"Won't you get your own vehicle?"

"I'll let you know. See you later, Pop."

Justice entered the station and greeted the officers milling around waiting for seven o'clock roll call. Sergeant Westfall met him and escorted him to his office.

"I prepared an agenda for you, Chief," she said. "There are a few things that need your immediate attention, and afterward I'll help you handle whatever comes up."

"I need a cruiser," Justice remarked as he scanned the agenda.

"A Ford Explorer is already in your spot."

He looked up, surprised by her efficiency. "Thanks."

"Are you going out in the field today?"

"Depends on what comes up. I'll play it by ear."

"If you do, take Officer Miguel Rivera with you. He was

born and raised in Laguna Beach and knows the streets better than anyone else."

"Got it."

"Ready for roll call? Captain Locke has graciously agreed to allow you to do it this morning."

"*Graciously?*" Justice repeated, arching an eyebrow.

"Graciously," she confirmed. Her lips twitched a little, trying to suppress a smile.

He rose to his feet. "Let's do this."

Including Tawny as they walked side by side to the roll call room felt right. She gave Justice the impression she would do everything in her power to support his leadership. Only time would tell.

* * *

Captain Everett Locke, a twenty-year veteran, stood at the podium, waiting for Justice. He'd met the older man at his swearing-in the previous evening, and though Captain Locke mentioned that the chief's position should have been his, he also said that Justice's service record and demeanor impressed him. He'd give Justice the benefit of the doubt. As long as the kid didn't step on his toes. Like now. This would be the first and last time he'd tolerate it.

Smiling, he shook Justice's hand and stepped aside.

Justice followed procedure, calling the officers' names and giving them their assignments.

"As always, stay safe. And take care of each other."

Choruses of "Yes, Chief" echoed in the room as the officers filed past him.

Captain Locke gestured toward four officers who hadn't been given their assignments. "What about them?"

"Officers Dooley, Carson, Morton, and Holcomb have a meeting with me."

"What about?"

"Sexual harassment."

"You're kidding. They're good officers."

"Maybe. But I witnessed it firsthand yesterday morning at Pop's Diner. Excuse me, Captain."

In order to avoid an argument with Locke, Justice didn't share what punishment he had planned for the officers. They followed him into his office, and he addressed them from behind his desk.

"I'll make this short and sweet. You're suspended for two weeks without pay. Turn in your badges and your guns."

Officers Morton and Holcomb looked stricken, and a little green, but they complied without protesting. Justice almost felt sorry for them.

Officer Dooley tossed his badge onto the desk and removed his gun from its holster. "This isn't the way you want to start your tenure," he remarked, his voice flat, his eyes unfriendly.

"Is that a threat?" Justice demanded.

Dooley shrugged. "Just sayin'."

He swaggered out of the office without another word.

Officer Carson's unemotional reaction to his suspension and the blankness Justice perceived in his dark eyes worried him far more than Dooley's bluster. It kicked him in the gut, and he sank into his chair. Logging on to his laptop, he pulled up Officer Carson's personnel file. He'd been with the Laguna Beach Police Department for a little more than two years, and his record was clean. Unremarkable, even. And that sent warning bells off in his head.

Exactly who was Officer Nash Carson?

# CHAPTER 5

Justice spent the rest of his morning handling paperwork and touring the facility at his leisure. Everyone he met welcomed him, eagerly discussed their positions with him, and offered their help.

At noon, armed with turkey sandwiches, chips, and two bottles of water, he made his way to the uniform shop, hoping to bribe Sally into having lunch with him.

After he greeted her with a hug, she chuckled. "You're still here."

He smiled. "Yes. I brought turkey sandwiches. Want to join me?"

"Of course."

"Is there somewhere we can talk privately?"

"My sewing room."

She cleared a space for them, and he unpacked the bag of food. God bless Tawny. She anticipated his needs before he knew them himself. He definitely wanted her on his team.

They ate in silence for a few minutes before Justice began, "What did you mean last night when you said that the mayor and Ferguson were a match made in hell?"

Sally popped a chip in her mouth and chewed it. "Because their disagreements were legendary until two years ago. Suddenly, Linda and Mayor Gage are best friends, supporting each other's initiatives and socializing when prior to that they couldn't tolerate one another."

*Right around the same time Officer Carson joined the force.* Justice kept that tidbit of information to himself, wondering if it held any significance.

"Why the about face? Do you think they're having an affair?"

She laughed. "Oh no! Both are totally devoted to their significant others. And to their kids."

Justice swallowed a bite of his sandwich. "So, do you have any theories?"

"Just one. Money. I read a lot of crime thrillers, and when you're in cahoots with someone you normally wouldn't associate with, it's always about money."

Justice smiled. "Follow the money, huh?"

"It generally leads to the truth."

He nodded, and they finished their lunch as Sally spoke about her family.

Contemplating Sally's comment about money being the root of Ferguson's relationship with the mayor, Justice tracked down one of the detectives in the department, Luca Martinelli. He found him in his office.

Tall and slim with dark hair and eyes, Luca greeted Justice in an open and friendly manner as they shook hands.

"Detective Luca Martinelli," he introduced himself. "Just call me Martini." He grinned. "Everyone does."

"Shaken, not stirred?" Justice inquired with a smile.

Luca laughed. "I like you, Chief. Now, what can I do for you?"

"I'm trying to get a handle on things. Tell me about your open cases."

"At the moment we're looking into a rash of stolen cars and B and E's and convenient store robberies. It's the start of the summer tourist season, so we'll see an increase in petty crime and domestic violence."

"What about cold cases?"

"We have our share of the usual. Missing kids and young people." Luca paused. "And then there's the perplexing case of Axel Anderson who disappeared off the grid two years ago."

"Axel Anderson? Who's that?" Justice frowned. This guy disappeared two years ago? Coincidence?

"Old California money. His family made a fortune in Napa Valley. He and his wife and children vanished into thin air. There hasn't been any activity on Anderson's accounts or social media. No digital footprint at all. Security cameras haven't caught hide nor hair of him or his family. The feds gave up looking for them after a year. It's a mystery." He shook his head. "Mayor Gage refuses to give up hope."

Justice's heart rate rose a little. "Mayor Gage? What does he have to do with it?"

"He and Anderson were close friends. Grew up together. Graduated from UCLA. The best man at each other's weddings, that sort of thing. Gage has offered a huge reward for any information regarding the family's disappearance, but so far nothing has panned out."

*Follow the money.* He understood Gage's connection to Anderson, but how did Ferguson fit into the picture?

"Thanks for the update, Martini. Will you keep me posted on the Anderson case if you learn anything new?"

"Absolutely, Chief. Just let me know if I can help you in any way."

Justice shook his hand again and left Martinelli's office. He wondered if Axel Anderson's disappearance had something to do with the reason why Madam Secretary wanted him in Laguna Beach. To keep an eye on the mayor perhaps? Pieces of a puzzle were beginning to take shape in his mind. He just wished he could see the big picture.

Justice slid behind the wheel of his brand-new black Ford Explorer decked out with the latest technology and grinned. "Cool." He called his father to let him know that he'd be driving himself to the beach house and pulled slowly out of his reserved spot. On his way home he stopped at a florist to buy flowers for Adrienne. He didn't know what kind she liked but figured he couldn't go wrong with a bouquet of red roses.

Parked in his driveway, his thoughts strayed toward the woman running on the beach, and he wondered if he'd see her again. So far, there'd been no sign of her. He let out his breath as he approached the front door. Better to focus on the job than on a woman.

He greeted Franklin with a hug and commented, looking around, "You did a nice job with the place, Dad. Thanks."

"You're welcome. The house needed a major cleaning. I bought you a few necessities and stocked the fridge and pantry. When I return to Connecticut, I'll send your personal things." He paused as he studied Justice. "That is, if you've decided to stay and run the police department."

Justice removed his gun belt. "I have. Last night was rough, I'll admit. I was overwhelmed. But today was better. I got a feeling for what I'm doing. Tawny, of course, is a godsend. I want her on my team."

He unbuttoned his shirt. "And I learned a bit of interesting information. An old friend of Mayor Gage's, Axel Anderson, and his entire family disappeared. Totally off the grid. Have you heard his name before?"

"Seems like I have," Franklin answered as he followed his son upstairs. "Rich family, right?"

Justice didn't reply. When he stepped into the master suite and saw the pink comforter and accent pillows, along with pink towels in the bathroom, he burst into hearty laughter.

Tossing one of the pillows at Franklin, he said, still laughing, "Great joke, Dad! I never knew you had a sense of humor."

"I couldn't resist."

"No kidding." Justice turned on the shower, finished stripping, and stepped into the stall. "To answer your question, yes, the Andersons are filthy rich. They own grape vineyards in Napa Valley. Old money."

"Odd," Franklin replied, mulling over the information.

"I thought so, too."

Justice finished his shower and dressed in a pair of black pants, a light blue shirt, and a black tie. He joined his father downstairs and found him holding the bouquet of roses.

"Flowers?"

"They're appropriate." Justice jerked his head toward a bottle of fine red wine. "For Adrienne?"

"It's appropriate," Franklin intoned, mimicking his son.

As they left the beach house, Justice ordered, "Please be nice to Adrienne."

"You sound like me."

"Yeah, well, there are times when I feel the need to parent you."

"Huh."

Justice glanced sideways at Franklin and grinned.

* * *

Nervous apprehension swept through Adrienne as she

double-checked her preparations for dinner with the McQuaids. She wanted everything to be perfect this evening. Not knowing whether or not there would be a Mrs. McQuaid joining them, she set an extra place at the formal dining room table. Just as she lit a couple of candles, the doorbell rang.

Smoothing her dress, a simple pale blue sheath, and patting her hair, Adrienne took a deep breath and opened the front door. She greeted them with a smile and said, "Welcome to my home. Come in."

The McQuaids stepped across the threshold and looked around with interest. The furnishings were comfortable and inviting.

Justice presented the bouquet of red roses. "For you, Adrienne. Thank you for opening your home to us."

"They're lovely. And you're welcome." Her soft gaze met Franklin's as she accepted his offering. "Red wine will go perfectly with our meal. I hope you like chicken parmesan?"

"One of my favorites," Justice assured her.

"I'm glad." She turned toward the kitchen, and they followed her.

As Adrienne arranged the flowers in a vase, she murmured, "I thought you might bring your mother with you, Justice."

She felt, rather than saw, Franklin stiffen, and the air suddenly grew tense between them. She knew she'd made a terrible blunder when she turned to face her guests. Franklin looked stricken with grief, but Justice just appeared sad.

"My mother died five years ago," he replied. "Cancer."

Adrienne's countenance reflected her sorrow. "I'm so sorry." She glanced at Franklin. "I'm sorry. I didn't know…" Her eyes flicked toward Franklin's wedding ring which caused her misunderstanding.

"Please, don't apologize. Here, allow me to pour the wine," Franklin offered.

His hand brushed hers. Little tingles of excitement rushed through her. She moved away from him, too confused by the feelings he aroused in her to stand close to him.

When they settled around the dining room table, Adrienne asked if they were opposed to saying grace. They shook their heads and reached for each other's hands. She kept her remarks brief because sparks were shooting up her arm, and she wanted to break the contact with Franklin as soon as possible. Even after she snatched her hand from his, she still felt its warmth seeping into her skin.

While they ate chicken parmesan on beds of spaghetti and fresh garlic bread, conversation flowed freely around the table. They shared their interests and spoke about their careers, and other innocuous subjects, carefully avoiding topics that were too painful or personal. Adrienne allowed the McQuaids to lead the direction of their interaction with each other, enjoying the banter between them. She appreciated their old-fashioned manners. These men understood how to treat a woman. They made her feel special and valued, something she hadn't felt in a while.

When she announced she'd made a sweet strawberry crème pie for dessert and rose from her chair, both Justice and Franklin leaped to their feet. Justice offered to help and followed her into the kitchen.

While a pot of coffee brewed and Justice cut slices of the decadent pie, he asked, ` "Adrienne, did you know Axel Anderson?"

"Oh, heavens, yes. Everyone knew him. It's a tragedy what happened to Axel and his family."

"Did you ever socialize with him and his wife?"

"At dinner parties and events hosted by Mayor Elliot Gage. My husband and I weren't close friends of his." She offered a slight laugh. "Not rich enough. I think we were included simply because Joel, my husband, was a colonel and lent them respectability they were otherwise lacking."

"And the mayor? What do you think about him?"

Adrienne made a face as she poured three cups of coffee. "Fake. About as fake as his wife's…" She broke off and glanced at Justice, who grinned at her. "Well, you get the idea. I haven't received a social invitation since Joel died. Elliot insisted on giving the eulogy at Joel's service just to make himself look good. I think he's disgusting."

Justice set the mugs of coffee and slices of pie on a silver serving tray. "Adrienne, what do you think happened to the Andersons?"

"I honestly don't know. If someone kidnapped the entire family, he, or they, went to a lot of trouble to make the Andersons' disappearance look as if they just left of their own accord. Not a shred of evidence to suggest otherwise."

"Is it possible that Mayor Gage…and former Chief Ferguson…know what happened and are keeping it a secret? Maybe because that's what Axel wanted?"

Adrienne met his inquiring gaze. "It's possible, I guess. The mayor and the chief did get very friendly with each other after that."

"Will you do me a favor and keep this conversation just between us?"

"What conversation?" She smiled at him.

After Justice and Franklin devoured the majority of the pie and drank multiple cups of coffee, they announced their leave. Justice held Adrienne's hands in his, leaned down, and pressed a platonic kiss against her soft cheek.

"Good night, Adrienne. Thank you for a wonderful dinner and evening."

"You're welcome. It was my pleasure. Please don't be

strangers." Adrienne looked at Franklin, expecting him to say something, but he merely inclined his head.

"Don't worry," Justice interjected in order to cover the awkward silence between Adrienne and Franklin. "I'll come over so often for a homecooked meal you'll get tired of me."

Adrienne offered a sweet smile. "I don't think that's possible."

* * *

At loose ends the following morning after Justice left for the station, Franklin decided to burn off his restless energy by going for a long run on the beach. Last night, Justice had noticed his reaction to Adrienne, damn him! He'd actually hugged him for being kind to their hostess. Justice mentioned they had the loss of their spouses to cancer in common, and maybe, just maybe, getting to know Adrienne and spending time with her would give Franklin a reason to stay in California. Justice wasn't too proud to admit, selfishly, that he wanted his father with him. He'd said he and Franklin may not always see eye to eye, but they loved one another unconditionally.

Pushing aside his thoughts, he stopped intermittently to introduce himself to the Laguna Beach cops on duty, most of whom expressed their acceptance of their new chief. By the time he returned to the house, he realized running on the beach hadn't helped to reduce the anxiety caused by the internal struggle between his need to remain faithful to his deceased wife and his need to feel a woman's arms around him. Swearing aloud, damning his soul to hell for what he was about to do, Franklin took a shower and dressed in a pair of jeans and a polo shirt. Before he lost his nerve, he grabbed his car keys and wallet and left the house.

A few minutes later he strolled into Laguna Beach Realty,

startling Adrienne who was speaking to a client on the phone. She lifted a finger to indicate she'd be a minute longer and returned to her conversation. After promising she'd have an answer for the client by the end of the day, she hung up and smiled at Franklin.

"Hi. What brings you by? Is everything all right at the house?"

Franklin quelled the rapid beating of his heart at the sight of her. She was as pretty as a bunch of wildflowers in bloom across a meadow in the springtime.

"Yes, yes, the house is great. I don't think Justice needs that much room, but it makes him happy." He paused, meeting her unwavering gaze. "I…I'd like to invite you to lunch. That is, if you're free."

"I am. Just let me get my purse."

Franklin opened the passenger door and helped Adrienne into the seat. Once he settled behind the wheel, he asked, "Where would you like to eat?"

"There's a wonderful bistro on the pier."

"All right, then. Sounds good."

Adrienne showed Franklin where to park, and they walked the short distance to the pier. A perky young woman wearing jeans and a bright yellow T-shirt advertising Sam's Beach Club led them to a table overlooking the water and took their drink order. When their waitress returned with two glasses of lemonade, they chose blackened mahi fish sandwiches and French fries and handed their menus to her.

Alone, they fell silent a moment before Adrienne began softly, "I have to admit I'm curious why you invited me to lunch. The truth is, I don't think you like me very much."

Franklin studied the knot holes in the wooden table, unable to look at her. "I'm sorry if I gave you that impression, Adrienne, because that's not how I feel. At all."

That surprised her. "May I ask how you *do* feel?"

Heat rose in him as his eyes finally met hers. "Alive."

She nodded. "What do you miss the most, Franklin?"

"This. Having lunch. Enjoying companionship with someone. Sharing all the small moments that make up a day."

Tears misted her eyes. "So do I. Do you recall that movie with Richard Gere and Susan Sarandon? *Shall We Dance?* There's a line in it that really hit me. Sarandon's character thinks her husband, Gere, is having an affair when he's just taking dance lessons, so she hires a PI to follow him. When she's told the truth, the PI asked why one gets married in the first place. Her reply? One gets married so we have a witness to our lives. *A witness to our lives.*"

Emotion choked her. Franklin reached out and touched her hand. Gazing at him through unshed tears, she concluded, "That's what I miss. Having a witness to my life. Sometimes... Sometimes I feel invisible."

Franklin opened his mouth to respond, but just then they were interrupted by the arrival of their meal.

By tacit agreement they dropped the subject of their spouses and moved on to other areas of their lives. Adrienne talked about her children, and though she proudly boasted of their accomplishments, a tincture of sadness echoed in her voice. Franklin got the impression they were unmindful of their responsibilities to her. It made him grateful for the relationship he had with Justice.

After they ate they took a leisurely stroll along the beach. Franklin held Adrienne's hand, allowing its warmth to seep into him. He hoped he wasn't misreading the signals she was sending him—the way she caressed his hand, the glow in her eyes, and the soft smile on her face. Well, he'd find out soon enough.

When they returned to his car, he cleared his throat and asked with hesitation, "Do you want me to take you back to work, or...?" His voice trailed off, and he held his breath.

"Or," she responded, her voice low and husky. She laid a hand on his thigh, and his muscles tensed beneath her touch. "Oh, please, *or*."

* * *

As soon as Justice joined his father in the kitchen after arriving home from the station and accepted a spicy Thai salad with a chunk of bread Franklin picked up for dinner, he sensed a difference in him. Franklin wore an expression on his face that Justice recognized all too well—sexual satisfaction.

*Holy shit!*

He wasn't about to ask for details, but Franklin volunteered them anyway.

"I did it," he suddenly announced, causing Justice to choke on a bite of salad. "I did it, and it was…incredible. But I betrayed your mother, so I…I have to leave, son. I can't face the temptation again. I don't expect you to understand this. My heart…my heart has always belonged to one woman, and damn…Damn!" Franklin lowered his head and held it between his hands.

Justice's gut tightened with disappointment and a small twinge of fear. He didn't know if he could do this job without his dad. "What about Adrienne? Does she know you're leaving?"

Franklin's eyes clouded. "Yes. She said she understands why, but…I feel like a… Please don't judge me for taking advantage of Adrienne." He paused. "I'm flying home Saturday morning."

Justice pushed his salad away. "I'm not hungry. Let's go to the gym. I need to work out." He just couldn't talk to Franklin right now. Maybe later, but not now.

# CHAPTER 6

Justice approached the front desk at the local YMCA in order to sign up for a membership. When the young man behind the counter realized Justice was the new chief of police, he said, "There's no charge for your membership, Chief. The Laguna Beach Police Department pays for cops to be members."

"Okay. Great." Justice accepted his membership card and added, "My father is my guest."

"No problem. Let me show you around the facility."

After a brief tour, Franklin started working out on a rowing machine while Justice headed toward a line of treadmills facing a bank of windows. He and another member stepped onto a treadmill at the same time. Glancing curiously to his right, his breath hitched, and he did a double take. It was the woman from the diner. As she began to run at an easy pace, her sassy ponytail swished back and forth. Justice set his speed to match hers; and although he looked straight ahead, his eyes darted toward her, drinking in her appearance.

A sports bra revealed her firm breasts and narrow torso.

Following her form, Justice admired her flat stomach, her small waist, her tight, muscular thighs and legs (imagining them wrapped around him caused his blood to pump even faster through his veins), and her soft, round, perfectly shaped bottom. His mouth went dry thinking about it, and he wished he could see her eyes. From her profile and incredible body, he could tell she was lovely.

At the end of the one-hour time limit on the treadmill, Justice and the woman next to him gradually reduced their speeds until they hit STOP on the panel. They turned toward each other…and Justice stared into the most amazing pair of eyes he'd ever seen.

Amber with brown striations.

Set in a heart-shaped face with high, delicate cheekbones and jawline, pencil-thin eyebrows, a pert nose, and a mouth designed for kissing.

Taken aback by the startling effect of those eyes and the arrangement of her other facial features, Justice stumbled backward off the treadmill.

The woman snickered in amusement.

"That first step is a doozy," she commented before she walked away.

It took several minutes for Justice's heart rate to return to normal, which didn't have anything to do with his workout on the treadmill. He watched the woman tackle the elliptical machine next; in fact, he couldn't tear his eyes away from her as she moved through her routine. Unable to focus on his own workout, he almost dropped a two-hundred-pound barbell, much to his father's annoyance.

"Pay attention!" Franklin snapped. "Before you hurt yourself." Following the direction of Justice's gaze, he added, "Better yet, just go introduce yourself so you can quit ogling that woman."

"No, no. I'm good, Dad. I'm good."

"Terrific. Now, get your head back into the game."

By the time Justice finished lifting weights, the woman was gone. Disappointed, he wrapped up his workout, and he and Franklin returned home.

Unable to sleep due to Franklin suddenly announcing his decision to leave, Justice lay awake, staring at the ceiling. Above the constant sound of the waves crashing against the shore, he detected the low thrum of a number of trucks. At first, he assumed teenagers were out raising hell, but the trucks were running without lights which would have flashed in his bedroom windows. And there was something stealthy about their movement on the beach. He didn't find any evidence of tracks the next morning, and that bothered him.

* * *

Every time she pictured the gorgeous, hunky man falling off the treadmill, Brielle laughed to herself. She'd felt his deep blue eyes on her during her workout, but that was nothing new. She was used to guys constantly checking her out. What *was* new, however, was her reaction to him. His sexy, muscular, well-toned body caused a slow, sweet heat to burn in her. She'd watched him, too, surreptitiously, and liked what she saw. He possessed a quiet and dignified demeanor that was hard to ignore.

Letting out her breath, she took a quick shower and dressed in a pair of cotton sleep shorts and tank top. Grabbing her cell phone and a bottle of water, she stepped outside onto her deck. A full moon shone high in the sky, reflecting its brilliance on the Pacific. Brielle admired the view for a moment before she glanced at her phone and saw that she'd missed a call from Brendan. Quickly, she pressed the CALL icon and waited for him to answer.

"Hey, Bri. I'm glad you returned my call. It's been awhile."

"Whose fault is that?" Brielle shot back. "What's going on with you? We used to be close. Now, you hardly speak to any of us, and you never visit during the holidays. Missing last Christmas really hurt Mom, though she wouldn't admit it."

"We're not kids anymore. Our lives are filled with duties and responsibilities." Brendan paused. "Besides, you're not named after a dead man. Jesus. *Brendan Stewart.* Mom actually used his last name as my middle name. It's a curse. That's how I feel. Cursed."

Brielle shook her head in disbelief. "It's not a curse. It's a blessing. Brendan Stewart loved Mom from the moment he met her when they were freshmen in high school. He was her champion then, and he protected her and loved her even though he either knew or suspected that a part of her heart belonged to Dad. It's a blessing," she repeated. "The Triple B will be transferred to you upon Mom's death. It's what Brendan would have wanted. And let's not forget that Trey is named after Mom's deceased brother. He doesn't complain about it."

Chastised, Brendan deftly changed the subject. "Speaking of Trey, I just spent the night with him and his family. We had a great visit."

"You did? Well, then, I'm glad. When are you going home to see Mom and Dad?" she demanded.

"I don't know. Madam Secretary is dealing with several irons in the fire right now and needs me. I can't get away anytime soon."

Brielle thought he was just making excuses but refrained from challenging him, fearing she might push him away. "I hope you'll make it home for the holidays this year, Brendan."

"I'll do my best," he responded noncommittally. Keeping

his voice carefully modulated, she noted, he continued, "By the way, Bri, how's everything out there?"

The bright lights of a luxury super yacht sailing south a couple of miles off the coast caught Brielle's attention. It was the same one she'd noticed on several occasions and belonged to Mayor Gage who allowed his cronies to throw lavish parties on it. According to gossip, the mayor and his wife sometimes joined their friends, and it was also noted that Chief of Police Linda Ferguson and her husband often attended those private parties. The Fergusons and the Gages made strange bedfellows, she thought.

Setting aside speculation about what was happening on the yacht, she replied, "Great. You know I'm training for SWAT. It's tough, but I'm determined to make it."

"You will," Brendan assured her.

"On my own."

Her implication was clear. With a single phone call from Madam Secretary, she'd be a shoo-in, and even more of a target. She wanted to earn her spot on the team through her own hard work and steely resolve.

"Of course. It's been great talking to you, Bri. I'll try to do a better job of keeping in touch."

"Please do. Love you, Brendan."

"Love you, too. Stay safe."

By the time Brielle pressed the round red STOP button on her cell phone, the super yacht had slipped beyond her sight. She tilted her water bottle to her lips. She'd done a fair job of hiding her frustration over her SWAT training from her brother. Earlier today she'd been thrown to the mat by the other officers, including Howie, so many times she'd lost track. Her sessions in the boxing ring were helping, but she couldn't gain an advantage. Loyal Howie tried to throw their match but ridicule from the others forced him to beat her.

As they'd filed out of the gym, her instructor had issued a

stern warning: if she didn't prove her ability to handle one on one combat, she'd be eliminated from the program. She'd taken down plenty of criminals on the street, but this was different. Tougher. With these guys she didn't have an edge over them.

Needing to talk to Faith about it, she pressed the keypad with her number, but her friend didn't answer her phone. After leaving a message, Brielle went inside, stretched out on her multi-sectional sofa, and found an old Bruce Lee movie on Netflix.

"Come on, Master Lee. Show me some moves I don't already know."

* * *

Music blared an upbeat tempo on the super yacht, fading into silence the farther the sound carried over the water. The privileged guests' raucous laughter as they consumed unlimited amounts of alcohol and danced and flirted and fornicated in the luxurious cabins below deck drowned out the subtle sounds of heavy wooden crates being transferred to a motorboat that tagged alongside the super yacht. No one noticed it, and if they did, they were too drunk to care. Once the motorboat was filled with stacks of crates, it headed toward a particularly rocky part of the coastline.

Several Ford F-250's waited for the shipment. Hands made quick work of moving the crates from the motorboat to the flat beds. No one spoke until someone stumbled and dropped one of the crates. It broke open, spilling its contents onto the sand.

"Fuck!"

The men grabbed the semi-automatic assault rifles and ammunition and threw them back into the crate. One man unobtrusively detached himself from the others and shoved one of the weapons into a crevice between the rocks. He kicked a box of ammunition a few feet away and stomped it into the sand. As soon as he had the opportunity, he'd return for them. But first he had to face the consequences of his stupidity.

When the trucks were loaded, they headed in different directions, but eventually they all turned north toward Oregon.

* * *

Hundreds of miles away in a dark, smoky dive deep on the south side of Chicago, Faith settled on a barstool with a bag that held her handgun and a can of pepper spray. Her driver's license and twenty dollars in cash were tucked inside her cell phone case. While she waited, she refused offers to buy her a drink. She knew better than to eat or drink anything here, though after she explained to the bartender that she was expecting company, he quit giving her crap about not ordering a drink.

At eleven-thirty a man wearing jeans and a dark hoodie perched on the barstool next to her and ordered a bottle of beer.

Looking straight ahead, he murmured, "What do you want?"

"Information. Where are the arms coming from?"

"China. North Korea. Russia. Syria. Take your pick."

"Okay, then. When is the next shipment due?"

"It's already arrived and on the move."

Faith cursed beneath her breath. "Get me inside."

He risked glancing at her. "No fucking way. You're an all-American girl. A patriot. They'll identify you as a plant the moment you step foot inside the compound. Anderson will know you aren't the type to turn against your own country.

And the methods they use…" He shook his head. "They'll kill you. *After* they dehumanize you. I'm lucky I got out alive. You won't see me again. I'm a dead man if they find me."

He drained his bottle of beer and threw a twenty on the counter. "You won't be able to contact me after tonight. My advice? Drop it. You can't stop them."

"I can try."

"You'll die."

Faith winced. "Then I'll die for a noble cause."

He snorted. "You're brave but stupid. Dyin' isn't easy. And Anderson will make it especially painful for you." With that final remark, he turned and left her alone.

A coldness crept through Faith. She had an incredible and frightening story to tell, but first she needed to be on Laguna Beach when the next shipment of weapons arrived, record it on her phone, and follow it straight to Axel Anderson's compound which she knew was located somewhere in Oregon. Only then would she alert the authorities.

*Brave but stupid.*

* * *

On Saturday morning Justice and Franklin decided to eat breakfast at Pop's Diner before heading to the airport. A couple of officers were having eggs and coffee at the end of their shift and greeted the McQuaids as they were seated. Justice looked around for the gorgeous, amber-eyed woman he'd seen at the YMCA, but she wasn't there.

After a waitress poured cups of coffee for them, Justice said in a low voice just in case anyone was listening, "I've only been on the job for a few days, Dad. I don't want you to leave. I need you."

Guilt swept through Franklin. Justice saw it in his eyes. Guilt over sleeping with Adrienne because he couldn't control his libido. Guilt over abandoning his son because he couldn't handle the feelings Adrienne invoked in him. He was leaving both of them and heading back to his empty house haunted by the spirit of his beloved wife.

"Son, I beg you, please don't make this any more difficult for me than it already is. You've got this. The department is behind you one hundred percent. I can tell the difference even in the short amount of time you've been chief. Don't ever underestimate your ability to lead."

Justice waited until they'd been served their breakfast before he replied, "Your love and loyalty and respect for Mom are admirable, Dad, and I hope I feel that way about a woman someday. But Mom made it clear she didn't want you to live a lonely, empty life. It's been five years. You've grieved. Every day. It's all right for you to find happiness again."

Justice saw the tug-of-war between Franklin's brain and his heart—his heart wrapped in old memories and a lifetime of loving just one woman—playing across his weathered face.

"Justice, I pray every day that you'll find a woman worthy of your love. A woman who will return your love and stand proudly by your side. That is my greatest hope for you."

What could Justice say after that? He couldn't change Franklin's mind. His father was dead set on returning to Connecticut. They finished eating in silence, lost in their private thoughts.

At the airport, though, Justice tried one more time to convince Franklin to stay with him.

"Dad, please consider moving to California. I can't stand the idea of your being alone. You don't have to sell the house that you and Mom built. If you discover you can't be happy here, you can return to Connecticut. At least you can say you tried, and I won't stop you from leaving. And you don't have to see Adrienne again, if that's an issue for you." To his great mortification, hot tears stung his eyes.

Seeing Justice's emotional reaction caused tears to spring to Franklin's own eyes. Swallowing heavily, he replied, "I promise I'll consider it. I may get home and feel those walls closing around me."

He pulled Justice into a tight hug. "I love you, son. Never doubt how much. You're going to do great things for this community."

"Thanks for that. Your faith in me means the world to me. Call me as soon as you get home. I love you, Dad."

"I will."

A voice over a loudspeaker announcing Franklin's flight interrupted them. He gripped his son's shoulders a moment, told him he loved him one more time, and hurried toward the boarding gate.

Needing to keep his mind occupied after Franklin left, Justice checked in with the dispatch officer who worked weekends, informing her that he was on duty patrolling the coastline, and changed into his beach uniform. He backed his department UTV, which he kept at the house, out of his driveway and drove down to the beach.

Clear blue skies and warm weather brought people to the beach in droves. Some surfed the waves; others tossed frisbees or played volleyball. Justice let two other cops on patrol know that he'd joined them and waved at the lifeguards. Behind his dark sunglasses he eyed pretty young women in bikinis who flirted with him, but he kept his distance. None of them appealed to him.

And then he saw her. Tiger Eyes. Running toward him on the beach. Justice sped up and turned sharply to his left, spraying sand as he brought the UTV to an abrupt stop right in her path.

She came up short and stumbled, nearly falling forward onto the UTV.

Yanking out her earbuds, she yelled, "Are you crazy? I could have been seriously hurt!"

Justice pointed at his head. "Brain injury. I'm a retired SEAL."

"And they let you drive this thing?" Incredulity laced her voice.

He flashed a broad grin. "I make this thing look good. Name's Justice McQuaid, Chief of Police, Laguna Beach."

She rolled her eyes. "Yeah, right, Beach Boy." She tucked her buds back in her ears and started to move past the UTV.

Justice leaped from the UTV and blocked her. "Not so fast. Name and ID, please." Behind his sunglasses his eyes shone with mirth. He didn't have the right to detain her of course; he just wanted to know her name, and he'd let her go in a minute.

She wasn't the least bit amused by his antics. "Okay, you want to play cop? Let's play, then. I don't have my ID or my badge on me, but I'm Sergeant Brielle McAdams, LAPD."

Justice ripped off his sunglasses and stared at her. In the sunlight her eyes glinted like pure gold. His heart slammed into his chest, and his stomach tightened with his attraction to her.

"Yeah, right, Beach Girl," he drawled, mocking her. "Impersonating a cop is a federal offense. Don't move." Speaking into his shoulder mic, he addressed Hutch. "Hey, I've detained a woman without any ID who claims she's Sergeant Brielle McAdams, LAPD."

"On it." Within moments Hutch whistled. "Oh, Chief, you just stepped in deep doo-doo. Sergeant Brielle McAdams, LAPD. Numerous medals and letters of commendation for bravery extraordinaire. Training to be a SWAT officer. Daughter of former U.S. Attorney Cameron McAdams and," he chuckled, "world-renowned historical romance author Brianna Birmingham. Noteworthy brothers are Dr. Trey McAdams, FBI profiler with the BAU, and Brendan McAdams, chief staff member to Secretary of State Barbara Washburn. As I said, you're in deep, deep doo-doo."

"Repeat that last part, Hutch."

"You're in deep…"

"No, before that," Justice interrupted.

"Brendan McAdams, who works with Madam Secretary, is Sergeant McAdams' brother. I'm sending you a photo of her now."

Justice's phone pinged. As he perused her photo, he thought, *Jesus Christ. Brendan McAdams is her brother. I might have known. I wonder if she's part of what's happening out here.*

His eyes met hers. God Almighty, they mesmerized him. "Sorry, Sergeant," he muttered. "A word of advice, though. Keep your ID and at least your badge on you from now on, if not your gun."

"Duly noted, *Chief.*"

Brielle took off running down the beach. Justice watched her until she disappeared around a large rock formation.

# CHAPTER 7

Out of his sight, Brielle slowed to a walk and caught her breath. *Chief of Police? No way.* She scrolled through her contacts and pressed the CALL icon for Tex.

"Hey, pretty girl, what's up?"

"Tex, I just met a cop who claims he's not only a retired SEAL but the new chief of police of Laguna Beach. Justice McQuaid. Will you look him up?"

"Don't need to. He's legit. I met him a couple of months ago at Walter Reed. Impeccable character. Superior service record."

"What happened to him?"

"You'll have to ask him yourself. It's not my story to tell."

"That's not likely. The chief and I didn't hit it off too well when he detained me on the beach."

Tex chuckled. "And so it begins."

"What's that supposed to mean?"

"You know what it means."

Brielle groaned. "Oh, jeez, now you're just talking a bunch of romantic nonsense. Okay, let's move on. Have you or

Melody spoken to Faith lately? I tried calling her a couple of days ago, but her phone went straight to voicemail."

"No, we haven't. Is something wrong?"

"I'm not sure. She sounded really strange the last time I spoke to her. You're tracking her, right?" Tex tracked everyone in his close circle of friends.

He checked one of his computer screens. A red dot representing Faith indicated that she was at the *Chicago Sun-Times*.

"Yeah, I've got her. She's at work."

"Maybe I'll try calling her later on. I appreciate your looking out for her."

"It's what I do. Take care, Brielle. Say hi to Justice for me." He laughed.

"Very funny."

After she and Tex promised to keep in touch, Brielle resumed jogging. Within a few feet, however, she tripped and fell face forward onto the sand. Assuming she'd stumbled over a rock, Brielle sat up and looked around. Half buried in the sand she discovered a white box.

"What in the world?"

Only guessing what it might contain, she removed the loose, flowing tunic she wore over her sports bra and used it to pull the box out of the sand. There weren't any labels on it, but she recognized its contents simply by the weight of the box. She decided to open it at home and rose to her feet, keeping the box carefully covered with her tunic. As she walked along the crowded beach, she searched for Justice but couldn't find him. If what she suspected was correct, the chief ought to know about it.

Brielle stepped inside her large, modern kitchen a few minutes later and slid a sharp knife along the edge of the box. Wearing latex gloves, she flicked open the lid and let out a small gasp of astonishment even though she knew what she'd find—a cache of 100 round Beta C-mags.

"Oh, my God," she murmured. "This can't be good."

She needed to inform Justice, but she was scheduled to teach a self-defense class at the YMCA in an hour. She locked the box of ammunition in her gun cabinet, showered, changed, and left the house.

\* \* \*

Justice went off duty at five-thirty. He changed into a pair of camouflage cargo shorts and an old Navy T-shirt and flipflops and headed down to the beach again. As he passed Brielle's house, he glanced up at the deck, but it was empty. He wanted to apologize to her for the debacle earlier that morning but was afraid she'd slam the door in his face.

Approaching one of the large rock formations that comprised the coast, he put Brielle out of his mind and focused on the task at hand. Hoisting himself onto the rocks, he looked down and nearly lost his balance.

"What the fuck?" He reached into the crevice and pulled out a military grade assault rifle. His heart pounded as he considered the implications. "How the hell did an HK416 end up on my beach?"

Although it would expose his Glock tucked in the small of his back, Justice removed his T-shirt and wrapped it around the assault rifle in order to preserve any fingerprints or other trace evidence that might be on it and to avoid scaring any beach-goers he'd encounter on the way back to his house. Now, he knew for certain that the trucks he'd heard on the beach were real, and he wondered if their drivers were just playing around or if something more sinister was afoot.

A few observant people on the beach noticed the object he carried, and in spite of his badge pinned to the waistband of his cargo shorts, they shied away from him.

As Justice drew parallel to Brielle's house, he heard her shout, "Hey, Beach Boy!" She gestured for him to join her.

His heart beat a little faster when he saw her. She looked hot in a long, flowing white skirt that sat low on her hips. A slit up the side revealed a shapely leg and thigh. The matching off-the-shoulder midriff she wore left a good deal of her torso bare, and his eyes devoured her.

Her gaze settled on his naked, muscular chest glistening with a light sheen of sweat and salt spray, and traveled downward, landing on his rock-hard abs.

Gesturing toward his T-shirt, she began, clearly uncomfortable, "Um, do you mind…?"

Justice chuckled low in his throat as he carefully set the assault rifle against the deck railing and pulled on his T-shirt. "Better?" he teased.

Brielle tilted her head. Her eyes sparkled as she offered a slow smile. "No. Just less of a distraction." Growing serious, she added, "Where did you find the HK416?"

"In between the rocks a quarter mile south of here. Looks like someone deliberately tossed it into the crevice."

"Wait here. I'll be right back."

She returned with the box of Beta C-mags. "I found this stomped into the sand a few feet past the rocks. I wanted to tell you about it as soon as I could, but I didn't see you." She paused. "By the way, Tex says hi."

So, she'd checked him out. He didn't mind. Not after the way he'd embarrassed her that morning. "You know Tex?"

"Friend of the family."

"Well, I'm sorry about this morning." He met her direct gaze. "Anyway, have you ever heard trucks on the beach?"

She appeared startled for a moment. "I thought I imagined them."

"You didn't. I heard them two nights ago. I guessed there was a bunch of teenagers carousing on the beach, but they weren't running lights or hootin' and hollerin'. No trace of them, either. This doesn't sit right with me. Something is definitely going on. I'm taking the HK416 to the lab and testing it for prints. See if anything comes up." He indicated the box of ammunition. "I assume you'd like to do the same with the Beta C-mags."

"If you don't mind. It's your jurisdiction."

"Nah, I don't mind. I'd like your input. Let me know what you find, and I'll do the same."

He started to remove his T-shirt again, but Brielle stopped him. "I just sat down to dinner. Want to join me?"

Justice glanced dubiously at her small tossed salad with slices of avocado on top, and she laughed.

"I have a thick rib-eye marinating in the fridge that's large enough for us to share. If you'll grill it, I'll add a couple of loaded baked potatoes."

"Deal."

Brielle handed Justice a bottle of beer, and while the steak grilled, they talked shop.

When she wanted to know if he lived on the beach, he nodded. "I'm renting a split-level a few hundred yards from your place."

"Oh? Just renting?"

He thought he detected a note of disappointment in her voice. "For the time being. I'm waiting to see if this works out before I buy a home." His eyes held hers.

Did she blush under his intense regard, or did he just imagine the color staining her cheeks?

She murmured, "I think the potatoes are done."

Alone, Justice turned his attention toward the steak. *I really like her*, he thought. In the past, he'd never dated women in the military, and he wasn't sure he wanted to get involved with a cop. But for Brielle, he'd make an exception. She'd captivated him.

She rejoined him a few minutes later with two plates bearing baked potatoes smothered with butter and sour cream and two more bottles of beer. They'd already eaten the tossed salad she'd prepared as an appetizer. Justice turned off the gas grill and plopped a piece of the rib-eye on each plate.

A cool breeze off the ocean caressed them while they ate, lifting loose tendrils of Brielle's hair. Her sleek side ponytail, hanging down one shoulder, drew his heated gaze more than once.

After complimenting his culinary skills, she said, "You know, I spoke to Tex about you this morning. He said if I wanted to know your story, I had to ask you myself. So, I guess this is me asking you to tell me how you ended up in Laguna Beach."

Justice's eyes clouded, and he took a swig of his beer. "My team and I were in Afghanistan to deliver supplies to a village of mainly women and children, so we were told. They were sick and dying, in need of medical attention. And then out of nowhere our Humvee was hit by a rocket launcher. My men, my friends, died instantly. I didn't. The next thing I remember was waking up in Walter Reed Hospital, my head swathed in bandages and my face so swollen I could barely see. And I was temporarily paralyzed." He paused and drank deeply of his beer. "I was their lieutenant commander. It was my duty, my *responsibility*, to protect them and I failed. *I failed.*"

His final words spoken so quietly must have stirred Brielle's compassion. Her eyes glowed like liquid gold as she reached across the table and covered one of his hands with hers.

"I'm sorry, Justice," she murmured. "I can't imagine how you must have felt."

The softness of her voice and the equally soft touch of her hand sent sparks of excitement shooting through Justice's body, but bitterness laced his voice when he resumed speaking.

"I hadn't recovered from my injuries when the Navy delivered the next blow—I was being retired. No explanation. Just a cavalier 'Thank you for your service. Oh, by the way, here's another medal. Another letter of commendation.'"

By this time he'd flipped the position of their hands. He caressed her palm and watched the gold light in her eyes grow slightly darker. When his thumb brushed the sensitive skin on her wrist, he heard her sudden intake of breath, and her pulse quickened beneath his touch.

"No explanation?" she repeated, a little breathlessly.

"None," he confirmed. "And then at my honor ceremony I received a job offer from your brother Brendan on behalf of Madam Secretary."

"What?" Surprised, she withdrew her hand from his. "You met Brendan?"

"Yes." He swallowed a bite of his steak. "You really have to laugh at how our government works. Brendan approaching me. Hinting at a job. Awaiting a call from Madam Secretary herself. All very clandestine, and as I said to my father, total bullsh—" He caught himself and flashed a smile. "Sorry."

"No need to apologize. So, the job offer. Police Chief of Laguna Beach, I presume."

"Correct." He waved a hand toward the HK416. "Madam Secretary caught wind of something happening and sent me out here to be her eyes and ears."

Brielle shook her head. "Forgive me, Justice, but that doesn't make any sense. I mean, I'm sure you're very good at what you do..."

"*Did*," he interrupted. "I was very good at what I did. I'm learning how to be a cop by the seat of my pants. But you're right. It doesn't make any sense, and the more I think about it the more I suspect Secretary Washburn wanted me focused on something other than the Navy."

"Because she's hiding the truth about what happened in Afghanistan."

"That's what I figure."

"My brother probably knows, too."

"That would be my guess." He saw the determined look in her eyes and wagged a finger at her. "Oh, no you don't, Sergeant. Stay out of it, please."

She shrugged, which he accepted as her acquiescence.

When they finished eating, Brielle offered dessert. "Peach cobbler," she enticed him.

"My favorite." He grinned at her. If she'd said she was serving tar, it wouldn't have mattered. She'd already ensnared him.

He was staring out to sea when she returned to the deck with two heaping bowls of warm peach cobbler topped with scoops of vanilla ice cream. Turning toward her, he smiled and accepted the dessert.

Justice shoved a spoonful into his mouth and groaned. "You baked this? It's the best peach cobbler I've ever eaten."

Brielle emitted a hearty guffaw. "Sorry, Justice, but I can't take credit for it. I hate cooking and baking. My mom made this. She freezes her cobblers and cookies and pies and sends them to me. It's an old joke in my family that she snagged my dad with one of her peach cobblers."

*You didn't need a peach cobbler to snag me*, he thought. "That sounds like a story," he commented.

"Oh, it is," she replied, and launched into her parents' love story.

"Wow. What an incredible tale," he remarked when she'd finished recounting it.

"How did your parents meet?" she asked, taking a bite of vanilla ice cream.

It lingered on her lips, and he wanted to lick it off. Swallowing heavily, he responded, "My parents' courtship and marriage were all very ordinary. They met in high school. Got engaged before my dad shipped out on his first tour of duty. Had me a couple of years after they were married." He smiled a moment before his eyes filled with sadness. "I lost my mom to cancer five years ago."

She touched his arm, briefly this time, he noticed. "You've been through a lot. Again, I'm so sorry for you and your dad."

"He's never gotten over it. I wanted him to stay here with me, but he left this morning."

Brielle didn't know what to say, so she offered him a cup of coffee. They drank the brew and watched the sun sink low in the sky, painting the horizon with glorious shades of pink and yellow. When darkness fell, Justice announced his leave.

"I have an idea, Brielle. Let's work on this mystery together. Why don't I pick you up in the morning around nine? We have a brand-new state-of-the-art forensic lab I'd love to show you."

Her face brightened with interest. "I'd like that."

"Breakfast at Pop's Diner?" he suggested.

She wrinkled her pert nose. "No, thanks."

Justice laughed softly. "Oh, I took care of that problem for you. I suspended the officers who disrespected you for two weeks without pay. Not only that but all sworn officers and civilian personnel are required to complete a minimum of six hours of sensitivity and sexual harassment training. They're not happy about it, of course, but there it is."

"You were there, and did this for me?"

"Yes, I did. I will not tolerate that kind of behavior from the men—or women—under my command."

Her eyes held his, a soft light turning them into molten gold. "Okay, then. Breakfast at Pop's Diner."

She helped him wrap the HK416 in a large black trash

bag, and as he started to walk down the steps toward the beach, he suddenly snapped his fingers.

"I almost forgot. I hope you don't mind riding on the back of a motorcycle. Other than my department vehicle, it's the only transportation I have. I picked it up yesterday afternoon, much to my dad's concern. He thinks motorcycles are dangerous."

A lovely smile crossed Brielle's face. "Come with me. I want to show you something."

He followed her down to the garage. Its glass windows afforded a spectacular view of the beach. Just as spectacular, though, was the Harley-Davidson Sportster XL883N parked proudly in its sacred spot.

"Awesome!" Justice exclaimed, running his hand across the handlebars and the seat. He checked out every inch of it, commenting on its features. "What a beauty." He glanced at her. *And so are you.*

She beamed with pride. "I love it. When I started commuting to LA, I wanted something economical that would also give me freedom. I hate being cooped up in a car for long periods of time." She let out a soft sigh of exasperation. "My parents, on the other hand, think I'm going to kill myself on it. That's not an exaggeration. I literally have to text them every time I head to work and again when I get home. They are more afraid of my being on a motorcycle than they are of my being in the field."

"They love you," he responded, his voice quiet.

"I know. I'm very fortunate. So, to answer your question, I can't wait to ride your bike."

She smiled at him. His heart somersaulted. *Oh, Christ. Hutch was right. I'm in deep, deep doo-doo.*

They returned to the deck. Moonlight glinted on the dark Pacific. Somewhere down the beach burned a small fire, and the strains of a guitar floated on the breeze.

"I think I'd better check that out after I lock this up," Justice remarked.

He took her hand and drew her toward him. Looking deep into her eyes, he kissed the palm of her hand, then her wrist. "Thanks. For listening. And for a great dinner." Leaning down, he pressed his warm lips against her soft cheek. "I'll see you in the morning."

* * *

It wasn't a date, Brielle convinced herself. Not. A. Date. The dinner she just shared with the hottest guy she'd ever seen. No. Not just hot. Sweet. Sensitive. Strong. His bulging muscles, even the veins on the back of his hands, were a testament of Justice's strength. And oh how gentle were those hands caressing hers. And oh how incredibly sweet were those lips pressed against her cheek. And oh how blue were those eyes watching her, assessing her, trusting her. No, it wasn't a date. Their meeting had been entirely an accident. Or Fate. But it was better than any date she'd ever been on. *Ever.*

In that moment the universe revealed itself in a vivid splash of color. For the first time she envisioned a future that didn't just include becoming a SWAT commander. She finally understood. And there was only one person who could reassure her that she wasn't crazy for feeling like this.

Collapsing breathlessly onto her multi-sectional sofa, she reached for her cell phone on the glass-topped coffee table and pressed the CALL icon.

"Mom, hi, I hope I'm not calling too late," she said in a rush.

"No, of course not," Brianna replied, her warm voice as soothing as always. "Your father is tending to a sick mare down in the stable, and I'm just puttering around in the kitchen. What's going on?"

"Puttering" usually meant Brianna was whipping up something fabulous to eat.

"It's true. It's *all true*. Every word you write in your novels. Everything you and Dad always said about looking into each other's eyes and just *knowing*, because...because it happened to me," Brielle declared, her voice rising with excitement. "Today. All he did was take my hand in his, look into my eyes, and kiss me on the cheek, and I thought I would swoon. *Swoon*, Mom! A swoon-worthy kiss on the cheek! When have you ever heard me say something like that?"

"Never," Brianna returned.

"I know, right? I've never felt like this about anyone. He's perfect, Mom. Not only is he gorgeous, he's so incredibly sweet, sensitive, and intelligent." She paused to catch her breath. "He has a quiet, commanding presence that makes me feel safe. *Safe*. I've never felt safe with any other man I've been with. That's important, isn't it?"

"Yes, it is, but there's something even more important, sweetheart." Brianna's voice held a teasing note.

"There is?"

"His name."

Brielle laughed self-consciously. "Oh, right. Justice McQuaid. Chief of Police, Laguna Beach."

# CHAPTER 8

"Dad, I really *have* to go," Justice insisted as he glanced at his military wristwatch for the tenth time.

"Hit the pause button, son. You've been alone for a long time. It's been years since you were in a serious relationship, and don't forget how that one ended. In a *Dear Justice* text message. I don't want that to happen to you again. All I'm suggesting is that you slow down."

"Okay, okay. May I please be excused now?" he demanded, half amused, half exasperated.

Franklin expelled his breath. "Call me later."

"Yeah, of course."

Justice pinned his badge to his belt and shoved his Glock into the small of his back. He picked up his helmet, wallet, and keys and headed outside. He hopped on his motorcycle and revved the engine. Pure power vibrated through him, filling him with energy. It exhilarated him, pumping him up for the day ahead. But thoughts of the woman who revved his *other* engine interrupted his concentration, causing his heart to slam against his rib cage. His father had the gall to caution him about Brielle when

Franklin jumped into bed with Adrienne after knowing her for forty-eight hours. At least he didn't have any plans to do *that*. Not yet anyway.

A couple of minutes later Justice pulled into Brielle's circular driveway. He hung his helmet on the handlebars and approached the double set of dark walnut doors. Ringing the bell, he waited, heart pounding and blood racing through his veins.

Brielle pulled open the door and smiled at him. "Hi."

She looked adorable in a pair of jeans and a light blue T-shirt with a fluffy white kitten on it. Her shiny dark hair hung loose this morning, parted on the side. Justice felt his gut tighten.

"Aw…sweet," he commented, staring at her chest.

Brielle grinned at him as heat rose in his cheeks. "What can I say? I love fluffy white kittens." She clipped her badge to her jeans and tucked her gun into her waistband.

Justice glanced around the enormous, airy living room. Its entire west side was comprised of glass which provided a magnificent view of the ocean. "Do you own a kitten?"

She reached for her helmet. "No. I haven't lived here that long, and, honestly, I've been too busy to adopt a pet."

"Oh? I just assumed you've lived in Laguna Beach since attending the police academy."

"No. I moved down here from LA several months ago." She saw the question in his eyes. "Long story, which I'll tell you over breakfast."

Justice followed her outside. When she saw his bike, she burst into laughter.

"You didn't tell me your ride was the same make and model as mine!"

He shrugged, smiling at her. "Yours is prettier than mine. I'm actually jealous."

Brielle chuckled, fastened her helmet and climbed on

behind him, wrapping her arms around his waist. His heart rate spiked.

"Hey, I almost forgot. Do you have the ammo?"

"It's in my backpack. Where's the HK416?"

"I locked it in the evidence room last night."

"You're learning, Beach Boy."

He smiled. "Hang on."

Out on the open highway, Justice went full throttle. Brielle clutched him tighter, her breasts crushed against his back. She pressed her hands against his abs and ripples of pleasure coursed through him. As he reveled in her touch, he was sure he'd just taken a nosedive off a cliff. Something that had never happened to him. Ever. He wanted the ride to Pop's Diner to go on forever and regretted its brevity.

As they entered the diner, choruses of "Hey, Chief!" and "Good morning, Chief!" greeted Justice. He took the time to shake hands and speak to everyone who addressed him.

When he and Brielle slipped into a booth, an odd feeling gripped him as he drowned in the gold depths of her eyes, glowing with admiration for him. Oh, God, what was happening?

After a waitress poured two cups of coffee and took their order of pancakes, scrambled eggs, hash browns, and bacon, Justice cleared his throat.

"So, how did you end up in Laguna Beach?"

Brielle took a sip of her coffee. "Two years ago my dad was invited to showcase his series of photographs of Maine's lighthouses at an art gallery in LA. Malcom, my ex, recognized my dad and fawned over him. That's how we met. Dad invited him to eat dinner with us after the showing. Malcolm is an artist and monopolized Dad's attention, much to my family's amusement.

"To make a long story short, Malcolm and I started dating, and two months later I moved in with him. Big

mistake. He had an artist's temperament, and, well. . . I just
didn't have the time, patience, or inclination to stroke his
fragile ego. Anyway, on the night of his big break, an exhibit
at The Broad, I'd spent the day involved in a gang war. By the
time I got home, I just wanted to crawl into bed. I totally
forgot about Malcolm's event. He came home sometime
during the middle of the night and ranted at me for being a
lousy girlfriend, and worse, emasculating him. Then he
threw me out of his apartment."

Justice frowned. Righteous anger swept through him.
"What? In the middle of the night?"

"Yes. I bought my house in Laguna Beach the next day. I
was sick of living in LA."

"Were you in love with him?" he asked, his voice soft.

"For about a minute." Her eyes pinned him. "Okay, Chief.
Your turn. What's your worst relationship disaster?"

Justice blew out his breath and rubbed the back of his
neck. "I got dumped in a text message."

Brielle choked on her coffee. "Seriously? What did she
say?"

"Uh…two words. *We're through.*"

They paused their conversation while the waitress set
their breakfast on the table.

"That's it?" Brielle asked. She reached for the butter and
spread it over her pancakes, followed by some maple syrup.

Justice nodded as she handed him the syrup, and he
smothered his pancakes in it. "That's it. Short and sweet.
Well, not so sweet. About two weeks later I found out she got
engaged to another guy. I figured Clara was cheating on me
at least part of the time we were together, maybe the entire
time. Who knows?" He shrugged, lifting a forkful of
pancakes to his mouth.

Brielle eyed him as if she wanted to taste the sweetness
on his lips. "Were you in love with her?"

His eyes sparkled with a devilish glint. "For about a minute."

She smiled and lifted her coffee mug. "Let's make a toast to relationship disasters."

Justice gently clinked his mug against hers. "To relationship disasters. May the last one really *be* the *last* one."

"I'll drink to that," Brielle murmured, and dug into her pancakes with relish.

While they waited for their check, Brielle excused herself to go to the restroom. When she returned to their table a few minutes later, her face was flushed.

"Are you feeling okay?" Justice asked. "You look feverish."

"I'm fine," she said. "I think I got overheated from the coffee."

He heard what she said, but the dazed expression in her eyes belied her words.

"It's warming up fast outside. How about I call for a cruiser?" He reached for his phone.

Her eyes widened. "No, really, Justice, that's not necessary."

He dropped the matter and paid the check but kept his hand beneath her elbow as they exited the diner.

Handing her helmet to her, he asked, "You're not going to faint on me, are you?"

She arched a delicate eyebrow, looking every inch like the cute kitten on her T-shirt. "Do I look like I'm the kind of girl who faints?"

Color crept into Justice's cheeks. "No, no, not at all. My mistake."

Both her stance and her expression softened. "You're forgiven. Thank you, though, for being worried about me."

"No problem. Let's head to the station and see if we can get any answers to our mystery."

* * *

Brielle wished she could get answers to the mystery of *him* as she pressed against Justice's back, arms wrapped around his hard torso. She'd gone to the ladies' room because thinking about kissing the maple syrup off his sexy mouth caused heat to rise in her cheeks, and a rosy hue unfortunately still stained them even after she'd splashed cold water on her face. What was wrong with her? She never blushed. She couldn't believe Justice noticed and thought she was feverish! She had a fever all right, one raging through her blood due to the closeness between them at the moment. A crazy yearning gripped her. She wanted to lay her cheek against his broad back. But, to her disappointment, her helmet prevented such intimacy.

Within a few minutes, Justice parked the bike in his reserved spot. When they removed their helmets, he perused her face.

"Are you okay? Your color looks normal."

Brielle nodded as she adjusted her backpack and followed Justice into the station. He greeted the officers on duty with his quiet authority and easy sense of fellowship, taking the time to introduce her. Once he'd been brought up to speed, he led her to his office where they deposited their helmets.

"I want to check to see if there have been any noise complaints or reports of trucks being on the beach after hours," he said, settling behind his desk.

He opened his laptop and logged on, but then his fingers froze on the keyboard. Color shot into his face.

Justice didn't say anything, most definitely didn't want her to know he was struggling, so she moved behind him and looked over his shoulder. In a quiet voice she told him what to type into the system.

"Law enforcement agencies across the U.S. are part of the

same network," Brielle explained. "It saves time while solving cases."

She helped him sift through complaints going back at least a year.

"There's nothing here," he declared, and closed his laptop in disgust. He rose to his feet and gazed at her, silently communicating his gratitude for her help. "Let's head to the lab. Maybe we'll have better luck pulling something off the HK416 and the Beta C-mags."

They left Justice's office and ran into Captain Locke. Brielle had never met the man personally, but she recognized him from when she'd volunteered at the toy drive he had organized last Christmas in conjunction with the LAPD. He didn't look happy as he addressed Justice.

"I was told you were here," he said, his tone somewhat tense. "I've been wanting to talk to you about Dooley, Carson, Morton, and Holcomb." His eyes shifted toward Brielle a moment before swinging back to Justice.

Justice drew himself up. "I'm surprised you waited this long."

Judging by the dark expression on his face, Locke didn't like his response.

"You didn't have to suspend them for two weeks without pay."

"Yes, I did. I'm not tolerating that kind of behavior from anyone in this department, and neither should you. Especially when it was directed toward a fellow officer."

Locke frowned. "What are you talking about?"

"This is Sergeant Brielle McAdams, LAPD. She's the officer they harassed. Officer Dooley actually put his hands on her. He's lucky I didn't fire him. I still might, depending on his attitude when he reports for duty in another week."

The captain relaxed a little. "I'm sorry, Sergeant. It won't

happen again." He looked at Justice. "Please do me the cour-
tesy of a heads up the next time you discipline my officers."

"I hope there won't be a next time, but if there is, I'll
discuss it with you first, Captain," Justice conceded.

"Fair enough." Locke nodded at them and moved aside as
they headed toward the lab.

"You handled that well," Brielle commented.

"I could have told Captain Locke what I intended to do
but chose not to. I wanted to avoid an argument with him,
and now he knows I don't have a problem asserting my
authority."

"Smart."

He flashed a smile. "We'll see."

At the evidence room, the sergeant on duty brought the
HK416, still wrapped in the garbage bag. Justice signed the
log, and they made their way to the new forensic lab. He
greeted the tech and introduced Brielle.

Presenting the garbage bag containing the assault rifle
and the box of Beta C-mags, Justice said, "We found these on
the beach and need you to run trace on them."

The tech whistled. "Let's see what we can find, Chief."

Using a pair of tweezers, the tech pulled a piece of
packing material from the barrel of the assault rifle. Next, he
scanned it for fingerprints, and as they waited for the results,
he lifted a partial shoe print from the box of Beta C-mags.

"Looks like our guy is about five feet ten and two
hundred pounds," the tech estimated.

"That's a military boot print," Justice observed.

The enhanced search system pinged its results.

"We have a hit on those fingerprints, Chief." His face fell.
"Oh no. This can't be right."

"Pull it up," Justice commanded.

The tech touched a couple of buttons and the information
appeared on a gigantic transparent screen. Justice stared at

the image in front of them, his jaw set and his eyes flashing in anger.

"Just as I suspected," he muttered low in his throat.

The tech glanced at Justice in surprise. "I'll run it again. Maybe..."

"No. You said our guy is probably about five feet ten and weighs two hundred pounds. It's right."

"Chief, there's got to be a reason..."

"Keep looking for anything that might yield a clue to where it came from," he interrupted. "Special markings or serial number, perhaps." He turned toward Brielle, gazing at him with concern in her eyes. "I can't return the HK416 or ammo to the evidence room. Not now."

"Chief," she addressed him, her voice soft but firm, "you must follow proper procedure. The chain of evidence needs to remain intact to make your case. When we get finished processing the rifle and the Beta C-mags, you have to log them in. It's the right thing to do."

He nodded, though he wasn't pleased with her advice.

The tech scoured the HK416 for more trace evidence, but other than sand from the beach and the piece of packing material and the fingerprints, nothing else could be discovered.

Running a hand through his golden hair, Justice addressed the tech. "You need to keep this confidential. I don't know what our guy may be involved in, and until I do, I don't want to tip him off. Do you understand?"

The tech appeared affronted. "It goes without saying, Chief."

Justice grabbed the trash bag with the HK416 in it and headed out of the lab. Brielle followed with the Beta C-mags and the piece of packing material, both in plastic baggies.

When they returned to the evidence room, Justice issued strict orders to the sergeant. "If anyone tries to sign this out, you need to let me know immediately. Make sure to inform the other two sergeants who have shifts after yours that no one gets access to this evidence but me. I don't care if it's in the middle of the night, I want to know."

"Got it, Chief."

"Very good."

Justice reached for Brielle's hand and led her back to his office. She felt the tension in his body as they walked briskly through the corridors. Though curious, she refrained from asking him any questions, letting him direct the conversation as soon as they were alone. He dropped her hand and closed the door. His eyes shone with worry as he rubbed his neck.

"Jesus. One of our own. Did you recognize the cop whose prints were on the assault rifle?"

"Yes. What are you thinking, Justice?" she asked, her voice quiet.

He shook his head, as if to clear the cobwebs. She waited for him to organize his thoughts. Moving toward the windows, Justice closed the blinds. He reached for a dry erase marker and wrote four names on the white board: *Elliott Gage. Axel Anderson. Linda Ferguson. Nash Carson.*

"Here's what I know so far. Axel Anderson is an old friend of Gage, and he and his family went missing two years ago." He drew a line connecting the two names and wrote MISSING above *Anderson*. "About the same time Gage and Ferguson became friendly after years of animosity." He drew another connecting line. "Add the fact that Nash Carson joined the department then, too. I looked into him. Not deeply. Just enough to learn that his service record is unre-markable."

He drew a question mark above Carson's name and jotted down a note about his fingerprints on the HK416, and more than likely his shoe print on the ammunition.

"Follow me, Brielle. The trucks on the beach were moving

illegal arms. Somehow Carson's involved. He's either part of an organization or he's infiltrated it. In which case he lost the HK416 and the Beta C-mags, possibly deliberately, possibly not."

"Okay, that makes sense. If he's undercover, wouldn't Ferguson have informed you?"

"You'd think. Unless, of course, she didn't know." He gazed at the white board. "Besides the trucks we heard the other night, can you recall anything else you might have seen or heard?"

Brielle frowned, searching her mind for something that seemed unusual. Then she recalled a detail that *appeared* ordinary.

"Justice, while I was speaking to Brendan that night, I saw the mayor's super yacht heading south. It probably isn't significant, except to note the parties on board are pretty decadent, from what I hear."

He tilted his head as he regarded her. "Now, that's interesting. Any chance with your family connections you could wrangle an invitation to the next party the mayor throws on his yacht? Gage dislikes me, by the way. He resents Washburn forcing me on his city."

Their eyes met. The warm blue heat Brielle perceived in them caused her heart to skip a beat. She swallowed the emotion rising in her throat and said, "Madam Secretary made a wise decision, even if she's keeping you in the dark about her true motive. Something is definitely going on here, and Ferguson is either part of it or turned a blind eye to it when she was chief. In any case, she's been ineffective for a while now. I think..." Her eyes grew soft. "I think you're good for Laguna Beach."

He smiled, revealing perfect, even white teeth, and her pulse leapt in her veins.

"Thank you. I appreciate your confidence in me. Now

about securing an invitation to the mayor's next party. Will you call Brendan?"

"Don't need to. I have a closer connection to Mayor Gage," she revealed, grinning at him. "His wife and fifteen-year-old daughter are taking my self-defense class at the Y."

Justice lifted an eyebrow. "Perfect. When is your next class?"

"Well, unfortunately, not until next Saturday. I'll see if I can wrangle an invitation. Care to be my plus one?" Brielle's eyes sparkled with a teasing light.

He chuckled. "The mayor might throw me overboard."

She laughed. "You're a Navy boy. You can swim. But I'd still throw you a life preserver."

"You would? Then, count me in."

Drowning in the dark blue depths of his eyes, Brielle didn't want to be saved. At all.

# CHAPTER 9

As they continued their discussion, Justice rubbed his forehead before he popped two Advil liquid-gels. He didn't complain about having a headache, but Brielle wondered if he was experiencing some pain. His thoughts and his speech were slowing down, too. After tossing around a few theories Justice recorded on the white board, they'd run out of ideas.

Brielle glanced at her watch and rose to her feet. "I have to leave," she announced with regret. "I scheduled training time at the police academy. Somebody should be there I can spar with."

"I can spar with you," Justice replied without hesitation. "If you don't mind my company."

*Mind his company?* If he hadn't offered to be her sparring partner, she would have suggested it herself. Oh, this was dangerous. Freefalling without a parachute.

Her eyes glowed with intense interest as she answered him. "No, I don't mind. I...I enjoy being with you...Beach Boy."

He laughed low in his throat, a gravelly, sexy laugh that caused her stomach to curl with a sharp stab of desire she'd never felt before. Certainly not with Malcolm. With her, he'd turned foreplay into art, like one of his paintings. But Justice aroused fluttery feelings in her with just one look. Or smile. Or throaty laugh. And she was hooked. She was afraid it wouldn't take much to reel her in.

"I brought a change of clothes with me," she continued, trying to cover her reaction to him. "What about you?"

"Wait here. I'll be right back."

Justice returned five minutes later with a pair of gray sweatpants and a white LBPD T-shirt.

"I raided the uniform shop," he explained, grinning. "I'll have to let Sally, our seamstress, know I took these. And this." He plopped a LBPD baseball hat on her head.

She returned his grin. "Aw, thanks, Chief."

"You're welcome. You look really cute, by the way."

He handed her the clothes to put in her backpack and reached for his cell phone. Justice took a picture of the white board before he erased it, which caused Brielle to wonder why he couldn't just memorize it. She already had. But she had no intention of asking him about any residual effects of his brain injury. If he wanted to tell her, he would in his own time.

However, when they reached his bike, Justice hesitated. He gazed at her, a stricken expression on his face, and opened his mouth to say something, but Brielle stopped him before he could get a word out.

"I think you should let me drive your bike up to LA. You command it like an old woman."

Relief and gratitude peppered his light laughter. He tossed her the keys. "Go for it, Beach Girl."

When Justice slipped his arms around her waist, Brielle's breath hitched in her throat and nearly choked her. Curls of pure pleasure spiraled through her entire body. The feeling of his muscled chest pressing against her back brought visions of him shirtless from the previous evening. Fantasies of running her hands over his naked torso, his naked body, occupied her mind on the ride up to LA. And if she leaned forward just a little, her breasts would brush his forearms. Oh, God! No! It was bad enough she'd actually caressed him when their positions were reversed.

By the time they reached the police academy, she felt a fire burning in her, and she knew her face was flushed again. She also knew Justice noticed, but merely quirked an eyebrow at her this time as a slow smile crossed his face. *He knew what caused it, too. Damn him.*

Quiet permeated the police academy on Sunday afternoon. Brielle and Justice changed their clothes in separate locker rooms and headed toward the training ring. A few trainees hit punching bags and jumped rope. Ducking beneath the ropes, the couple squared off in the center of the ring.

"Show me what you've got, Sergeant," Justice challenged her.

Brielle executed a series of kicks and punches, but Justice parried every single one. She couldn't even get close enough to him to land a blow. He refused to strike her, though, remaining on the defensive.

Frustrated, she called a time out. In between heavy breaths, she complained, "You're holding back, Chief. Don't. I can take it." Lifting her LAPD T-shirt, she showed him a bruise on her torso, which she knew he'd already seen. "The guys I'm training with don't mess around. Some of them want to see me fail."

Justice's eyes darkened a little before he nodded. "All right, Tiger Eyes. No more messing around. Let's do this."

She attacked him. He parried, and struck her when he had the advantage, which was during the entire time they worked out. Brielle found herself thrown to the mat on her back more often than not.

Each time, Justice leaned over her, offered his hand, and ordered, "Get up, Tiger Eyes. Let's go."

Brielle fought with vigor and took everything Justice threw at her. Once, when she didn't think she could handle any more pain, her muscles crying for mercy and she wanted to quit, Justice said with his quiet authority, "SWAT doesn't quit."

That's all it took for her to take his hand, jump to her feet, and go another round with him. She knew the limits of her own body, though, and when she absolutely had nothing left to give, she told Justice she was done. He didn't argue with her.

As they climbed from the training ring, Brielle caught sight of Finnigan smirking at her.

"Pathetic. I guess that smack down we gave you last week wasn't enough to convince you that you don't have what it takes to be a SWAT officer. After what I just saw today, you're through. Out of time. Why don't you quit and save Commander Mattox the hassle of dropping you?"

Too embarrassed to respond, Brielle felt Justice stiffen next to her. She wanted to move past Finnigan, but Justice stopped her when he grabbed her hand.

"It's a mistake to underestimate Sergeant McAdams. She has more grit and determination than most men I know. That's what you saw here today."

"Who the hell are you?"

"Retired Lieutenant Commander Justice McQuaid, Navy SEAL. Currently, Police Chief of Laguna Beach."

Finnigan chortled. "A shitty job! You make quite a pair. Well, McAdams, when you're dropped from the SWAT program, you can always get a job with your boyfriend. Laguna Beach is better suited to your skill set."

Justice squeezed her hand and clenched his teeth. "When my *girlfriend* kicks your ass, I'll be there. And I'll laugh *my ass* off as you're staring up at her from the flat of your back." Without another word, he dragged Brielle toward the locker rooms with him. She felt heat seeping from every pore of his body.

Brielle never cried. The last time she recalled breaking down was the day Ben and Trey were shot ten years ago. Since then, she'd been a stoic go-getter. Now, however, hot tears filled her eyes and ran unimpeded down her cheeks, mingling with the warm water of the shower as she envisioned losing her opportunity to join SWAT. It was a hard, crushing reality for a woman who'd never failed at anything in her entire life. And part of her cried from sheer embarrassment over the disrespectful way Finnigan treated her in front of Justice. He'd been so sweet to defend her, actually calling her his girlfriend. How could she possibly face him now?

* * *

Justice's fury dissipated as he took a shower. He'd wanted to smash his fist into the face of the guy who'd hassled his girlfriend. *His girlfriend.* Well, that wasn't quite accurate, but the words rolled off his tongue before he could stop them. And besides, he liked the way it sounded. Not to mention he wanted it to be true. He wondered how Brielle felt about the guy assuming he was her boyfriend. Did she like the way it sounded? Did she want it to be true, too?

When he met Brielle outside the locker rooms, he thought he'd find her spitting mad, like a kitten. He never expected to see her face splotchy and her eyes red-rimmed from crying. Justice's heart dropped into his stomach. He didn't know what to do except open his arms. She moved into his embrace and allowed him to comfort her. Thank goodness she didn't cry. If she had, he'd have been at a complete loss.

"Who was that guy?" he asked, his voice gentle.

"Marcus Finnigan. He wants me gone."

"Why?"

"I honestly don't know. He's either a complete sexist, or he really doesn't believe I can make it. He sure as hell doesn't like me."

"Hmm…" Justice pondered that as his eyes suddenly began to sparkle with a mischievous glint. "Maybe the opposite is true. Maybe he's crushing on you and hiding his feelings by being mean to you."

Laughter bubbled inside her and escaped in a rush of breath, and his eyes fastened on her incredibly sexy mouth. He wondered how it would taste beneath his.

"Very funny, Justice."

He loved the way his name fell from her lips. Hearing her introduce him as her boyfriend would sound even better. So much for his father's warning. He was already wrecked by this siren's call.

"Where to now?" he asked, hoping she wasn't ready to dump him yet.

"Would you like to do a few touristy things while we're in LA?"

"Sure." So, she wanted to spend the rest of the day with him!

Their first destination was a food truck. They both declared they were hungry after their sparring match. While they devoured pressed Cuban sandwiches and bags of potato chips, Justice wanted to know if he'd been too rough with her.

"I would feel horrible if I gave you any more bruises."

"I'll let you know tomorrow," she replied, offering a smile. "But even if I am bruised, it was worth it."

Sensing the subject was unpleasant for her, he dropped it, and they discussed the sights Brielle planned to show him as they finished their sandwiches.

They toured LA, strolling along its famous boulevards and laughing over the exorbitant price tags of items displayed in windows. Brielle waited until an hour before sunset to take Justice to the hills above the Hollywood sign. There, they watched the sun sink low in the sky until it disappeared, and the city below them glowed brilliantly with light.

"Breathtaking," Justice murmured.

Brielle slipped her arm around his waist, and he drew her close to him. They stayed like that for several minutes, enjoying the comfortable intimacy between them.

"There's one more place I want to show you," Brielle said, eventually moving toward the bike. "The Griffith Conservatory. It's spectacular at night, and we have just enough time to get there before it closes."

They were too late to get into the planetarium, so they spent an hour wandering through the other areas.

As they left, Justice rubbed his stomach and exclaimed, "I'm starving! What about you?"

"I'm ravenous," she confessed. "I know a great place to eat that serves the best food in LA."

Thirty minutes later, Brielle pulled into the parking lot of Vinny's Bar and Grill. As soon as they stepped into the dimly lit, noisy restaurant, Vinny rushed from behind the bar to meet them. The short, stocky owner pulled Brielle into a bear hug and kissed her on both cheeks.

"Brielle! What a surprise! It's been too long." Vinny quickly appraised Justice and offered a knowing grin. "She's my avenging angel. A year ago, I was left for dead in the alley behind my restaurant. Not only did Brielle find me and save my life, she chased the thief and got the cash deposit back. Now, he's rotting in prison."

Turning toward her, his grin grew even broader. "I'm so glad you're not with that whiny, artsy-fartsy weasel anymore, and found yourself a new boyfriend." Thrusting his hand out, he continued, "I'm Vinny Bono."

Justice shook his hand with a firm grip. "Justice McQuaid." He didn't bother to correct Vinny's assumption that he was Brielle's boyfriend.

Neither did she. In fact, she boasted, pride resonating in her voice, "Justice is a retired lieutenant commander, a SEAL. He's just been appointed Chief of Police of Laguna Beach."

Beaming, Vinny looked from one to the other. "Well, it's about time you found someone worthy of you. Come on. I'll show you to a table and bring you a huge platter of barbecued ribs. Once you've tasted my ribs, Justice, you'll never be satisfied with anyone else's. Mine are the best in LA."

He brought them two bottles of beer and promised to be back with their appetizers.

When they were alone, guilt swirled through Justice for not being completely honest with Brielle about his brain injury. Although she didn't mention any of the difficulties he experienced throughout the day, he knew they were on her mind, and she deserved an explanation.

He took a long swig of his beer and cleared his throat. "Brielle, there's something I neglected to tell you yesterday about my brain injury. I…I'm not fully recovered. And it's highly unlikely that I ever will be."

Justice shared his primary issues with her and studied her face as he spoke, looking for signs of rejection, or worse, pity. Neither appeared in her expression. She drew closer to him, leaning forward, caressing his forearm, and asking questions about his condition when she needed clarification.

He fell silent as Vinny set two salads and fresh bottles of

beer on the table and made a few teasing remarks before he returned to the kitchen.

Meeting Brielle's eyes, he began awkwardly, "Um...I... don't know what you're thinking right now."

"No? Well, I'm thinking that it took a lot of courage for you to be honest with me. You're the bravest man I've ever met, and...perfect boyfriend material." Her tiger's eyes sparkled with a teasing light as she grinned at him.

Justice relaxed, though his heart flipped. He resisted the urge to cup her face and kiss her senseless. He kept that in the back of his mind for later.

Smiling, he replied, "According to Vinny."

After enjoying Vinny's succulent barbecued ribs and baked beans and sharing a rich, decadent piece of chocolate cake, they complimented his culinary skills and promised to visit again soon.

When they reached Justice's motorcycle, Brielle handed him the keys. "You've got this. I'll tell you step by step how to get to the highway, and from there it's a straight shot down to Laguna Beach."

He nodded, fastened his helmet, and started the engine. Brielle's arms around him and her voice in his ear boosted his confidence as he followed her directions. Justice drove without haste beneath black velvet skies dusted with twinkling stars because he didn't want their time together to end. He couldn't recall a day more perfect than this one.

All too soon he turned into Brielle's driveway. He shut off the motor; they climbed from the bike and removed their helmets. Floodlights illuminated their faces as they regarded each other.

"Thanks for giving me the best day of my life to date," Justice murmured. He took her hand and drew her toward him. "I probably should have asked you this last night, but since you didn't slap me, I figured it was okay. May I kiss you good night again on the cheek?"

Her chest heaved and she expelled her breath. "No," she answered. Her soft voice trembled. "I want you to kiss me like you mean it. Kiss me like my boyfriend would kiss me."

Momentarily stunned by her boldness, Justice didn't need any further encouragement. Wanting their first kiss to be special and tantalizing, his fingers traced her delicate jawline and brushed against her lips before he tilted her chin upward to meet his mouth. He nibbled, he tasted, then he molded his mouth to hers, reveling in its softness, its sweetness.

Justice increased the pressure as heat rose between their bodies, and Brielle's arms crept around his neck and toyed with his hair. Her lips parted, inviting his tongue to slip inside her mouth. She moaned low in her throat as their tongues swirled around each other, and he drew hers into his warm mouth. His hands spanned her waist, holding her against him. Justice kissed her harder, sucking on her bottom lip. The frantic thrusting of his tongue deep into her mouth imitated what he longed to do with her in bed.

Afraid of losing control, Justice lifted his head and released her. Breathing heavily, he touched her cheek. "Get a good night's sleep, Brielle. Training begins at five tomorrow morning on the beach. Sharp."

Confused, a sexy haze in her amber eyes, she stammered, "Wh—what?"

"Oh, didn't I tell you? I'm taking over your training. You have a slim chance of making it into SWAT without my help. You fight great, but you're predictable. I anticipated every single one of your moves and was already five moves ahead of you. I'm going to teach you skills, Brielle, and believe me, Finnigan and the others won't see them coming until you unleash them. I wasn't kidding when I said I want to be there when you knock Finnigan on his ass."

She let out a strangled laugh before she hurled herself against him and kissed him hard, fisting his T-shirt in her hands. Several long moments later, she looked up at him and smiled.

"See you in the morning, Justice. Sleep well."

*Sleep well?* How could he when he couldn't get their steamy kisses off his mind? Tossing back the covers, he went into the bathroom and took a cold shower. It reduced the heat in his body but didn't help with his erotic dreams that night.

Eager to see Brielle the following morning, Justice gulped a cup of hot black coffee, gobbled a banana, and headed down to the beach. Jogging easily along the water's edge, he saw Brielle already waiting for him as she stretched her muscles.

"Good morning!" he called. "Are you ready to get down to some serious work?"

"Absolutely, Chief. What's first?"

He put her through a tough routine of calisthenics without any equipment. Afterward they ran side by side until Justice kicked up their speed. She ran fast, in perfect form, but his strides outpaced hers, and she soon lagged behind him.

Justice turned around, running backward, and yelled, "Pick it up, Sergeant!"

Brielle gritted her teeth, and with an incredible burst of energy, she caught up to him and kept pace with him for the duration of their run.

During their cool down, Justice asked, "What is your schedule like today, Brielle?"

"I have to report to my precinct and check in with my squad. After I get off duty, I'm going to the Main Street Gym."

She'd showed it to him the previous day. "I'll meet you

there to continue your training."

Brielle nodded. "I'll text you." She took his cell phone and programmed her number in it.

Unable to resist, Justice slipped his hand around her neck and leaned down to capture her mouth with his. After his erotic dreams about her, he couldn't get enough of her and kissed her deeply, his tongue sparring with hers. Kissing her until they ran out of breath, he finally broke away from her.

"Stay safe, Justice," she murmured, her eyes soft and luminous.

He could hardly tear his gaze away from her sweet mouth, bruised and swollen with passion.

"You, too. See you at the gym later, Brielle."

Justice turned and jogged toward his house. Whistling his favorite tune, he showered and shaved, dressed in his uniform, and headed to the station.

# CHAPTER 10

After roll call Justice met Officer Miguel Rivera, who'd been informed that he was riding with the chief today.

Rivera shook Justice's hand, offering a friendly smile. "It's an honor to be your partner, Chief."

"Likewise. I heard you're an expert on Laguna Beach."

"Born and bred." They reached Justice's Explorer. "Do you want me to drive?"

"Yes. I want you to drop me off so I can walk the streets and meet the residents and business owners. You know, get a feel for the community."

Rivera slid behind the wheel. "Understood."

As they pulled away from the station, Justice asked, "So, what's your story, Officer Rivera?"

"Livin' the American Dream, Chief," he replied. "My grandparents crossed the border illegally from Mexico. They hid in a peach shed where the owner found them, half dead from exhaustion and starvation. He spoke Spanish and offered them jobs picking peaches. He said they could stay in the shed. It wasn't ideal, but they made it work. Eventually my grandfather turned it into a small home.

"The owner and his wife loved my grandparents and sponsored their path to citizenship. As time passed the owner placed my grandfather in charge of the day to day operation of the business, and then made him his partner. When the owner and his wife passed away, my grandfather inherited the peach grove."

Rivera paused and glanced sideways at Justice. "My grandparents were so fortunate. They were able to provide a good life for my father and my aunts and uncle. My parents are immigration lawyers who own a firm in D.C. Believe me, they're a pain in ICE's ass. One of my aunts works for Doctors without Borders, and the other is a social worker who spends her time helping migrant children. And my uncle is a software developer in Silicon Valley."

"That's an incredible story, Officer Rivera. What about you? Why'd you choose law enforcement?"

"Call me River. It's a nickname that sorta stuck. To answer your question, my parents taught me and my brothers and sisters to offer our lives in service. My siblings have moved away, but I stayed behind in order to help the kids in this community. I work with them on social skills and reading skills if they're struggling."

"Wow. That's awesome. Are you married?"

"Nah, man. You?"

"No." Justice broke off, thinking about the hot kisses he'd shared with Brielle.

*But I want to be. I'm tired of being alone.*

"Well, one thing about Laguna Beach. There are plenty of women to choose from!" He grinned.

"Yeah. I've already met someone."

"You have? That's great. Hope it works out, Chief."

River pulled into the parking lot of a 7-11. "We call this intersection Four Corners. Olivera Street runs east and west, and Oak Street runs north and south. I keep a close eye on this area because teenagers like to hang out at the Taco Bell."

They climbed out of the Explorer.

"Ready to walk the beat, Chief?"

"Absolutely. Let's start here at the 7-11."

After spending eight hours on the beat with River and watching and listening to him deal with everyone they met, Justice realized how indispensable he was to the department. He reminded him of a guy on his SEAL team—the one who drew others to him because of his humble, down-to-earth personality. Thinking of his dead teammate brought a sadness to his countenance.

"Hey, Chief, thanks for the opportunity to ride with you today."

"No. Thank *you*, River. I learned a lot being on the street with you. You're an asset and a credit to this department."

"I do my best." River handed Justice the keys to the Explorer. "Look, Chief, I just want to say that I'm sorry about your team. Losing your brothers-in-arms—I can't imagine how difficult that must have been for you."

"Not unless you've lived through it. But I appreciate your sympathy."

"I know this isn't much consolation, but the other officers have said they're glad you're here. They're behind you, Chief."

Feeling less uncertain about the job he was doing by River's encouraging words, and especially by Brielle's promised text message, Justice changed into civilian clothes in the locker room before he stopped at Tawny's desk to let her know he was off duty.

Anxious to meet Brielle at the Main Street Gym, he left his Explorer in his driveway and hopped on his Harley. He thought he'd be able to recall the directions Brielle had added to her text, but if he got lost, well, he'd just plug the address into his GPS.

Caught in heavy late afternoon traffic, Justice worried that Brielle would think he wasn't coming. Several times he resisted the urge to text her as he sat at red lights and inched his way through the streets. At least he didn't get lost, he congratulated himself as he pulled in front of the gym. He checked his phone, relieved to find another message from Brielle.

Brielle: If you're stuck in traffic, don't respond. I'm not going anywhere.

She'd added a happy face emoji, which caused *his* current happy face. Smiling broadly, he sent a reply.

Justice: Just got here.

Entering the gym, Justice's eyes lit on Brielle working out with a punching bag. Damn. She was both the cutest and hottest woman he'd ever met. He wanted her in the worst way. And not just for sex, though he imagined it'd be spectacular. No, he wanted her to be a permanent part of his life. He wondered what she'd say if he asked her if she'd like to date him.

When she caught a glimpse of him watching her from the corner of her eye, Brielle steadied the punching bag and offered a bright smile. "You made it, Chief."

"I did." Justice advanced toward her. "You've got great form, by the way."

"Thanks. But I've got a lot to learn from you."

"Can we use the ring?" A pair of boxers were currently sparring in it.

"Yeah." Brielle whistled boyishly. "Hey, guys! My turn!"

They turned toward her and lifted their gloved hands in acknowledgment.

"No problem, Sarge!" one called as he and his buddy ducked through the ropes.

Justice and Brielle squared off in the center of the ring. Boxing taught her to be quick on her feet, but she needed to combine speed with new techniques. Focused and stern, Justice demonstrated each sequence of strike and counter-strike he wanted her to learn. She followed through, impressing him with her agility and attention to detail. No matter how hard she tried, though, Brielle couldn't take Justice down.

Sensing her discouragement as they headed toward the locker rooms, he commented, "You'll get there, Brielle. You're already better than you were yesterday. You know you're going to have to work hard to knock me off my feet. But when you do, I'll be cheering for you from the ground."

Brielle didn't say anything. She just stared at him through her glorious amber eyes a moment before they separated to take showers and change clothes.

As they rode their twin motorcycles side by side down to Laguna Beach, Justice thought about how he would approach asking Brielle if she'd like to date him. The truth is, he'd never dated much in the past. He'd slept with a handful of women and had two serious relationships that went nowhere. How did one go about asking someone to date him or her nowadays, anyway?

Hey, baby. Want to go steady? Nah. Too old-fashioned.

Hey, sugar. Want to hang out sometime? Nah. Too vague.

That just might be the fuel Brielle needed to toss him on his ass before she slammed the door in his face.

When she welcomed him in her arms as he moved in for a slow, thrilling kiss outside her house, Justice made up his mind to throw caution to the wind and risk humiliating himself. He ravaged her mouth first, though, plunging his tongue into its sweet depths again and again. That might make it harder for her to reject him.

Brielle   responded   without   inhibition,   her   hands

exploring the broadness of his chest and back, her fingertips feeling his rippled muscles beneath her touch. Justice's breath caught in his throat when she hooked her fingers in the belt loops of his jeans and tugged him closer to her. It was now or never.

Lifting his head, he cleared his throat. "Brielle, uh, I—I wanted to ask if you, um, if you..."

"Want to be your girlfriend?" she interrupted him with a soft smile. "The answer is yes."

Shocked, Justice stepped back from her. "Whoa. Wait. What?"

Confused by his reaction, color shot into her cheeks. "Oh. I, um, I'm sorry. I misunderstood. I guess I shouldn't have cut you off..."

He cut *her* off, crushing her against him and kissing her hard. His hands cupped her bottom, and he lifted her, encouraging her to wrap her legs around him. Their bodies clung together as their kiss deepened.

A hungry fire ran rampant through him. On the verge of losing control, Justice broke their frantic kiss. "You didn't misunderstand. I just couldn't believe you beat me to it."

"You're sweet." She caressed his rough cheek.

"And you're cute when you blush."

Justice captured her lips again with his. Her taste intoxicated him. Drunk with her in his arms, his mouth left hers and traveled down her neck, nibbling her soft skin.

"Justice," she murmured, her voice husky.

"Hmm?" His tongue circled her delicate ear. He felt her shiver in his arms.

"Well, um, are you going to put me down or take me to bed? Or both? Because..."

His face turned red. He held her pressed against the hard bulge in his jeans. Sweet Jesus! Justice set Brielle on her feet.

"Oh. I'm—God, I'm so embarrassed."

She chuckled low in her throat which caused his stomach to tighten as he grew harder. "Don't be. It felt nice and...*impressive*."

He guffawed. "Just wait."

"How long?"

Justice threw his head back and let out a roar of laughter. "Well, I've never measured it, but I think it's probably..."

She slapped him playfully on the arm and chortled. "You know damn well that's not what I meant! Though," she cast her eyes downward, "I *am* curious."

He grew serious as he brushed her hair off her forehead and trailed his fingers down her jawline. "So am I. I want to know if we'll be combustible in bed."

Justice wrapped an arm around her and drew her into his embrace. His lips skittered across her eyes, her cheeks, her nose, and finally possessed her mouth in a hot, erotic kiss.

"My guess is combustible," Brielle murmured when they drew apart.

"We'll know soon enough. Good night. I'll see you in the morning."

She grabbed one more kiss. "Good night."

\* \* \*

The next day Justice checked in with the forensics tech, who didn't have any new information to report, on the case involving the HK416 and the ammo. Afterward, he headed down to the beach, patrolling it himself, learning the rhythm of the Pacific and searching the rock formations for more evidence without any luck. He observed the rhythm of the beach-goers, too, getting to know the regulars and subtly asking them if they'd seen anything suspicious or out of the ordinary. No one had.

That night Justice stood at his bedroom window,

watching and listening for trucks, though the area where he and Brielle discovered the assault rifle and ammo was about a mile south of his place. When he'd asked Brielle if she'd heard or seen anything lately, she said she hadn't, either.

During the rest of the week, Justice worked out with Brielle every morning, and on Wednesday and Friday he met her at the Main Street Gym where he guided her training with a single purpose. To teach her how to handle herself like a SEAL. When they parted in her driveway, he didn't do anything more than span her waist with his hands, holding her against him as he ravished her mouth with his. He ached to explore her body fully, to cup her perfect breasts in his hands, to consummate his growing passion for her. But he was afraid of being on the receiving end of another *Dear Justice* text message if he took Brielle to bed too soon.

By Friday he'd ridden along with a few of the other officers and decided it was time to put his team together. He had four individuals already in mind, with one spot left. Moving forward with his investigation was his top priority. Justice couldn't wait for Officer Carson to report for duty on Monday. He wondered if Carson knew he'd found the assault rifle and the ammo.

Exhausted from a full, hectic week, Justice fell into bed. Two hours later an emergency call from the station roused him.

"Chief, there's been a shooting at the 7-11, Four Corners. Two fatalities. The suspect is still at large."

Wide awake, he leapt out of bed. "I'll be there in ten."

He pulled on his jeans and a T-shirt and shoes. Justice grabbed his badge, gun, and keys and sprinted toward his Explorer. Backing out of his driveway, he flipped on the siren and flashing lights.

When he arrived at the gruesome scene, an officer waved him through, and he parked the Explorer. Ducking beneath crime scene tape, he approached the medical examiner bending over a pair of teenage boys. Around Justice, lights flashed as emergency personnel conducted their duties, and Laguna Beach police officers kept order and the looky-loos at bay.

Crouching next to the ME, Justice asked, "What have we got?"

"Several shots to the upper torso, Chief McQuaid. .38 caliber. The shells have been recovered."

Luca approached them. "I just interviewed witnesses who claim that this is a drug deal gone bad. Our victims, Theo Ames and Pedro Martinez, owed our suspect, Arnold Dewitt, money for moving bricks for him. It sounds like they kept the money for themselves."

River arrived at the scene and pushed his way toward them. Staring in horror at the lifeless teenagers, he cried, "No! No! It can't be possible!" Helplessly, he shook his head. "They were clean, Chief. I swear it. Theo and Pedro were on the right track at last. I helped them find jobs and get caught up on their credits so Laguna Beach High School would allow them to return to graduate with their class. Jesus! They didn't deserve this! They were only seventeen years old. Seventeen!"

Justice draped a comforting arm across River's broad shoulders. "It's going to be okay." Turning toward Luca, he continued, "What do we know about Dewitt?"

"He's a small-time drug dealer, twenty years old. In and out of jail since he was fourteen for various petty crimes."

"Not this time. Dewitt just graduated to murder. Okay, people. No one goes home until we catch this guy. Luca, stay here and finish working the scene. River, come with me. We'll hit his house first. Don't worry. He's going to pay for this."

River told Justice that Dewitt lived with his parents, so

they headed there without the siren or flashing lights in order to prevent his discovering them, though neither believed they'd find their suspect hanging around waiting for them. When they approached the modest home, darkness enveloped it. Justice parked a few houses away, and they climbed from the Explorer, guns drawn. Communicating silently with River, Justice took the lead.

He pounded on the door. "LBPD! Open up!"

At that moment a light came on inside, and they heard the distinct cries of a child.

"That's Dewitt's little sister, Rosie," River whispered. "We have to go in. He may be holding his family hostage."

Justice nodded. "On three. Cover me." He tried the knob, and it turned in his hand. "It's Chief of Police McQuaid! I'm coming in!"

Slowly, he pushed open the door, and before he could step over the threshold, he caught a blur of bright pink as a young girl launched herself at him, stopping short when she saw the gun in his hands, tears streaming down her sweet face. Startled, Justice lowered his gun, and River moved around him, his dark eyes alert for trouble. He called out, identifying himself as he swept each room.

When River returned a couple of minutes later, shaking his head, Justice squatted in front of the girl and asked in a kind voice, "What's your name, sweetie?"

She hiccuped and sniffed. "R…Rosie."

"Hi, Rosie. I'm Chief of Police Justice McQuaid." He shook her small hand. "It's nice to meet you. How old are you?"

"H…hi." Rosie swiped at her tears. "I'm ten."

"Rosie, are you home alone?"

"I…I woke up. Something scared me. I…I looked for Mom and Dad, but they're not here." Fresh tears ran in rivulets down her cheeks.

"What about your brother, Arnie?" Justice used the drug dealer's nickname.

Rosie made a face and her eyes grew wrathful. "He's not here, either. I don't like him!" she blurted. "Arnie's always in trouble and makes Mom cry and that makes Dad mad. Do you know where my parents are?" She glanced from Justice to River.

Justice shook his head. "No, Rosie. But I promise Officer Rivera and I are going to find them."

He started to rise to his feet, but Rosie grabbed his arm.

"Wait! You're not going to leave me alone, are you?" She swiped at her tears again.

The distraught child tugged on his heartstrings. He had some experience with children. He'd tossed around a football with his teammates' kids and babysat a few times. Stunned by Rosie's trust in him, though, he really didn't know how to react. Once again, he communicated without words to River, who left the room in order to call child services. Then he called Tawny to ask her to stay with Rosie until a social worker arrived.

"Rosie, we'll stay with you until another officer gets here, but then we have to go look for your mom and dad."

"Do you think...they're okay?" she asked.

"I hope so." Needing to change the subject, Justice asked brightly, "Hey, do you have a favorite doll or stuffed animal you'd like to show me?"

She frowned at him. "I'm not a baby."

"My mistake. Anything else you'd like to show me?"

"Maybe." She headed upstairs.

When they were alone, River chuckled. "Wow. It took ten minutes for Rosie to wrap you around her little finger, Chief."

Justice shot him a dark look. "Don't be silly. I'm just doing my job."

"Right," he drawled.

A moment later Rosie rejoined them with an iPad in her hands.

Justice smiled. "That's a really nice iPad."

"Yeah. I like it."

"Hey, are you hungry? Want a snack? Let's see what's in the kitchen."

"Can I have chocolate milk and some cookies?"

"Sweetie, you can have whatever you want."

River chortled, and Justice offered a helpless shrug of his shoulders with a broad smile.

# CHAPTER 11

Tawny arrived within twenty minutes, though both Justice and River fretted at the delay. She wore casual clothes beneath her Kevlar vest, with her gun belt strapped to her waist. This frightened Rosie, although she hadn't been afraid of Justice or River. Maybe she intuitively understood Tawny's presence, which meant something bad for her, or possibly her parents.

Years of training kicked in, and Justice felt a hard knot form in his stomach. Trusting his instincts, he pulled Tawny aside and murmured, "I don't like this. Take Rosie to the station and wait there for child services."

"Yes, Chief. I'll call them with our new location."

Turning toward Rosie, he said, "C'mon, sweetie. You're going to the police station with Officer Tawny. Let's go upstairs and pack a few things."

Rosie still looked scared, but she led Justice to her bedroom. He told her to put on a pair of pants and a shirt and socks and shoes. He found her backpack and stuffed it with clothes and other necessities. When he saw her comb and mirror, his heart lurched for the child. He tucked them inside the backpack and asked if there was anything else she wanted to take with her. Rosie shook her head, and they rejoined Tawny and River.

Full of nervous energy, bouncing up and down on his feet, River declared in a low voice, "Chief, we gotta move now. A tip just came in. Our suspect is at his aunt and uncle's place."

"Tawny, please don't leave Rosie alone. If she's placed in foster care, I want you to go with the social worker to the foster parents' home. Check it out. If you get a bad vibe, don't leave her there. Bring her back to the station, and I'll try to figure something out."

"I have a better idea, Chief," Tawny replied. "My parents are guardians in the foster care system. I'll arrange with child services to have her placed with them until this situation is resolved."

Justice's body relaxed as relief swept through him, but only for a moment. From the corner of his eye, he saw the look of impatience on River's face. "Thanks, Tawny. We've got to go."

As Tawny and Rosie followed behind them, River remarked in a low voice, "I called for backup. Neighbors reported several shots fired at the aunt and uncle's home."

He'd barely finished speaking when an old white Toyota Corolla screeched to halt in front of the house, and their suspect leapt from the vehicle.

Covered in blood, Arnold Dewitt brandished his .38 and screamed, "Rosie! It's time! Time to be part of the New America!" His wild eyes pinned them as he took menacing steps toward them.

Rosie cried out in terror. Tawny drew her gun and pushed the child behind her. Justice and River trained their guns on Dewitt, too, never taking their eyes off him.

"Drop your weapon, Dewitt!" Justice ordered. "Get down

on the ground! Now!"

"Rosie!" Dewitt yelled. "Get over here! I just want to take you to Mom and Dad! We're all going underground…"

Out of his mind on some drug, he charged toward them. Justice fired his gun a couple of times. Dewitt's body jerked, and he fell dead onto the grass. Tawny shoved her gun into her holster and grabbed Rosie, shielding her from the grisly sight.

Several squad cars converged on the scene as Justice directed Tawny, "Get Rosie out of here."

"Yes, Chief." She took Rosie by the arm and guided her toward her cruiser.

One of the newly arrived officers approached Justice and said, "Chief, you need to head to the Swifts' place right now. I'll handle this situation until Captain Locke gets here."

Justice nodded. "River and I were on our way there when Dewitt showed up." He inclined his head. "Let's go, River." Glancing at Dewitt, he felt sick to his stomach. What a waste.

When he and River pulled up in front of Rosie's aunt and uncle's house ten minutes later, first responder vehicles covered the driveway and the lawn, along with CSU. A detective Justice hadn't met yet made his way toward him and River, a grim expression on his face.

"Chief McQuaid, I'm Detective Caleb Yarin. I got here a few minutes ago. Come with me. I'll take you through the crime scene."

Justice's gut clenched as he gazed at the blood-spattered living room, and Detective Yarin explained in unemotional and clinical terms what occurred in the Swifts' home.

"According to phone records, Mrs. Swift placed a call to her sister at approximately one-fifteen this morning, and she and Mr. Dewitt rushed over to find their son Arnold holding his aunt and uncle at gunpoint. He shot his parents first and then Mr. and Mrs. Swift."

Bile rose in Justice's throat. He found it difficult to accept that they couldn't have prevented this from happening. But the worst was yet to come. Detective Yarin led him upstairs where Arnold's cousins lay in their blood-soaked beds. Justice nearly retched. He held on to the door frame to steady himself when he saw the last of three children—a little girl a year younger than Rosie. The thought entered his head that killing Arnold Dewitt had been too easy after the atrocities he'd committed tonight. And Rosie, sweet Rosie, would have died tonight, too, if he and River and Tawny hadn't been there to protect her. How in God's name was he supposed to tell that little girl who'd trusted him instinctively that her entire family was gone? Who would take her in? He wondered if she had any other family members, grandparents, perhaps. Justice's head pounded and his stomach roiled.

Detective Yarin must have read the sick, guilt-ridden expression on Justice's face. "Don't beat yourself up, Chief. No one saw this coming."

Justice didn't find the detective's words comforting even if they were true. He remained at the scene of the gruesome murders until the Crime Scene Unit finished processing it and the bodies had been loaded into fire rescue trucks and transported to the morgue.

Weary and heartsick, he and River rode to the station in silence. Alone in his office, Justice dreaded calling Tawny. He delayed for as long as possible, writing reports and answering questions, until he couldn't avoid the inevitable any longer.

When Tawny answered on the third ring, he asked in a quiet voice, "Where's Rosie?"

"Here with me at my parents' house."

"Is she awake?"

"Yes. Waiting for news."

Justice heard the question in her tone. "Her parents didn't

make it. Neither did her aunt and uncle and...her three cousins." His voice broke.

"Oh, my God," Tawny murmured.

"I'm on my way to tell her. Rosie shouldn't hear this from anyone but me."

"Of course."

"The press is expecting a statement. I'll be right over after that."

Flanked by River, Captain Locke, and Detectives Martinelli and Yarin, Justice made his way to the press room and took his place at the microphone. Sally, God bless her, stood off to one side. She must have heard about the mass murders and come to offer his support.

Drawing a deep breath, Justice explained how the victims met their demise at the hands of Arnold Dewitt, who'd been killed by the police when he attempted to murder his sister, too.

Grilled for an hour by the press, Justice's head ached incessantly, and he felt tense and on the verge of exploding by the time he ended the press conference. He didn't blame the reporters for wanting answers. Hell, he wanted them, too. He wanted to know what went wrong, why Dewitt went on a murderous rampage, why he yelled some nonsense about a New America. But the only ones who might shed some light were lying on cold slabs in the morgue.

On his way out, Justice took a call from an irate Mayor Gage.

"Just what the hell is going on in my town, Chief McQuaid? How could you let something like this happen? Ten people are dead, for God's sake!"

Justice wasn't in the mood to be polite or political. "Back off, Mr. Mayor. I'm not having this conversation with you right now. Unless you intend to tell Rosie Dewitt that her entire family is dead, which I'm about to do myself, then I strongly suggest you shut the hell up. I'm not in the mood to listen to your bullshit."

When the mayor remained silent, Justice snorted in disdain. "Yeah, that's what I thought." Without another word, he ended the call.

Sally waited for him next to the Explorer. "Let me go with you to the Westfalls' place," she said, her voice soft with empathy.

"No, Sally. I have to do this by myself."

"Want a hug?"

"Yeah, that'd be nice."

She wrapped her arms around him, and he inhaled her grandmotherly scent before he dropped a kiss on the top of her head and detached himself.

"It's going to be okay, Justice."

"I hope so."

* * *

Tawny's parents lived on the beach a couple of miles north of Justice's home. He rang the doorbell and stepped inside a wide foyer leading to a large living space. Tawny introduced him to her mother, Cynthia, and her father, Beau. Cynthia offered a comforting hug, and Beau shook his hand in a firm grip while clasping his shoulder.

"It's good to finally meet you, Chief McQuaid," Beau commented. "Although, I wish it were under different circumstances. Tawny raves about you all the time."

"Thank you, sir. And you have an extraordinary daughter. I honestly don't know what I would do without her." Justice paused. "How's Rosie?"

"She's scared. And anxious," Tawny replied. "Right now, she's watching a Disney movie. Follow me."

She led Justice into a cozy family room. Rosie lay on her

stomach in a pair of pajamas as she watched a movie about a Disney princess who lived in a world of make believe, while the child's reality was about to crash down on her. Hearing footsteps behind her, she leapt to her feet and rushed toward Justice. Something in his eyes, sorrow and regret, perhaps, stopped her dead-still in her tracks.

"Mom and Dad?" Her voice ended on a sob.

Justice scooped her up into a hug. "I'm sorry, sweetie. So sorry."

Rosie burst into heart-wrenching cries. Within a few minutes, though, she sniffed and declared, "I want my aunt Beverly!"

Justice held her even tighter against him. Swallowing the hard knot of emotion rising in his throat, he said, "Rosie, honey, Aunt Beverly and Uncle Clint and...and...your cousins, well, they're...they're with your mom and dad in heaven."

The child emitted a loud wail followed by a flood of hysterical tears. She kicked and hit Justice, but he refused to let her go. He held on to her, murmuring soothing words of comfort. Rosie's tears soaked his shirt. Eventually, the worst of the tempest passed, reduced to whimpers, until she fell into an exhausted sleep in Justice's arms.

He followed Tawny upstairs to a pretty bedroom decorated in soft shades of rose and cream. After he laid her gently on the bed, he sank into a white wicker rocking chair next to her.

"Chief, you don't have to stay," Tawny whispered. "She's completely wiped out."

"I'm not leaving her," he stated in a firm tone. "I can't. I feel responsible for her."

"Okay."

Tawny stayed up with him, bringing him cups of hot coffee throughout the next few hours. She offered him something to eat but he declined. The thought of food made him ill.

Dawn broke. Justice felt shaky from the pain in his head and too much caffeine, but at least Rosie slept peacefully, not plagued by any nightmares. As the sun rose higher, it cast its rays through the window, and Rosie slowly opened her eyes. At first she was confused and disoriented, until she wiped the sleep from her eyes and noticed Justice watching her. Her chin quivered and tears filled her eyes.

"Chief," she mumbled. "So...I wasn't dreaming."

"No. Smell that? Breakfast is almost ready. Are you hungry?"

She nodded.

"Good. So am I." Justice rubbed his stomach. "How 'bout you change out of your pajamas and we go downstairs?"

Rosie offered a small smile, climbed from the bed, and headed into the bathroom with her backpack. She dressed in a pair of shorts and T-shirt, brushed her teeth and her hair, and joined Justice.

After the Westfalls and Justice and Rosie feasted on eggs, bacon, and blueberry muffins, the adults stayed in the kitchen to discuss the situation while the child headed into the family room to watch Saturday morning cartoons.

"So, what's going to happen to Rosie? Were you able to locate other family members?" Justice inquired.

"Sadly, no," Cynthia answered. "Her maternal grandparents passed away a few years ago, and her paternal grandparents are in an assisted living facility."

"What about other siblings her parents may have?"

"None, that we know of. Here's what we thought we'd do. On Monday we'll file a petition with family court to become Rosie's permanent guardians. After that, Beau and I will probably adopt her. We don't want her crushed time and again when she doesn't get chosen to be adopted by potential parents who want a baby instead of a ten-year-old little girl."

"I'd like to adopt her," Justice blurted, startling himself and them.

Tawny and her parents gaped at him. His face turned red, and he rubbed the back of his neck in his typical manner.

"Well, it was just a thought. Besides, I just started dating someone, and though I'm hoping this relationship works out, only time will tell."

Tawny's jaw dropped even further. "You have a girlfriend?"

A grin crossed his face. "Yeah. We met on the beach. Sergeant Brielle McAdams, LAPD. She's training for SWAT," he added. Pride echoed in his voice.

"I've heard of her, though we've never met. Nothing but good things," Tawny responded. "I'm happy for you, Chief."

"Thanks. I'm a lucky man. Now, about adopting Rosie. Is there a chance I might be able to?"

"There's always a chance," Cynthia replied. "Let's get guardianship of her first."

"All right." Justice rose to his feet. "Thanks for breakfast, Mrs. Westfall. I'll say goodbye to Rosie and see myself out."

After promising Rosie he'd see her again whenever he was able, Justice headed into the station to check in with his squad. A somber mood prevailed, especially when the officers learned he'd been up all night watching over Rosie Dewitt in the aftermath of her brother's bloodbath. They encouraged him to go home, and two hours later he finally took their advice.

* * *

Justice stripped down to his boxers and fell into bed with images of the slaughter he'd seen dancing in his head. It didn't take long, though, for pure exhaustion to overcome him, and he slipped into a deep sleep. But not for long. Within an hour the repeated ringing of his cell phone penetrated his foggy brain.

"Chief McQuaid," he croaked, barely able to focus.

"Oh, my God, Justice!" Brielle exclaimed. "I just heard the news. Are you okay? You sound terrible."

Justice leaned against the headboard and scrubbed his face with his free hand. "Yeah. Yeah, I'm okay. I've been up all night and just went to sleep a little while ago."

He must not have been convincing because Brielle replied, "You definitely don't sound okay. I'm cancelling my self-defense class and coming over."

"No, please don't do that, Brielle. We need to stick to our plan to get an invitation to the next party on the mayor's yacht. I just need to get some sleep. Will you come over for dinner? I'll cook."

"I'd love to. See you tonight. Rest, Justice."

"I will. Looking forward to seeing you later."

Getting ready for her self-defense class, Brielle heard Justice's voice coming from her television. Drawn at first by its familiar, deep tones, she listened in absolute shock as he described the shooting spree that occurred in Laguna Beach during the wee hours of Saturday morning. That her first instinct had been to drop everything and rush over to take care of him surprised her. In one week Justice had affected her like no other man before him. She suspected in another month or two she'd be utterly lost. And anticipating being lost in his arms, in his eyes, in his body, caused her blood to race through her veins. Putting aside her romantic ruminations, she grabbed her things and left the house.

At the YMCA Brielle heard some of the members buzzing about what happened during the night. Most of them praised the LBPD, but a few blamed the officers for not doing enough to prevent the tragedy. A couple of women in her self-defense class broached the topic with Vivian Gage, who expressed her concern but nothing else. Brielle saw her frown at the women's backs, clearly displeased by their comments. She wondered if Vivian shared her husband's attitude toward Justice, and if she'd manage to finagle an invitation to the Gages' next party on their yacht.

After ninety minutes of instruction, the women dispersed. Before Brielle had the opportunity to speak with Vivian, the woman headed into the workout area. Sighing because she'd literally have to stalk the mayor's wife, Brielle started to pack her gym bag.

"Hey, Brielle, do you have a minute?" Shawna Gage asked from behind her.

Turning toward the fifteen-year-old, Brielle smiled. "Sure. What's up?"

"I aced my geometry test yesterday," the teen bragged. "Thanks to those tips you gave me."

Brielle had spent extra time with Shawna after her self-defense class every Saturday to tutor her in math, and they'd bonded. "That's great, Shawna."

"And I have a boyfriend!" she confessed, blushing to the roots of her light brown hair. "We met in the computer lab. Drake's on the baseball team. Wanna see a picture?"

"Absolutely."

Shawna scrolled through the pictures in her gallery on her cell phone until she found the right one. She handed it to Brielle, who grinned at the blond-haired boy with a perfect California tan and bright blue eyes. He had a sweet air about him, and Brielle could see why Shawna liked him.

"Oh, he's really cute, Shawna."

She giggled. "I know, right? Drake's a junior and really popular. But he's not stuck up like the other popular kids. He's down-to-earth and genuine. More to the point, he doesn't make a big deal about my dad being the mayor."

"That's important," Brielle agreed. "You know what? I have a boyfriend, too." She reached for her cell phone and pulled up a picture of her and Justice taken at the Hollywood sign. The sunset lit his golden hair, making it blaze, and emphasizing his deep blue eyes. Looking at him like that made her heart beat faster. "His name is Justice."

"Wow! He's such a hunk, Brielle," Shawna declared. "I like him so much better than your last boyfriend."

Brielle chuckled. "So do I."

"I'd really like to meet him. Wait, Justice? Justice McQuaid? He's the new chief of police, right? I want you to meet Drake, too." Her face brightened, and she snapped her fingers. "Hey, I have a great idea! Mom's birthday is next Saturday, and we're throwing this huge bash for her on the yacht. Why don't you come with Justice?"

Brielle's heart rate kicked up a notch. "I'd love to, sweetie, but we need to ask your mom if it's okay first."

"Oh, yeah, sure, Brielle. She's working out. Let's go ask her right now."

Brielle followed Shawna into the workout area where they found Vivian on the elliptical machine.

"Hey, Mom, is it okay if Brielle and her boyfriend attend your birthday party next Saturday?"

"Yes, that's fine!" Vivian panted. "I'll add Brielle plus one to the guest list."

"Thanks, Mom! I really want to introduce Brielle to Drake." Beaming, the teen turned toward Brielle and high-fived her. "I'm so happy you'll be there. By the way, it starts at seven-thirty, and it's formal wear only."

Brielle smiled. "Perfect."

# CHAPTER 12

With several hours to kill before dinner with Justice, Brielle went for her usual run on the beach and searched for signs of suspicious activity. No luck. When she returned home, she showered and dressed in a denim skirt and a sleeveless pink blouse with a scooped neckline. Grabbing an apple from the bowl of fruit on the kitchen table, Brielle touched base with her parents. As she munched, her father grilled her about the new man in her life. She tolerated his questions because, well, he was *the* Cameron "Hurricane" McAdams, a force to be reckoned with, even if he was no longer a U.S. attorney. And besides, she absolutely adored him.

After he cautioned her to be careful with losing her heart too easily, Brielle ended the call and spent another hour exchanging a flurry of text messages with her four older brothers and her sister, Brooke, a doctor in Portland, Maine, who was getting ready to head to Ecuador to treat needy children. When Brendan responded to her first text, she berated him for not telling her that something strange was happening in Laguna Beach right beneath her nose. And then he played dumb, which irked her.

Brendan: Is there? Don't know what you're talking about.

Brielle: Don't treat me like an idiot. Justice McQuaid and I are dating. Both of us found arms and ammo right on the beach.

A long pause.

Brendan: Leave it to you to get involved. I didn't want you to be a part of this.

Brielle: Too late. So spill.

He shared what little information he knew.

Brielle: That's it?

Brendan: Yeah.

Brielle: Well, we're on it now. I'll keep you posted.

Brendan: Ok. Stay safe. I love you.

Brielle: Love you back.

After their brief conversation, Brielle headed into her office and booted up her laptop. She Googled Axel Anderson and began the tedious task of reading and sifting through the online articles about him.

Part of America's elite one percent, Anderson accepted his powerful position and continued his family's legacy. On the surface nothing appeared off or out of the ordinary about him. Yet the more she delved into his life and his past, the more suspicious she became.

Brielle dug deep, using whatever resources were available to her, and fell short of calling a cyber tech she knew to hack into Anderson's business and personal bank accounts. Her patience paid off, though. Buried deep in his social media posts and little-known articles published about him, she found decidedly anti-America comments. The hate speech directed at the country she loved and served caused her blood to boil. A hunch, a gut reaction, prompted her to call Faith.

When her friend answered in a low, breathless voice, Brielle frowned. Something was definitely up with Faith.

"What's wrong? This is the first time I've been able to reach you in days. Now you're talking in whispers, and I can barely hear you. And don't give me that crap about a boyfriend. I know that's not true. Don't make me fly to Chicago, Faith, to drag the truth out of you. You know I will."

Faith blew out an exasperated breath and raised her voice a little. "All right. I'm in the middle of an investigation and don't want to be noticed. Happy?"

"Happy that you're basically yanking my chain? No. But, listen. I've got a story for you. It's about Axel Anderson."

Faith issued a string of soft curses at Brielle. "Whatwhat about him?"

Brielle's stomach clenched, as if she'd just been punched in the gut. During all the years they'd known each other, Faith had never cursed at her. And that caused hackles to rise on her neck. "Look, Faith, I'm sorry if I'm bothering you, but this is important. I think he's mixed up in something fishy here in Laguna Beach, and I'm investigating…"

A shriek followed by another round of curses stopped Brielle mid-sentence. "I can't talk to you right now!" Faith declared. "I'm busy. In the middle of an investigation as I said. Forget Anderson. He's probably dead."

Brielle stared slack-jawed at her cell phone when she realized Faith hung up on her. Speaking barely above a whisper, cursing at her, hanging up on her—nothing about Faith's behavior made sense. A cold chill ran up her spine. In her profession she'd learned to rely on her instincts, and every instinct screamed that whatever Faith was investigating wasn't good. Not at all.

She'd just about made up her mind to fly to Chicago when her phone pinged with an incoming text message.

Faith: Sorry about that. I'm investigating allegations that a high-ranking judge is visiting prostitutes. About to blow it wide open along with a CPD detective.

Her timing couldn't have been more perfect. And for that reason alone, Brielle didn't believe a single word in the text message.

Brielle: No worries. Can't wait to read the story! LOL! Be safe. Love you.

Faith: Be safe. Be careful. Love you, too.

The triple heart emojis at the end of Faith's text only partially reassured Brielle. She still didn't believe the story Faith fed her. But for now, she'd let it go.

Brielle researched Mayor Gage, Nash Carson, and Linda Ferguson until six-thirty. She'd gathered plenty of information she wanted to share with Justice.

*Justice.*

She thought about him as she applied mascara, a little blush, and pale pink lip gloss. He'd dealt with his first crisis as chief of police, and in her opinion, he'd handled it well. She hoped he'd been able to get some much-needed rest after a terrible night on the job.

After grabbing the strawberry cheesecake she'd picked up on her way home from the YMCA, Brielle strolled up the beach to Justice's place. She made her way around to the front and rang the doorbell.

Justice yanked it open a moment later, and Brielle's heart sank. His tousled hair, dark, tragic, red-rimmed deep blue eyes, and pale face filled her with sympathy and concern.

"Oh, Justice," she murmured as she crossed the threshold.

She set the cheesecake on the coffee table, took him by the hand, and led him to the sofa. "Lie down."

He obeyed and she cradled his head in her lap. Stroking his forehead with gentle fingers, she said in a soft voice, "It's going to be okay."

Justice trembled. "Jesus, Bri. Ten dead. *Ten.* And there wasn't a damn thing I could do to stop it."

She whispered again before pressing a warm kiss against

his lips. "No, don't think like that. Focus on what you *were* able to do. You said in your press conference you shot and killed Arnold Dewitt. You saved his sister's life, and probably countless others, too. That's what matters."

Her voice, her words, soothed him. Reaching up, he pulled her head down to meet his mouth in a long, thrilling kiss that set passion aflame between them. And although he only had to slightly turn his head to nuzzle her breasts, Justice didn't take advantage of her. Disappointment swept through her. She wanted him to touch her so badly!

Emitting a soft sigh, Brielle murmured, "You stay here on the sofa. I'll cook dinner."

"No, no. I got this." Justice rose to his feet. "I already stuffed a couple of Cornish hens, and they're roasting in the oven. You can help with the rest of the meal, though." He eyed the cheesecake. "My favorite, next to your mom's peach cobbler. Did she make the cheesecake, too?"

Brielle smiled. "Not this time. I stopped at a bakery after I left the Y."

"Oh. Well, I bet she makes an awesome cheesecake."

"She does."

"Want a tour before we eat? The hens won't be done for another fifteen minutes."

"Sure."

Justice proudly showed her his home, pointing out the features he loved about it. When they reached the top level, though, he adamantly refused to show Brielle the master bedroom.

"It's a mess," he explained.

Brielle shot him a funny look but didn't comment.

By the time they finished touring the house, the oven timer buzzed. Justice removed the pair of juicy, golden-brown Cornish hens from the oven as Brielle tossed the ingredients for a salad. Working together, throwing teasing comments about whose culinary skills were better, they finished preparing their meal and set everything on the kitchen table.

Justice grasped her hand. He said a quick prayer for the souls they'd lost during the night, and especially for Rosie as she grieved for her family. Brielle echoed his "Amen" and squeezed his hand before they began to eat.

After commenting on the succulent meat, Brielle continued, "I've got great news, Justice. You and I are attending Vivian Gage's birthday party next Saturday on the yacht."

His face brightened. "Perfect. I knew you could do it."

"Well, actually it was their daughter Shawna's idea, but Vivian approved and added me plus one to the guest list."

Justice swallowed a bite of salad. "Plus one, huh? Get that life preserver ready, Bri. The mayor already gave me hell about last night."

She warmed to his use of a nickname for her. It was her mother's too. "I told you I'd save you," she reminded him in a teasing tone of voice. "There's more, though."

While they ate, Brielle shared her research on the principal players in their mystery. Impressed by her thoroughness, Justice fired questions at her, and they discussed possible theories based on their new information. A terrifying picture formed of what might be happening, but they lacked proof.

"And you couldn't get any information from your brother?" Justice inquired as their discussion drew to a close.

"No. Closemouthed as ever." Brielle cleared the table and cut slices of the delectable cheesecake.

Justice closed his eyes as he savored the first bite. "Mmm. This is really good."

He looked so damn sexy as he licked his lips just then that Brielle felt her stomach tighten with desire. God, she wanted him so much!

"I love your house," she commented randomly to get her mind off sex. "It's a lot of room for just one person, though, since you don't have a large fam..."

Brielle clapped a hand over her mouth as color shot into Justice's face. "I'm so sorry! I didn't mean to..."

He waved his hand. "Don't apologize. My dad made the same remark." His eyes bored into hers. "The truth is, I rented the house because of you."

She frowned in confusion. "What? I don't understand."

"I saw you running on the beach as Mrs. Bosco, the realtor, was showing us the house. When I realized you lived a few hundred yards down from it, I snatched at renting the place," Justice confessed.

She smiled. "I see."

His eyes grew deep and unfathomable like the ocean. He cleared his throat. "I'm ready to settle down," he began in a soft voice. "I want a real home and a family. I had a great career in the Navy, and now I have a second one in law enforcement, and I'm tired of being alone. I want to share my life with someone. Someone who shares my values. Someone who's loving, kind, compassionate, funny, and smart." Justice continued to hold her gaze. "But more importantly, someone who's strong and independent. Not afraid to speak her mind or set me straight when I need it. Someone who loves kids. Last night reminded me that I'm pretty good with them. Rosie Dewitt likes me and trusts me. So, I..." his voice trailed away.

While he'd been speaking, Brielle's heart melted, drawn into the future he described. She'd never heard sweeter words. "Go on," she encouraged him.

"Well, I... I think I want to adopt her," Justice blurted. "And I guess... I need to know if...if that's okay with you. And if you're in this with me for the long haul. I mean, I'm all in with you. And I just wonder if...if you think I'm a man worth having...worth loving..."

At the stunned expression on her face, he broke off and groaned. "Oh, God! I just blew it, didn't I? I blew it! I spoke too soon about what I want, and I've scared you off. Oh, man, I'm such an idiot."

Brielle's mind whirled, making coherent thought impossible. Her heart slammed into her chest as pure longing curled in her stomach. She rose to her feet on shaky legs and planted herself in his lap. He sat stiffly, probably unsure of what she planned to do, like slap him silly, for instance. She cupped his scruffy face and molded her mouth against his in a gentle kiss. It lasted mere moments before she rained butterfly kisses on his cheeks, his nose, and his forehead. She encircled his ear with her delicate tongue and blew her breath into it. She took his mouth again, then began to travel a path down his neck, nipping and lightly sucking. Brielle inhaled deeply of his scent—a combination of earthy spices.

Wanting to feel his warm skin beneath her fingers, she pulled his T-shirt over his head and ran her hands up and down his bare chest devoid of any tattoos. Her mouth followed her hands. When her tongue flicked across his nipples, Justice drew in a sharp breath, and she felt his full arousal beneath her.

"Bri," he muttered. "What—what are you doing?"

Her hand dipped lower and rested on the waistband of his jeans for a moment. He sucked in his gut as she unfastened his Levi's and slipped her hand inside to caress him. His breath came hard and fast.

"What does it *feel* like I'm doing?" Brielle countered.

Justice gritted his teeth as she continued to stroke him and press kisses against his chest. "Um, uh, it feels like you're making love to me." He groaned. "Ahh...God, Brielle!"

She captured his mouth with hers, and when his lips

parted in an open invitation, she slid her tongue inside and swirled it around his in an erotic dance. He grew rock hard under her ministrations. Brielle took his hands and placed them on her rib cage just below her breasts. Though he kissed her deeply and hungrily, his hands remained still instead of roaming over her body as she desired.

Lifting her head, she murmured, "Yes, I'm making love to you." She paused. "I love the fact that you're an old-fashioned gentleman, but I swear to God, Justice, if you don't touch *me*, the woman who may bear your children someday, I will leave."

His eyes widened a moment before her threat galvanized him into action. His hands slipped beneath her blouse and teased her nipples, already hard and throbbing and pressing against the flimsy material of her bra.

And then he took control of their lovemaking. He rose to his feet with her in his arms and started to move quickly toward the stairs.

"I'm taking you to bed, Miss McAdams. Any objections?" he demanded, his voice thick with desire.

"None. It's about time, Chief," she answered, humoring him.

He chuckled, but his mirth left him as they reached his bedroom door. "Um, you can't go in there," he declared, setting her on her feet.

"Oh, why the hell not, Justice? It can't be *that* messy. After all, I grew up with four older brothers."

She pushed open the door and burst into laughter when she noticed the pink comforter. "Oh, my God! Are the sheets pink, too?"

Justice's face flushed to the roots of his golden hair. "Uh, yeah. Pepto-Bismol pink. My dad's idea of a joke. If you'll wait a few minutes, I'll change them."

"Uh-uh. I want to see you naked on those pink sheets."

Brielle maneuvered him backward until his knees bumped against the side of the bed. "Sit down, Navy Boy."

Justice obeyed and pulled her between his legs. With enticing slowness, he unbuttoned her blouse and tossed it aside. His eyes feasted on her rosy nipples, peeking through her lacy pink bra. Leaning forward, he drew one nipple into his mouth, teasing it, then the other. The warm wetness seeping through the material, incredibly erotic, caused Brielle to groan aloud with pleasure. In one fluid movement, Justice reached behind her and unhooked her bra, dropping it next to her blouse. He cupped each breast, bringing them close to his face and sucking hard on those puckered nubs.

Brielle closed her eyes, threw her head back, and buried her hands in his hair. Justice's mouth moved from her breasts down her torso, licking and nipping her smooth skin until he reached her navel. He teased it with his tongue as he unzipped her denim skirt, and it fell to her feet. She kicked it aside and inhaled sharply when Justice rolled her lacy pink panties down her hips.

"You're so beautiful," he murmured before he pressed his mouth right above her mound.

Brielle pushed Justice back on the bed and pulled his jeans from his hard, lean body. "Mmm. Boxers. Good choice," she noted with a smile before they landed on the floor.

When his full erection sprang free, Brielle's eyes grew wide in appreciation of his male beauty. "Oh, wow!" she exclaimed as she ran a hand up and down his long, hard shaft. "I think it's about eight or nine inches."

Justice let out a strangled cry, a half laugh, half gasp as Brielle took him in her mouth. She used her tongue and her hands to stroke him in rhythmic harmony. His moans of pleasure and the tensing of his body alerted her to his fast-approaching orgasm. Very deliberately, her tongue slid across his slit, and that was his undoing. His body exploded, shaking with waves of intense pleasure.

"Jesus, Brielle!" he panted.

Noting he was still rock hard, she rose to her feet and smiled at him. "Don't move. I'll be right back. And then I'm going to rock your world, Chief."

When she returned after refreshing herself, Brielle leaned down and murmured, "I'm clean, Chief. I just had a check-up two weeks ago, and I haven't been with anyone for months. Malcom always used a condom, and I'm on the pill."

"I'm clean, too," Justice assured her. "I, um, haven't had sex in, uh, over a year, and I always used protection."

"Well, then, I don't expect we'll get any sleep tonight." She straddled him, sighing with satisfaction as his hard shaft fully penetrated her. He moaned, gripping her hips.

"Bri, don't you want..." he muttered.

"Oh, yes, I *want*, Justice. I want everything you've got to offer. But right now I'm taking care of *you*."

"Jesus!" he swore again and thrust upward, fast and furiously.

Her moans fueled his desire, and he rolled her beneath him. Capturing her mouth with his, he kissed her hard, his tongue sliding in and out, imitating the rhythm of his lower body. She took him fully inside of her, her inner walls stretching to accommodate him. Justice slipped his hand between them in order to stimulate her. The friction of his shaft and the stroking of his fingers drove Brielle to the brink.

"Oh, God, Justice! Now! Please, now!" she begged him, clutching his back.

With one final thrust, they freefell together into a passionate abyss. Brielle bucked against him, squeezing him and drawing out his pleasure. Breathing heavily, Justice collapsed on top of her. A moment later he rolled away from her and onto his feet.

Holding out his hand, he said, "Come."

Her legs felt like jelly as he led her into the bathroom and turned on the water in the shower. He adjusted the temperature, and they stepped into the stall as water like raindrops fell gently on them. Justice sensuously lathered Brielle's body with soap, pausing often to kiss her and suckle upon her breasts. She did the same for him, using her skillful hands to arouse him. The combination of the slick soap and her long strokes caused soft moans of pleasure to escape from his throat.

Lifting her hips, he thrust into her, making sure his angle hit her most sensitive spot. When her breathing grew ragged, he knew she was ready to come again. He increased his rhythm until she cried aloud, and he let himself go. They cleansed each other again, and after they dried themselves with Pepto-Bismol pink towels, Justice carried Brielle back to his bed.

He covered her body with his, and tenderly brushed the hair out her eyes. Justice claimed her mouth in a hot kiss before he whispered, "What you did for me, well, now it's your turn, baby. Let me take care of you."

# CHAPTER 13

He nibbled, tasted, and savored the sexy curves of her mouth before taking it fully with his own. His tongue slowly probed inside, swirling and sparring with hers. He lifted her arms above her head and threaded his fingers through hers as his mouth slanted across her lips. When he sucked her bottom lip, her body writhed beneath his. Justice broke the sweet, tortuous kiss and trailed a fiery path down her neck, licking and grazing it with his teeth. He focused attention on her perfect breasts, devoting equal time to each one, flicking his tongue across her nipples, nipping them with his teeth and drawing hard upon them.

Brielle's breath caught in her throat at the incredible sensations he aroused in her. "Justice," she moaned. She tried to caress him, but he wouldn't let her.

"No, baby. I haven't rocked *your* world yet."

He placed openmouthed kisses along her toned torso and moved further down her body until he reached the tantalizing apex between her thighs. He stopped short then, to caress and kiss her feet, slide his hands up her legs, and press his mouth on the sensitive spot behind her knees. Justice made her breathless with anticipation as he pulled her legs apart and ran his hands along her inner thighs. He teased her mercilessly as he slid a finger inside her hot, wet folds before he lowered his head and used his tongue to excite her. Long, slow strokes with pauses in between each one caused Brielle to whimper and moan low in her throat as she tossed her head from side to side. When his tongue flicked her clit, she gasped and arched her back.

"Oh, God, Justice!"

He blew softly into her and continued those slow, measured strokes, every so often teasing her clit until the sweet pleasure building inside of her exploded in the most powerful and intense orgasm she'd ever experienced. At that moment Justice sucked hard on her clit, and Brielle cried his name, gripping the sheet beneath her.

When her body stopped shuddering, he flipped her over, moving her hair aside so he could kiss her neck and her shoulders. One finger traced her spine followed by feather-light kisses. He squeezed her softer, rounder, more tempting curves, and lifting her up a little, inserted one finger, then a second into her slick opening.

Her soft mewls of pleasure excited him, and he couldn't hold back any longer. Justice turned Brielle onto her back and sank deep inside her, groaning as she took all of his hard, pulsing length. Wanting to prolong their penultimate climax, wanting to please Brielle more than himself, he thrust slowly and steadily, then changed his rhythm, sometimes pulling nearly all the way out before pumping against her.

Raking her nails lightly down his back, Brielle practically sobbed as she demanded him to move faster and harder. As she reached her climax, she cried, "Yes! Oh, God, yes!"

Justice cut her off by capturing her mouth with his, moaning his own pleasure deep in his throat. He kissed her hard until their bodies stopped quaking from the ecstasy they shared. Afterward, they lay, limbs entwined, as Justice guided Brielle's head onto his chest.

"My answer is yes," she told him in a soft voice. "To everything you wanted to know. If you want to adopt Rosie, I'll support you. In fact, let's visit her tomorrow so you can introduce me. And," she pressed a warm kiss against his skin, "I think you're definitely a man worth loving. You're amazing, Justice. Both in and out of bed."

His arms tightened around her. "So are you. I've been waiting my entire life to meet a woman like you. I know this happened fast, but I've never felt like this about anyone else. Thanks, by the way, for not slapping me or shoving the cheesecake in my face or running out the door earlier. And mostly, thanks for the way you made love to me. You made me feel, I don't know…"

"I hope I made you feel wanted. Appreciated," she responded. "Because that's how you made me feel. And I've never felt like this about anyone else, either, which is why I trust it. Trust *you*."

Justice grinned. "We lit this bed on fire."

Brielle leaned up on one elbow. "Ready for round three?"

"I think it's four, but who's counting?" Justice drawled as he rolled her beneath him and molded his mouth to hers.

After a long night of lovemaking, they finally fell into a deep, sated sleep.

* * *

Brielle awoke mid-morning. She yawned and stretched before glancing down at Justice. She smiled as she recalled the incredible things they'd done in his bed all night. He proved to be a fantastic lover, generous and giving, always caring more about her pleasure and satisfaction than his own. But she took care of his needs, too, as they explored each other's body and learned what pleased them the most.

Expelling a soft breath, Brielle didn't have the heart to wake Justice. He looked so peaceful and boyish with one arm resting on the pillow above his head. Quietly, she slipped from the bed and took a quick shower. Her body still tingled from making exquisite love for hours. Honestly, she didn't think she was capable of having multiple orgasms, one after another, until Justice learned the secrets of her body.

After rummaging through a dresser drawer, she found one of his Navy T-shirts and pulled it on. It fell to her knees, and she smiled.

Downstairs in the kitchen, Brielle brewed a pot of coffee and poured herself a cup, enjoying those first few sips as she gazed at the Pacific. The sun shining gloriously on the water reflected the brightness deep in her soul this morning. But nothing compared to the man sleeping upstairs and his place in her life. In her heart.

Turning away from the view, she found eggs, link sausage, and pancake mix. Humming to herself, she fried the sausage while flipping pancakes. When the sausage was done, she scrambled half a dozen eggs.

Just as she flipped the last pancake onto a platter, she heard Justice's rich, deep voice. "You look damn sexy in my T-shirt."

Brielle set the platter of pancakes on the granite counter and sidled toward him. "Good morning." She offered her mouth for a kiss.

"Good morning." Justice crushed her against him. His mouth slanted relentlessly across hers, his tongue plundering again and again as he lifted the T-shirt.

"Aren't you hungry?" she whispered against his lips.

"Starved. But breakfast can wait."

He swept her into his arms and took her upstairs for a

quick romp in his bed and again in the shower. Laughing, they chased each other downstairs to the kitchen.

After they devoured every single bite of food, several cups of coffee and glasses of orange juice, they discussed their plans for the rest of the day. Justice called the Westfalls and arranged to see Rosie around two o'clock that afternoon.

"Let's have a picnic on the beach," Brielle suggested. "Nothing fancy. Just sandwiches, chips, cookies, and lemonade. I'll pack a basket."

"I really like that idea."

He wrapped an arm around her waist as he walked Brielle back to her house.

Before they parted, Justice kissed her. "Have I told you that I think you're the most beautiful woman I've ever met? And I'm not talking about the way you look."

She shook her head. "No."

He cupped her face and gazed at her, eyes smoldering with a dark blue heat. "You are. Without a doubt. And I'm lucky to have you in my life."

"I'm lucky, too," she murmured before she melted into him.

* * *

After checking in at the station, Justice called his father to discuss what occurred with Arnold Dewitt and the latest development in his relationship with Brielle.

Franklin offered his support of the rough situation regarding the deaths of nine innocent people, ten including Dewitt, but cautioned his son not to invest so much of himself in one woman.

"This is what you do, Justice. Go all in with your heart, and before you know it, it's ripped out of your chest. Have you forgotten what Clara did to you? How many times do I have to say this before you listen to me?"

Justice ran his free hand through his hair. "Dad, you're right. I've done it again. Jumped in without thinking. But this time I laid out my expectations, what I wanted, and Brielle didn't run for the nearest door. She's the one. I feel it in my gut. If you could just see us together, you'd agree. So, when are you coming out to California for a visit?"

"I don't know, son. Maybe next month."

"Perhaps for the first time in your life, you leapt before you looked, and now you regret it," Justice gently chided his father. "Have you thought at all about Adrienne? Or spoken to her?"

"Yes and no. Look, just take care of your own life, and I'll take care of mine," Franklin snapped.

"Okay, Dad. No need to bite my head off. I'll call you in a few days."

"Sure. I'll talk to you then."

Justice shook his head. He wished his dad would move on with his life and find some measure of happiness.

While he waited for Brielle to rejoin him, he searched online for military surplus stores. There were a couple in the general area, but unfortunately, they were closed on weekends. At the first opportunity, he planned to show them a picture of Nash Carson and see if they could ID him. He didn't find anything in Carson's past to indicate he'd been in the military, but that didn't necessarily mean it wasn't true. Looked like he'd have to call Tex and ask him to check out Carson.

When Brielle sent a text to let him know she was on her way, Justice quickly changed into a pair of board short swim trunks and a tank top. He met her on his deck, and his eyes lit with admiration. She wore a pair of navy shorts and a white tank top over her bikini.

Pulling her in for a kiss, he commented, "You look hot."

Brielle tilted her head as she eyed him. "Where's your badge and your gun, Chief?" she teased.

"I'm off duty today. Completely. I'm all yours."

Earlier they'd decided to walk up the beach to the West-falls' house, and as they started down the steps of the deck, Brielle grabbed his warm hand.

"Yes, you certainly are. In every way."

Her words caused his heart to soar. Though he suspected Secretary of State Washburn's true motive for sending him to Laguna Beach, he'd have to thank her one day. He'd found his reason for living.

When they climbed the wooden steps to the Westfalls' deck, Rosie shuffled out of the house and plopped into a chair.

"Hi," she mumbled.

She wore a cute one-piece bathing suit, anticipating their picnic on the beach. Justice hugged her and dropped a kiss on her head. "Hey, squirt."

"Who's this?" Rosie asked, looking with interest at Brielle.

"This is my girlfriend, Brielle." No need to mention she was also a cop just yet.

Brielle held out her hand, which Rosie accepted. "Hi, Rosie. It's nice to meet you."

"You, too." She eyed the picnic basket. "I'm kinda hungry."

Justice chuckled. "So am I! Let's head down to the beach."

He grabbed a huge beach umbrella, a few towels, and the blanket the Westfalls' provided, and the trio tramped down the steps. They found their perfect spot, and Justice set up the umbrella while Brielle spread the blanket and set the picnic basket on it. He attached a brown hexagonal Blue-tooth speaker to one of the spokes in the umbrella and pulled up a playlist of Disney tunes on his cell phone. They listened to the soundtrack from the *Moana* as they devoured ham and cheese sandwiches, potato chips, and nearly the entire container of homemade chocolate chip cookies.

Afterward, Justice helped Rosie build an elaborate fortress in the sand. He flashed Brielle a smile as he lugged sand and water to create their architectural wonder. His eyes kept straying toward her because she'd removed her tank top and shorts to reveal her body clad in an emerald green bikini. God, she was killing him!

Hot and sweaty and covered in sand, Justice and Rosie decided to take a dip in the Pacific after they built their sand-castle. Brielle joined them, and they enjoyed frolicking in the powerful, rolling waves. Rosie could swim, but Justice and Brielle kept a close eye on her.

Later, they returned to their blanket and finished the rest of the lemonade and cookies before heading back to the house.

After Rosie hugged and thanked them for spending the afternoon with her, Justice and Brielle turned to leave.

"Wait, Justice!" Her chin quivered a little. "Aren't there supposed to be funerals for Mom and Dad? For my aunt and uncle and cousins? And…and Arnie?"

Startled by her unexpected question, Justice looked help-lessly at Brielle.

She sat on a deck chair and pulled Rosie close to her. "Rosie, honey, how do you know about such things?"

Big tears filled her brown eyes. "I'm not a baby, Brielle. I'll be eleven in July. I've been to funerals. I know we're supposed to bury the dead."

Brielle glanced up at Justice and saw the stricken, heart-sick expression on his face. She tightened her arms around the little girl. "I'll tell you what. Justice and I and the West-falls will make all the arrangements for the services. Tomorrow after school Mrs. Westfall can take you home so you can get the rest of your things and pick out clothes for your mom, dad, and brother. And maybe some pictures, too. Justice and I will go to your aunt and uncle's house and do the same. It may take a couple of weeks, though, for everything to be settled. Does that sound okay?"

Those big tears pooling in Rosie's eyes now rolled down her cheeks. She threw her arms around Brielle's neck and mumbled, "'kay."

"Do you want to go to school tomorrow, sweetie? There's only three weeks left. Mrs. Westfall could pick up your assignments for you."

Rosie lifted her head. "Yeah, I'm good to go to school. I *need* to."

"Well, if anyone bothers you, tell them you've got Chief Justice on speed dial," Justice chimed in. "I'll be there in a flash to set them straight."

She grinned. "Thanks, Chief, but I'll be okay."

He ruffled her hair. "All right, kid."

As he and Brielle walked back to his house, he said, "Bri, maybe it's just me, but do you think Rosie is, well, far too calm after what's happened?"

"It's not you. I don't think reality has hit her yet, and when it does, you need to be prepared, Justice. There's no telling how she will react."

* * *

Justice and Brielle spent a romantic evening making sweet love and talking and caressing while they lay in each other's arms on his pink sheets. Before it grew too late, however, he escorted Brielle home, and they kissed for long moments on her deck, loath to part.

"I'm gonna miss your warm body next to mine tonight," Justice murmured, tracing her jawline with a finger.

Brielle uttered just one word. "Stay."

He couldn't resist her invitation. They made love one more time before falling asleep, wrapped securely in each other's arms. By four-thirty, though, they were up and out on the beach to continue Brielle's training. An hour and a half later Justice kissed Brielle farewell, told her to be careful, and promised he'd see her at the Main Street Gym after their shifts ended.

Justice's first order of business at the station that morning was to deal with his four officers returning from their suspension. He dealt quickly with Morton and Holcomb, partnering them with older, more experienced officers and sending them on their way.

Officer Owen Dooley, however, posed a different problem. From the scowl on his face, Justice presumed his attitude toward him remained unchanged.

Leaning back in his leather swivel chair, he asked, "Why did you become a cop, Officer Dooley?"

"To serve and protect." Dooley smirked.

"Cut the bullshit. You and I both know that's not true. You haven't earned a single commendation the entire time you've been on the force. In fact, you have a file full of complaints. So, either get real with me or get the hell out of my department. I'm on the fence about firing you, anyway."

"You want real? All right, I'll give you *real*. My sister was murdered fifteen years ago, and her killer has never been caught. She was eighteen, just graduated from high school, when Hayden was snatched right off the beach in broad daylight. *Our* beach." Dooley paused, shaken by the memory.

"I was sixteen, and I remember that day as if it were yesterday. It's burned in my memory. When she didn't come home, my parents went ballistic trying to find her. Cops swarmed our house, but I remember one who took the time to notice me and what I was going through. Officer Miles Bryan."

"The officer for whom the forensic lab is named?"

"Yeah, that's him. He vowed to find my sister's killer after her body was found in the Redwood National Forest. God, he devoted hours of his own personal time to follow the leads, but nothing ever panned out. When the FBI and local authorities finally gave up, Officer Bryan kept on looking until the day he died in a gunfight. He never forgot me, either. We kept in touch. He and my sister are the reason I became a cop."

Justice studied him, wondering what went wrong. Why he became so ineffective and apathetic. But he also saw an honest part of Dooley he could mold into something better.

"Well, Dooley," he addressed the officer as he tapped his pencil on his desk, "today's your lucky day because I'm not going to fire you. Instead, you're joining a team of five I'm creating. But," he leaned forward, "you need to get in better shape, so your training starts tomorrow morning on the beach. 5 AM. My place."

"Oh, hell no," he growled. "That's not happenin'."

Justice rose to his feet. "You know, I'm sick of your insubordination. I'm giving you an opportunity to work with an elite team, and trust me, we'll look for your sister's killer, and to be a credit to Officer Bryan, and you're turning it down?" He shook his head. "Looks like I'm firing you after all. Get out of my office."

Dooley panicked. "Wait, Chief. Please. Give me another chance. I want to find Hayden's killer. If you and this team can help, I'm in."

Justice expelled his breath. "Fine. Go to the conference room and wait for me."

Accustomed to holding his cards close to his chest, Justice's expression revealed nothing when he met Carson next. He noticed, however, faint yellow and purple bruises on Carson's face, and oddly, he wore a long-sleeved shirt in spite of the heat. Peeking beneath the cuffs, Justice observed partially healed ligature marks.

Frowning, Justice asked, "What happened to you, Officer Carson? Have you been in a fight? Let me see your wrists."

Carson pulled back his cuffs to give Justice a brief glimpse of the marks. "Yeah, Chief. I've been in a fight with a beast of a horse. I flew home to Texas where I'm from, and a wild stallion threw me. I got caught up in the reins, and he dragged me all over the corral until my dad's ranch hands caught him."

Justice gave him credit for his creative lie. He suspected Carson had been brutally punished by someone for losing the assault rifle and ammo. "Well, Officer Carson, you're going to have to be more careful around wild stallions. Can't afford to lose you. I hope you've learned your lesson, though."

"I have, Chief, and I'm ready to get back to work."

"Excellent. I can see an improvement in your attitude already. For the time being, I want you to ride with Officer Rivera. I think you can learn a lot from him. He has a meeting with me in a couple of minutes, so you'll be heading out after that."

"Okay, Chief."

When they left Justice's office, they headed in opposite directions.

*Cool as a cucumber. No more blank, empty looks. What's up with that?* Justice thought.

He put aside his concern over Carson as he entered his conference room and faced Tawny, River, Martini, Dooley, and Hutch. All five looked at him, a common question in their eyes. Why were they there?

"Good morning. I can see you're wondering what's going on. The simple truth is, I need you to help me do this job and to have my back. I know this is unorthodox, but I'm forming a team. Each of you brings something unique to the table which we will definitely utilize moving forward. We have a situation, a dangerous one, but before I get into it, I have to share some information about myself."

In the silence following his explanation of his brain injury and its effect on him, Justice waited, holding his breath for their response.

One voice eventually broke the heaviness in the room. "I've got your back, Chief. Whatever you need from me, I'm in," River declared, his tone firm and confident.

Four others echoed the same promise.

# CHAPTER 14

Grateful for their support, Justice straightened his shoulders and took command. He handed everyone a file folder Brielle had prepared and methodically laid out the situation he believed he'd been sent to investigate.

"As you can see, we have few facts and a lot of conjecture," he finished. "Something is brewing, none of it good. We need to find out where those arms are coming from and who's stockpiling them."

"And why and where they're being kept," Luca added. "Jesus. This is nuts."

"What do you need from us, Chief?" Hutch asked.

"I need you and Luca to work together on the Anderson angle. River, you'll be keeping a close eye on Carson now that he's been assigned your partner. Chat him up. See if you can get him talking. Dooley, I want you to hit the military surplus stores in the area. Show Carson's picture. In the meantime, I'll find out if he has a military service record. And, um, my girlfriend Sergeant Brielle McAdams with the LAPD and I will be checking things out on Mayor Gage's yacht on Saturday while we attend his wife's birthday party."

Dooley's eyes grew wide a moment, and he muttered under his breath, "Fuck me."

Justice heard him and hid a small smile. Dooley would be lucky tomorrow morning if Brielle didn't kick his ass!

"Okay, team, you know what you have to do. Tawny is my eyes and ears, and my second-in-command. You need anything go through her. She runs this place, anyway." He tossed a grin at her. "One more thing. We're working on a cold case. The murder of Dooley's sister, Hayden. We're gonna get this guy, dead or alive. Luca, that's a top priority for you. Understood?"

Luca glanced at Dooley's red face. "Understood, Chief. I'll pull the case files right away."

Chairs scraped against the tiled floor as they rose to their feet.

"It goes without saying that complete confidentiality is required. What is shared and discussed in this room *stays* in this room."

"Copy that, Chief," they repeated one after the other.

Alone in the conference room, Justice sent Brielle a text giving her the heads up about Dooley training with her.

She sent back a perplexed emoji.

Brielle: If that's what you want. By the way, got word today my final eval is next Monday. I've got one week to prove myself.

Justice: Don't worry. I've got you. You'll be ready. See you later.

Thinking about contacting the ME's office to find out when the bodies of the Dewitts and the Swifts would be released, the last person on his mind this morning was the mayor, but he found him pacing outside his office.

"Mr. Mayor," Justice acknowledged him with a slight nod of his head and closed the door behind him. "Care to sit?"

"No, I don't care to sit!" Gage fumed. "Do you know how

much backlash I've faced since your screw-up on Saturday? You've got plenty to explain, Chief McQuaid!"

"I don't give a damn about your issues with the media or your public image, if that's what you're griping about. My concern is for the families of two dead teenagers and a ten-year-old little girl who will never get over what her brother did. And, furthermore, I'd like to know how I or this department screwed up. As far as I'm concerned, every officer who worked those crime scenes followed procedure. We took Arnold Dewitt down. Will we ever know why he snapped? Depends on the ME's report and eyewitness statements which we're still sifting through.

"Later today I'll be visiting Theo's and Pedro's parents. Concerned about your image, Mr. Mayor? Why don't you come with me? It'll be a perfect photo op."

Fury poured off Mayor Gage in waves. Their eyes clashed in a battle of iron wills. Justice had no intention of backing down. In fact, it took every ounce of his self-control not to demand information from Gage about the movement of arms on Laguna Beach. He stood firm with his powerful arms crossed over his chest, daring the mayor to further criticize him and the department. His body language and the hardness of his eyes must have convinced Gage he didn't hold any sway over Justice because the mayor physically backed away from him.

"I'm sorry, Chief McQuaid. What happened shocked me. Shocked the community."

Justice wondered if the mayor truly realized he'd gone too far or if he was just playing a game with him. "If you're truly shocked, Mr. Mayor, then do something about it. Go talk to the community. Spend some time on the beach. Eat lunch at Pop's Diner. Do something other than giving me a hard time about it." He made a point of glancing at his watch.

"Now, if you'll excuse me, I have phone calls to make. To the morgue, for one."

Without another word Mayor Gage left the office.

Justice spent twenty minutes getting an update from the ME on the progress of the autopsies. Satisfied with the information he'd been given, he called Tex to ask him to check into Carson.

"McQuaid, hi. How's it going?"

"A lot better than when you saw me two months ago."

"Glad to hear it. So…you and Brielle McAdams, huh?"

Justice grinned. "Yeah. She's quite a woman."

"Uh-huh. I could be wrong, McQuaid, but I don't think you called me just to shoot the breeze. What's up?"

"Something that Brielle and I are looking into. Will you run the name Nash Carson through your system and tell me whether or not he's ever been in the military?"

"Sure. Hold on."

Justice heard Tex typing furiously on his keyboard and a couple of minutes later he said, "Nah. No record of anyone by that name being in any branch of the service. And by the way, your guy is nearly a ghost. He doesn't have much of a digital footprint."

"Yeah. He just appeared out of nowhere two years ago. If you don't mind, could you continue looking into him?"

"No problem. I'll let you know what I find."

After Justice ended the call, he spent the rest of the morning dealing with issues as they arose and any loose ends regarding the murders that occurred over the weekend. Toward one o'clock he asked Tawny if she wanted to ride along with him on patrol and visit the grieving families of Theo and Pedro, but she declined. He wondered why she preferred to be a desk sergeant when he'd seen for himself just how well she handled herself in the field. As he headed toward his Explorer, he made a mental note to ask her about it.

Worried about Rosie's first day of school, he pulled up in front of Top of the World Elementary School and waited for her to be brought to the parents' loop after he spent time with Theo's and Pedro's parents. Listening to them tell stories about their boys through laughter and tears drained him.

Cynthia Westfall was there to pick up Rosie, but when the child caught sight of Justice, she waved and hurried toward him.

"Hi, Chief!" She hugged him and waved at Cynthia.

"How was your day, squirt?"

"It was good. Everyone was really nice to me. The lunch lady gave me an extra cookie!"

Her girlish giggle warmed Justice's heart. "That's awesome. Okay, go on now. Mrs. Westfall is waiting for you. Do you have any homework?"

Rosie made a face. "Yeah. Pages and *pages* of math. Yuck!"

He chuckled. "All right, then. Get to it."

Justice hung around with the school resource officer, making sure the students were safe getting into their parents' vehicles and crossing the street if they were walking home. Over the next two days he thought he should make similar visits to the middle school and high school. Maybe talk to the kids. No pressure. Just a *want to get to know you* approach.

He drove through Laguna Beach, checking on things, until his shift ended at five o'clock. Exhausted by his emotional visit to the teenage boys' families, he was ready to call it a day. Tawny had created a group chat and sent out her first text.

Tawny: Report in, guys.

Martini and Hutch texted they'd made little progress on their investigation. River reported that Carson had been friendly though not forthcoming about himself. When Dooley didn't respond, Tawny sent out another text.

Tawny: Put down that donut, Dooley! We need a status report.

Dooley: Give me a freakin' break! I was doing my job. You know? Writing a speeding a ticket?

Justice: Any luck?

Dooley: No. Went to every military surplus store in a twenty-five-mile radius. No one recognized our guy.

Justice: Great job, team. See you tomorrow. Especially you, Dooley. Don't forget!

He replied with an unhappy face emoji.

Justice chuckled to himself and hopped on his bike.

When he arrived at the Main Street Gym, Brielle looked both serious and scared. She wasn't attacking the punching bag with her usual verve.

Pulling her aside, Justice got right down to business. "We've got one week to whip you into shape, Bri. So, tell me, are you whipped right now?"

Her head snapped up. "No. Why would you ask that?"

"Because you look defeated to me."

"I just—I just don't want to let you down."

He didn't think that was it but didn't want to contradict her. "You won't. Not if you try. If you try and fail, that's one thing. Not trying, though? No excuse for that." His voice softened. "And just for the record, Bri, there's nothing you could ever do or say that would let me down except…"

"Except what?"

"Tell me we're through in a text message. That would hurt. A lot. Worse than getting hit in the head with a piece of steel."

Her radiant smile warmed his heart. "Not likely." She lifted her chin. "Let's go, Chief. I'm ready."

After a tough session, Justice and Brielle showered and dressed and met outside the locker room.

"Any thoughts about dinner?" Brielle asked as they headed toward their motorcycles. "We could go to another one of my favorite restaurants."

"Actually, Bri, if you don't mind, I'd really love a quiet dinner at home."

"That sounds perfect to me."

By the time they stepped into Brielle's living room, Justice felt wiped out. Brielle told him to lie down on the sofa while she prepared a light supper of tomato soup and sandwiches. As soon as his head touched the throw pillow, he fell asleep.

Several hours later he jerked awake, heart pounding from his usual nightmares, made worse by the killings over the weekend. Disoriented, it took a few moments for him to realize he was at Brielle's house. She'd thrown a blanket over him and removed his shoes. Touched by her tender thoughtfulness, he headed upstairs to join her in bed. He wanted to make love to her, teased by the scent and softness of her skin, but she lay sleeping so peacefully, he didn't have the heart to wake her, especially after what he'd put her through earlier at the gym. Molding his naked body against hers, he dropped a kiss on her shoulder and promptly fell into a sleep devoid of any more nightmares.

In the darkness of morning, Brielle roused him with warm kisses and the magic of her skillful hands, mouth, and tongue. Justice rolled her beneath him and began a slow, erotic exploration of her body. Enthralled with each other, they made love, took a shower, and dressed. Justice had just enough time to change into his workout clothes at his house before he met Dooley and Brielle on the beach.

When Dooley saw Brielle, he declared, "I know she's your girlfriend, Chief, but what the hell is she doing here?"

"She's training for SWAT. Now apologize to her, Dooley."

"Sorry." He mumbled his apology and held out his hand. "No hard feelings?"

"None." She gripped his hand.

"All right, you two. Drop and give me a hundred push-ups."

Dooley's eyes went wide. He dropped to the sand and grunted as he used muscles he hadn't exercised in years. After he did ten, he started to struggle. Justice crouched next to him, urging him to keep at it, to reach deep, until Dooley couldn't do one more push-up. He made it to thirty before he collapsed.

"Sorry, Chief!" he panted. "Can't do it!"

"On your feet," Justice ordered. Brielle had finished her push-ups by the time Dooley hit thirty.

Dooley scrambled to his feet. He did better with jumping jacks and squats but running as fast as Justice and Brielle wasn't an option. He jogged a couple of miles, with them keeping pace beside him, until he couldn't breathe. Justice told Brielle to finish her run while he walked with Dooley back to his house.

An hour later when he reported to the station, Justice found Dooley waiting for him.

"Uh, Chief?" He looked uncomfortable.

"Yeah?"

"Just wanted to say thanks." Dooley offered his hand.

Justice repeated what Tex had said to him in the hospital. "No thanks necessary, Dooley. Ever." He emphasized the last word. "Ready to meet with the team?"

"Yeah. By the way, I never got a good vibe from our guy."

"I want to hear about that."

A few minutes later when the team assembled in the conference room, Dooley opened the meeting by discussing his early impressions of Carson. River added his from the previous day, going into more detail.

"I couldn't get a handle on him. You know? Who he is at his core. It's like he's not really Nash Carson."

"That gives me an idea," Hutch interjected. "I'm going to do a deep dive into the dark net and see if there's any chatter about domestic threats to America. This might just be about mercenaries buying arms for covert operations overseas."

"Even if," Justice added. "I ran into some of those groups when I was a SEAL. They're in it for the money. Those mercenaries negatively affect the reputations of legit security firms helping to rescue Americans who are trapped in life-threatening situations."

Murmurs of agreement echoed through the team.

When their meeting concluded, Luca pulled Dooley aside. "Let's talk about your sister's case. I'd like to show you the files and get your perspective."

Dooley looked at Justice. "Chief, is that okay?"

"Absolutely." Justice nodded his assent.

As soon as he left the conference room, he received a frantic phone call from Cynthia.

"Chief, Rosie's in crisis at school. She's locked herself in a bathroom and refuses to come out. We can hear her crying and screaming."

"I'll be there in five," he promised as he sprinted toward his Explorer.

Punching the gas, he flipped on the siren and tore out of the parking lot. He cursed himself for not anticipating this sooner. She was *ten*, for God's sake! He knew her stoicism was just a façade.

The principal, Cynthia, Rosie's teacher, and a custodian were gathered outside the single stall bathroom in the classroom. The students who were freaked out by Rosie's breakdown had been ushered into another teacher's classroom.

Hearing Rosie's pitiful cries broke Justice's heart. He signaled for the custodian to unlock the bathroom door and called, "Rosie, sweetie, it's Chief Justice. I'm coming in, okay?"

Cautiously, he pushed open the door and found her huddled against the far wall, shaking and crying. Instead of hurtling herself at him, she stayed rooted to the spot, her eyes wild. He crouched on the floor next to her, and she whirled on him in a fury.

"He killed them! He killed them all! Mom! Dad! My aunt and uncle and cousins! Arnie did it! And he was going to kill me, too, but...but..." Her eyes grew even wilder as the shock of what she'd witnessed finally hit her full force. "You! You shot him! You shot him!"

Rosie let out a loud wail that ended on a choking, guttural sound as she struggled to breathe. Recognizing the signs of a panic attack, Justice tamped down on his helplessness over her accusation and shoved her head between her knees.

"Breathe, kid. Breathe. With me. In...out...in...out... That's it. You're doing great."

When her breathing partially returned to normal, Justice lifted her into his arms and rushed out of the bathroom. "She's had a panic attack," he reported, his voice grim. "I'm taking her to the hospital."

"I'll follow you," Cynthia replied.

Two hours later Justice stood with Cynthia and the pediatrician outside Rosie's room in the pediatric wing of Mission Hospital.

"You're right, Chief McQuaid," Dr. Gregory addressed him. "Rosie suffered a major panic attack. She's in fight or flight mode, and her anxiety is high. I'm keeping her overnight."

"She needs to see a therapist," Justice stated.

"I agree. I've got a call in to the best child psychologist in the area. I expect to hear from her within an hour."

"I don't want the kid medicated," Justice declared in a voice that would brook no argument.

"I'm sorry, Chief, but that's not up to you," Dr. Gregory replied. "You're not Rosie's guardian."

"I'm her guardian," Cynthia interjected. "And I agree with Chief McQuaid. We're not pumping Rosie full of meds."

"If that's what you want. She is sedated at the moment, though."

"May I see her?" Justice asked.

"She's sleeping due to the sedative we gave her. And under the circumstances it might be best to wait until after Dr. Chichester has evaluated her. She associates you with what happened, Chief. She saw you shoot her brother."

Justice's heart dropped into his stomach. The thought that she might not want anything to do with him now that she'd begun to process the traumatic events of Saturday killed him. He looked at Cynthia. "Keep me posted?"

"Of course. And don't worry. She knows how much you care about her."

He nodded but didn't take comfort from her words.

Later, Justice's day got worse when Cynthia called him with an update. Dr. Chichester diagnosed Rosie with anxiety and recommended she avoid school and, unfortunately, Justice, too. Not being able to visit Rosie caused him such anguish that he endured a miserable week. And the lack of progress on the team's investigation increased his frustration. When were they going to get a break?

During the shift change on Friday, Justice received a call from the sergeant on duty in the evidence room.

"Hey, Chief," he said in a low voice, "Officer Carson is here asking if an HK416 and a box of Beta C-mags were taken into evidence."

"Tell him no," Justice ordered.

"Copy that."

Justice headed toward the evidence room and met Carson, who wore an apprehensive expression on his face, in the corridor.

"Something I can help you with, Officer?" Justice asked. "You look worried."

"Nah. I was just checking on some evidence. I'll be testifying in court next week."

"Oh, okay. Are you on this weekend?"

"No."

"Got any plans?" Justice grinned and winked.

"Not really. Just hangin' out with some friends, I guess."

"All right, then. See you Monday."

In his current mood it took a great amount of effort on Justice's part not to slam Carson against the wall and beat the truth out of him.

* * *

Justice wasn't looking forward to spending any time with Mayor Gage until he saw Brielle, dressed in a silky brown and gold evening gown which enhanced her skin tone and the unique color of her eyes, on Saturday night. His heart skipped several beats and his jaw dropped. In her three-inch stilettos, they were eye level, and he couldn't stop staring at her.

"You look…stunning," he finally managed to say.

Brielle smiled as she straightened his white satin tie "So do you," she complimented him. "You look elegant in your black suit."

He offered his arm. "Ready?"

"Yes. Just let me grab my evening purse."

Earlier in the week Justice had leased a Chevy Equinox. He helped Brielle into the passenger's side and fastened her seat belt. He'd been in the area long enough to know how to get to the marina, and they arrived within twenty minutes. He parked, assisted Brielle out of the SUV, and held her hand as they made their way toward the Gages' luxury super yacht, a Spectrum worth over a hundred million dollars. One of only a handful of its kind, a futuristic model that only the wealthiest could afford. Justice whistled when Brielle shared that tidbit with him.

"And where do you think the money came from to pay for this?" he inquired in a low voice.

"It bears investigating," Brielle murmured.

A crew member dressed in a crisp, well-tailored black and white uniform greeted them at the gangplank. "Names, please."

"Brielle McAdams, plus one," she answered.

He nodded as he found her name on his list. "Welcome aboard. Cocktails are being served on the second deck."

The long sleek lines of the Spectrum impressed Justice. It sported multiple levels with sections that jutted over the water on a lower deck, making it easy for a motorboat to pull alongside it. The middle level contained a pool and a hot tub. Several couples were already swimming or relaxing in the hot tub with drinks in their hands. From the interior Justice and Brielle heard strains of live music. A piano player performed Billy Joel's classic "Piano Man." Surrounded by distinct Italian décor and opulence, they ambled toward the open bar and ordered two glasses of white wine.

"Shall we find our host and hostess?" Justice asked with a mischievous grin. "I can't wait to see Mayor Gage's face when he realizes I'm your plus one."

# CHAPTER 15

White Italian leather low-backed seats with black accent throw pillows adorned the lounge, arranged in groups of two and four. A few couples milled around them. Next to the shiny black Steinway piano a set of polished hardwood stairs led to the other levels.

"Shall we try the upper deck first?" Brielle suggested. "That's where the Gages' private suite is located."

"Why not? They're probably waiting to make their grand entrance."

As Justice and Brielle approached the stairs, Shawna descended them, holding hands with a teenage boy, who took each step awkwardly, constricted by his suit and tie. Justice thought Shawna resembled her father. They shared the same color of eyes and facial features. She looked lovely in a black beaded cocktail dress.

"Brielle!" Shawna called and waved.

Amused, Justice watched them share air kisses.

"You look absolutely beautiful!" Shawna gushed.

"So do you," Brielle replied with a smile.

Shawna turned toward Justice. "You must be Brielle's

boyfriend. Nice to meet you, Chief McQuaid. My dad, um, speaks a great deal about you."

Justice shook her hand and winked. "I'm sure he does."

Shawna drew the blond-haired boy forward. "This is Drake Shelton, my boyfriend. Drake, this is Sergeant Brielle McAdams, my self-defense instructor, and Chief of Police Justice McQuaid."

He shook hands with them and said with solemnity, "Sir. Ma'am."

"Shawna, where are your parents? We'd like to personally wish your mother a happy birthday. We also have this for her." Brielle removed a birthday card from her evening purse. Inside was a gift certificate which entitled Vivian and a guest to spend a day at one of LA's upscale spa resorts.

"Oh, Mom and Dad aren't going to make their appearance for at least another hour. Not until after all the guests are on board and we're at sea." She rolled her eyes. "I'm supposed to greet everyone along with my brothers, but they're nowhere in sight. Probably holed up in their cabin playing video games." She reached for the card. "I'll take this, though. There's a table set up on the dining deck for cards and gifts. Please make yourselves comfortable. Plenty of appetizers are being served by the pool and on the other decks, too."

"Thank you, Shawna. We will."

When the girl and her boyfriend were out of earshot, Brielle murmured, "You were right. Vivian is vain but expecting your fifteen-year-old daughter to play hostess isn't cool."

"No, but it gives us an opportunity to explore and note who's here. I just spotted Linda Ferguson and her husband. I'd like to avoid her for the time being."

"All right." She grabbed his hand. "Let's go to the lower level."

* * *

The Spectrum cut the water smoothly as it cruised at ten knots parallel to the California coast. When all the guests were gathered in the lounge, the pianist began to play the Happy Birthday song, and everyone sang as Vivian and Elliott descended the stairs. She looked regal in a silver beaded evening gown. Elliott wore a black suit with a silver dress shirt that coordinated perfectly with her dress. He made a great spectacle of wishing her a happy birthday and kissing her as everyone applauded.

Since Justice stood head and shoulders above the guests, he was easy to spot. He watched the mayor's eyes widen in disbelief and offered a humorous grin while lifting his wine glass in salute. Justice caught a flash of momentary anger, and something else, too, in the mayor's eyes as his gaze slid away. Fear.

An announcement was made that a full sit-down dinner was being served to the nearly seventy-five guests on board, and they moved en masse to the dining area. Two long dark walnut tables, elegantly set with delicate china and sparkling glass and silverware, sat twenty-five guests at each. The Gages' closest friends joined them on the upper deck for a private meal. Justice wryly noted that he and Brielle weren't among the chosen ones.

Although the Gages were eating outside their private suite, Shawna preferred to join Brielle and Justice on the dining deck. Justice enjoyed teasing Drake as they discussed sports and the teen's goals for the future. Dinner was an elaborate five-course affair prepared by a renowned chef at one of LA's finest restaurants. Again, Justice wondered where the money came from for such a fancy meal. This particular chef did not come cheap.

After dinner, guests moved about the various decks,

drinking and dancing to piped-in music. When a slow song played, Justice took Brielle into his arms, loving the way she fit perfectly against him. They swayed, thoroughly engrossed in each other, yet aware of everything going on around them. Alcohol flowed freely, but they didn't imbibe except for the glasses of wine they drank earlier and at dinner. As the guests grew tipsy and louder, Justice and Brielle decided it was time to search the super yacht.

"I'll take the cabins," Justice whispered in Brielle's ear and nipped lightly on it.

She shivered in his arms. Turning her head, her mouth met his in a hot kiss. "Lower deck."

After they separated Justice meandered toward the cabins two VIP and four double. He started with the four double cabins and knocked on the first one to his left. Trying the door, he found it locked. Behind it someone panted.

"Wait your turn, man! It...will...only...be...another... Ahh!" Someone moaned in pleasure.

Disgusted, Justice turned away and moved on to the next cabin. This one was open, and he entered, glancing around. It was obviously the Gages' sons' quarters, for clothes lay strewn across the beds and on the floor. A video game system was hooked up to a large screen TV. He searched it thoroughly but didn't find anything of interest. The third cabin belonged to Shawna, and unlike her brothers', hers was neat and tidy with all of her personal possessions in their proper place. Nothing there, either. The last cabin was empty and his search proved fruitless.

The VIP cabins were larger and lavishly decorated. His search of the first one took longer than the double cabins. A couple was using it, for he found clothing belonging to them, but no information about their identity. Given the identity of the occupants in the second VIP cabin, Justice was surprised to find it unlocked. Linda's purse sat on the dresser. He rifled through the clothes hanging in the closet and the dresser drawers, but they yielded nothing. None of the cabins had loose floorboards or hidden spaces.

Expelling a disappointed breath, Justice stepped out of the cabin and found himself face to face with Linda. Her eyebrows shot up.

"What in God's name are *you* doing here?" she demanded, her voice a mixture of surprise and something akin to dread.

"Do you mean in this spot or in general?" he replied flippantly.

"Don't play dumb with me, McQuaid. You're sharper than you'd like us to believe. How'd you end up on the yacht? Elliott can't stand you."

"My girlfriend Brielle McAdams is Mrs. Gage and Shawna's self-defense teacher. They invited her to this lovefest, and I'm her date."

"I might have known you'd hook up with her." Linda rolled her eyes. "Now what the hell were you doing in my cabin?"

* * *

Brielle spotted the Gages' personal security detail dressed alike in dark suits and placed strategically throughout the decks. She slipped by a couple of them and entered the massive lower deck. Guests loitered, talking and laughing and drinking. No one noticed her as she pushed open the door to the gym. In this area of the super yacht, the side jutted out into the water where guests could enjoy the view on comfortable lounge chairs. Brielle surmised how easy it would be to transfer arms this way and glanced around the gym. Rectangular compartments with leather lids lined the walls. Typically, they should contain life jackets. Brielle lifted the lids and discovered they didn't. Instead, snuggled inside, she found wooden crates that could easily hold the arms. She took pictures with her cell phone. Looking down, she saw a piece of packing material and picked it up. She dropped it, along with her cell phone, into her evening purse and hurried from the gym.

\* \* \*

Linda glared at Justice as she waited for a response.

"Actually, I, um…" Justice floundered for an answer.

"Oh, there you are!" Brielle hailed him. "Did you find a bathroom, baby?"

"Yeah, I did." He grinned. "In Linda's VIP cabin."

Brielle placed her hand on his chest and kissed him fully on the mouth. Turning to Linda, she smiled. "Nice to see you again."

Linda frowned at them, suspicion shining in her eyes. "So, Brielle, now that you're dating the chief are you planning to transfer to the LBPD?"

Brielle shook her head. "No. On Monday I'll find out if I made SWAT or not. Even if I don't, I'm staying with the LAPD. It's not a good idea for either one of us to be in a position of power over the other. Besides, there's no place for me in the LBPD." She reached for Justice's hand and started to pull him toward the stairs. "Come on, Chief. They're serving birthday cake in the lounge."

"Can't refuse cake." He flashed a helpless grin at Linda.

"McQuaid, take my advice. Don't go looking for trouble, or it just may find you instead."

He held up his free hand. "I swear I'm not looking for it, Linda. Thanks for the warning, though."

\* \* \*

Justice and Brielle couldn't wait to disembark from the yacht. The rowdy, drunken behavior of the guests made them uncomfortable, especially when they saw how it affected Shawna. Her face burned with embarrassment. And the dirty looks Vivian kept shooting at Brielle indicated she didn't approve of her bringing Justice as a guest given Elliott's attitude toward him. It didn't bother Brielle, but it upset Shawna when she figured out what was going on. Brielle assured her it didn't change their relationship.

Both remained silent during the short drive to Brielle's house. She kicked off her stilettos while Justice tossed his jacket onto the multi-sectional sofa and removed his tie and partially unbuttoned his shirt. He followed Brielle into the kitchen where she brewed a pot of coffee and handed him a cup.

"So, you go first. Did you find anything?"

"No. The cabins were clean, well, except the one where I interrupted a couple having sex. And honestly, Bri, the way you look in that dress I was tempted to lure you into one of those cabins, rip it off your body, and make love to you." He grinned and took a sip of coffee.

She laughed lightly. "Later, baby. What else?"

"I noticed the Gages employed heavy muscle. Far more than necessary, if you ask me. No way I was getting near the upper deck to search their private cabin. I get Gage is the mayor, and maybe he's worried about his family's safety, but those guys weren't your run-of-the-mill security guards," Justice commented.

"No, they weren't," she agreed, lifting the mug to her lips.

"What about you? Any luck?"

Her eyes glowed with triumph as she smiled. "Yes. Look at these." She removed the piece of packing material from her evening purse and pulled up the photos she took on her cell phone.

Justice studied the pictures and whistled. "So, we were right. Somebody is using Gage's yacht to move arms. Who would suspect it, right?"

"Not just *somebody*," she added. "Axel Anderson. I'm sure of it." Brielle paused. "The only place around here where the rich can dock their super yachts is Del Rey Landing. Security is tight. There's no way the arms are being loaded onto the Spectrum at that location. We don't even know where the arms are coming from."

"We need to find out where the Spectrum's been lately. I'll have Hutch look into it." He drained his coffee mug and set it in the kitchen sink.

Brielle presented her back to him as she placed her own mug in the sink, and the sight of her bare skin enflamed him, turning his thoughts from their investigation to making love with her.

His eyes began to burn with an intense fire.

"Come here, Nancy Drew."

Justice tugged her into his arms. He reached behind her and unzipped her dress. Her body melded into his.

He molded his mouth to hers, his tongue sliding between her parted lips. The simple contact of their tongues seeking and exploring exploded into fiery passion. Brielle's fingers frantically finished unbuttoning his black dress shirt. He'd been amused watching her amber eyes slide over his almost bare chest while they'd been talking. And as far as he was concerned, her cleavage had enticed him all evening.

Their clothing landed on the floor as they fell as one upon the multi-sectional sofa. Arms and legs entwined, Justice eased into Brielle, groaning his pleasure as her wet warmth enveloped him. They moved rhythmically together, in sync, in harmony, in tune with their bodies. Making love, making music, what was the difference?

Sated, their desire spent, they lay wrapped in each other's arms, unmoving, until they fell asleep.

After Sunday morning breakfast on Brielle's deck, they headed to the Main Street Gym for a final training session.

Facing each other in the ring, Justice began, "You've got this, Bri. You're in superb physical shape, and you've got the heart of a warrior." He touched her chest and felt her heart pounding beneath his palm. "Now all we have to do is get your mind in sync with your body and heart."

"Meaning?" she questioned in a soft voice.

"Take me down."

Unlike their other sessions Justice didn't coach her. He attacked her with the ferocity of a deranged, desperate criminal, determined that she use the skills he taught her to stop him.

Justice watched her center herself as she parried each one of his strikes. He wanted to give her verbal encouragement, tell her exactly how to gain the advantage, but he kept quiet. And then she executed a move that took him by surprise. She dropped her left shoulder instead of her right one, spun around behind him, grabbed his waist, and swept his legs from under him. His forward momentum took them both down, but Brielle quickly leapt up again. She bounced up and down on the balls of her feet, breathing heavily from physical exertion and excitement over her victory.

Justice flipped over onto his back and gazed up at her, a silly grin on his face. And then he burst into hearty laughter. "You did it!" he gasped, rising to his feet. "You did it! I knew it! I knew you could do it!"

He picked her up, spun her around, and kissed her soundly. Laughing, she wrapped her legs around him and hugged him.

"Oh, my God, Justice! You were right! I just needed to get my head in the game."

"Come on, Tiger Eyes. Let's get something to eat. I've worked up an appetite."

They went to Vinny's again, who was thrilled to see them.

"You two look really happy," Vinny commented.

Justice met Brielle's eyes aglow with a mysterious light and felt his heart thump against his chest. He reached for her hand and brought it to his lips. "We are."

A huge smile crossed his face. "Well, that makes me happy for you. How about pulled pork today? I smoked it for hours."

"Sounds great," Justice replied, still caressing Brielle's hand. His eyes never left hers. She held him spellbound. Trapped in a golden net.

When they returned home, they strolled leisurely on the beach, holding hands. As they spoke quietly, Justice expressed his concern for Rosie. Brielle urged him to call Cynthia to check on her.

"She's struggling," Cynthia told him. "But she's a fighter. She'll make it through this."

"Has she asked about me?" Justice wondered.

"No. I'm sorry, Justice. Give her time. Be patient."

Justice shook his head as he pressed the END button on his cell phone. "I don't think Rosie is ever going to forgive or forget my part in killing her brother." His heart ached.

Brielle wrapped her arms around his waist and pressed her cheek against his chest. "I'm so sorry," she murmured. "Don't despair, Justice. I know in my heart Rosie will forgive you."

"I honestly don't know how I got so lucky to have you in my life, Bri," he replied, tucking her hair behind her ear. "I— I'm in awe of you."

She offered her mouth for a sweet kiss. Without a word they turned toward her house where they spent the remainder of the day in bed.

The following morning Justice urged Brielle to sleep as long as possible and offered last-minute advice.

"Don't give yourself away too soon, Bri. You know all their moves, and they think they know yours. Let them. You'll know when the moment is right to turn the tables on them."

"You're still going to be there, right? Ten o'clock?"

"Hell, yeah. Wouldn't miss it." He leaned down and captured her mouth in a sensual kiss. "You're going to kick ass."

Brielle smiled and yawned. "Hope so."

* * *

Justice held a brief staff meeting the following morning, and by eight-fifteen he pulled onto the highway and headed north to LA. The SWAT command center sat in the LAPD's headquarters downtown, an impressive glass and cement building. Since he was wearing his uniform, he was greeted with respect and taken to SWAT's training area. All of the officers who were training for SWAT wore similar T-shirts and sweatpants. They stood at attention in a straight line listening to the commander of the unit. This was it. They'd reached the end of the program and during the past two weeks the number had dwindled to just these eight officers. Only three would be permitted to fill the slots SWAT needed.

Their instructor paired them up, and, of course, he paired Brielle with Finnigan. The final pair to enter the ring, they squared off in the center. In the face of Finnigan's sneers and taunts, Brielle remained calm. Justice watched, in awe of her, as she deliberately led Finnigan through a dance of her own design. And then, when he believed he'd beaten her after knocking her to the mat, she pulled a move on him he never anticipated. He landed hard on his back, staring up at her in shock, and partially in pain. One could have heard a pin drop in the cavernous space.

Brielle leaned over Finnigan with a smile playing about her lips. Holding out a hand, she said, "Welcome to the New World Order, Finny."

His face red with embarrassment he allowed Brielle to help him up.

From his spot several feet away, Justice clapped and cheered. "Way to go, Sergeant!" His heart exploded with pride, and something else—something deep and powerful.

Macklin echoed his own congratulations, followed by the others' praise as Brielle ducked out of the ring and jumped into Justice's arms. They kissed deeply and hungrily in front of her fellow officers while they looked on in amusement.

Laughing, Brielle cried, "It worked! Just like you said it would! Oh, God, Justice! I'm in shock right now!"

"So is Finnigan," Justice remarked. "Here he comes."

"You knocked me on my ass, McAdams," Finnigan declared, half grudgingly, half admiringly. "I didn't think you had it in you. So, congrats."

"And I told you I'd laugh my ass off when she did," Justice reminded him.

Finnigan shot him a dirty look. "You can beat it now, Chief. Commander Mattox is ready to announce who's in."

"Consider yourself damn lucky *I* don't kick your ass, *Finny*." He kissed Brielle one more time. "We'll celebrate tonight at my place."

"If I made it," Brielle added.

"You did," Justice replied with confidence before he turned and left.

He had just reached his Explorer when his cell phone pinged with a text message.

Brielle: I'm in! So are Finnigan and Macklin!

Justice: Congrats, baby! See you tonight.

* * *

When he arrived at the station, he went to see Hutch.

"Hey," Justice greeted him. "Do you have any information about where the mayor's yacht has been recently?"

"I do. But first tell me if Brielle made SWAT or not."

Justice grinned. "She did. Watching her in the ring was like watching a perfectly choreographed dance routine. So, whatcha got?"

"Once a month the Spectrum anchors off the coast of Nicaragua."

Justice frowned. "Not good."

"No. The thing is, I've been poking around the dark net posing as a prospective arms buyer, and I've encountered several nasty organizations. Someone is dealing with North Korea and arms are coming through Nicaragua. There's lots of ugly chatter, Chief, about a revolution right here in America." Hutch paused and met Justice's grave expression. "Are you sure Homeland Security knows about this?"

"I'm not sure of anything at the moment. You have any more information?"

"Yeah. There's been discussion about a nosy *Chicago Sun-Times* reporter asking a lot of questions. She's kicked a hornet's nest, and they're not happy."

"Did they mention a name? Brielle told me her best friend Faith is a reporter for the *Chicago Sun-Times.*"

"No, but they tend not to."

"Okay. Keep on it. See if you can make a deal. In the meantime, I'll call Brendan McAdams."

Brendan didn't answer his cell phone, so Justice left a message. Two hours later Brendan returned his call. "Thanks for calling me back."

"You said you have news?"

"I do." After he explained what little information they'd

gleaned, he stated, "Surely Homeland Security already knows this." He kept the part about the mayor's yacht to himself.

"Some of it."

"What about the *Chicago Sun-Times* reporter? Do you think it's Faith Stoker?"

Brendan let out his breath. "If I had to guess? Yes."

"Well, you'd better keep an eye on her, then."

"Eyes are already on her. The best. Tex Keegan is tracking her."

"What? You're kiddin' me. What's their connection?"

"She's the niece of Tex's former FBI commander. Tex keeps tabs on everyone in his, I mean, Tex's, inner circle. Tex's former SEAL team are often in danger and need his help, and he always has their back. I hope to God I'm wrong about Faith being involved in this mess. If anything happens to her, there will be hell to pay."

# CHAPTER 16

Justice set a vase of fresh flowers for Brielle on the table on his deck and checked to make sure everything was perfect. After all, it wasn't every day your girlfriend made SWAT. The grilled salmon lay on a bed of jasmine rice along with a combination of sautéed squash and zucchini. A bottle of fine French champagne chilled in an ice bucket. He'd actually bought fancy china and silverware, too, at Tawny's insistence. The setting, however, wasn't complete until the woman he'd been waiting for his entire life joined him.

Wearing a yellow and white checkered sundress, she glided up the steps to his deck. Backlit by the sun, she looked like a goddess rising from the sea.

Suddenly tongue-tied, aware for the first time of strange, new feelings she invoked in him, he just gazed at her, soaking up her beauty.

"Wow. Um, you look really lovely."

Her eyes swept the table. "You did this for me." It was a statement, not a question.

"Yes. I hope you like salmon."

"I do." She leaned over to smell the flowers. "These are beautiful."

"They're for you."

When she lifted her eyes, they glittered with unshed tears.

"Allergic?" Justice teased her, smiling gently.

Brielle let out a little laugh and shook her head. "My first bouquet of flowers."

He lifted an eyebrow. "Aw, come on. You mean what's-his-face never gave you flowers?"

"No. The prevailing attitude among the few men I've dated in the past was that they preferred not to waste their money on something that was going to die in a week or sooner. Or maybe they thought I wasn't worth it." She shrugged.

"Fools. I think you're worth more than a bouquet of flowers. Far more." Cupping her face, he caressed her mouth with his.

Several long moments later he seated her and popped the cork off the champagne bottle. He poured two glasses and offered one to her.

"Congrats, again, Bri. I'm so proud of you."

"I wouldn't have made it without you, Justice. I…" She broke off, unable to speak as she swallowed the hot emotion swelling in her throat. "Thank you. For helping me. For believing in me."

He didn't know what to say. The idea that he'd fallen in love with her popped into his head, but he forced it aside. Instead, he took a sip of champagne. "You're welcome. Now, let's eat before the salmon sprouts fins and swims away."

*What an absolutely lame thing to say!*

If Brielle thought so, she didn't voice her opinion aloud to him. She cut into the salmon and remarked on its flaky texture and flavor. After she pronounced the main course delicious, Justice surprised her with a special cake in the shape of a shield. It had her name scrawled across the top and the SWAT anacronym on the bottom. This time, when a drop of ice cream with the cake lingered on her lips, he didn't hesitate to lean forward and lick it off. That led to a heavy round of kissing, ultimately landing them in his bedroom. On fresh, clean, and manly gray sheets.

With their lovemaking being hotter than ever, Justice didn't want to ruin it by discussing the job, but Brielle needed to know what Hutch had told him earlier.

As they lay in the afterglow of earth-shattering sex, he said, "Bri, I found out something today. There's talk on the dark net about a *Chicago Sun-Times* reporter snooping into arms deals. It might be Faith."

Brielle disentangled herself. Without a word, she reached for his discarded shirt, hurried downstairs, and found her cell phone. Justice followed her, pulling on his pants.

"Faith, dammit! You need to call me and stop fucking around! This is important!"

Worry filled her eyes as she punched up Tex's number. "Tex, sorry to bother you, but where's Faith?" Tension and fear rang in her voice.

"Hold on." A beat. "She's on the move. Driving toward her apartment from what I can see. What's the problem?"

"Not answering her damn phone, Tex! Has she mentioned anything dangerous she might be investigating?"

"No. Now I'm curious. Spill."

She looked at Justice. He held a finger to his lips. "There's something fishy going on that Justice and I are investigating, and we thought Faith might know about it."

"Huh."

"Just keep an eye on her and let me know if she goes off the grid."

"Whatever you and Justice are involved in you should share with me."

"Not now, Tex. Maybe later." She disconnected the call before he could badger her into giving up the truth.

Brielle met Justice's steady gaze. "Faith is investigating Axel Anderson. I feel it in my gut. She knows what's going on and that's why she's been avoiding me and warning me to drop it. My God, Justice. What if Faith has all the answers? Her life could be in danger."

Justice trusted her instincts. "What do you want to do, Bri? Fly to Chicago to confront her?"

"I can't. Not now. SWAT is always on call. Let me try her number again."

Just as she hit the number, her cell phone rang. "Thank God," she muttered. "Faith…" She hit the SPEAKER PHONE icon so Justice could hear the conversation.

"We may be best friends, Brielle," Faith addressed her in an abrupt tone of voice, "but that doesn't give you the right to treat me like a kid. For your information I was driving home when you called, and I didn't need to be distracted by talking to you. Now, what the hell is so important?"

Justice saw heat rise in Brielle's cheeks. "I'm not treating you like a kid. I'm worried. You need to be honest with me, Faith. Are you investigating Axel Anderson?"

"Are we back to that?" Faith parried. "I told you the guy is dead."

"He's not. At least we don't think so. Some evidence has come to light that casts doubt on what happened to him."

"Doubt? No one knows for sure what happened to begin with. Look, I don't know of any new evidence, but I do know this. You're chasing a ghost."

Brielle fell silent. Justice watched her struggle with wanting to tell Faith the truth and keeping it to herself. "Watch your back, Faith. Please," she finally said.

"I've got Tex watching my back, thank you very much. Now, please stop parenting me, Bri."

Brielle sucked in her breath. "I'm sorry. I—I made SWAT. Just wanted to share my good news with you."

"That's great! I'm really happy for you." Faith paused. "Sorry for snapping at you. I know your heart's in the right place."

"You're like a sister to me. I love you, and I just want you to be safe."

"Same here. Listen, I just walked in the door, and I'm tired. We'll talk soon, okay?"

"Yeah, sure. Good night, Faith."

"'Night, Bri."

Her face filled with dread as she faced Justice. "We've never kept secrets from each other until now. Faith point-blank lied to me. How can we protect her if she won't tell us what she knows?"

Justice enfolded her in his arms and kissed the top of her head. "I updated Brendan earlier today. I didn't tell him everything, but he assured me that Faith couldn't have better eyes on her than Tex's. You know that's true, right?"

Brielle nodded. "He won't let anything happen to her."

"Wanna go back to bed?" he asked, brushing her lips lightly with his thumb.

"I'm too keyed up. Let's take a look at our investigation. Maybe it's time to shake Carson down."

"Or Linda Ferguson."

For the next couple of hours, they examined their evidence and facts but didn't make any decisions regarding how to proceed from this point. Justice escorted Brielle home and took her to bed for another bout of hot lovemaking.

* * *

Two weeks later Brielle and Finnigan entered the Royal

Business Bank on Sunset Boulevard. Within the last few days, a trio of armed, masked men had hit several branches of the RBB, leaving behind six dead and more than a dozen critically injured victims. They'd received a tip that the branch on Sunset Boulevard was next. The vault housed several billion dollars' worth of diamonds and gold bricks.

Beneath Brielle's casual clothes, she wore a Kevlar vest and her gun tucked into the back of her pants. The rest of their team waited in an armored vehicle behind a diner a block away. Their commander, Isaiah Mattox, called the shots from headquarters.

Brielle and Finnigan loitered in the lobby, keeping an eye on the entrance, the customers, and the tellers. From the corner of her eye, Brielle noticed a security guard locking the double glass doors. Her pulse kicked up a notch.

"It's happening," she murmured into her earpiece.

"Copy that," Macklin's voice crackled in her ear. "We've got eyes on you."

The words barely left his mouth when three masked, heavily armed gunmen appeared out of nowhere. They sprayed the lobby with bullets, striking a man in the leg and his wife in the stomach, and narrowly missing Brielle and Finnigan, who yelled simultaneously, "Stop! LAPD!"

"Drop your weapons!" Finnigan shouted.

All three swung their semi-automatic assault rifles toward him, directly aiming at his head, and pulled their triggers. Brielle reacted without hesitation. She fired, killing one of the them, as she threw herself in front of Finnigan. He dropped to the floor, unhurt, and fired his own weapon. Another gunman dropped dead. Glass shattered. Macklin and two other members of SWAT rushed into the lobby and took out the third gunman.

Brielle felt a burning sensation underneath her left arm and in her leg, but she ignored it as she knelt next to the male victim and assessed his wound. She removed his belt and used it as a tourniquet.

"You're going to be...okay," she assured him, gasping a little. She felt strange. Her heart fluttered.

He grabbed her hand. "Officer, you've been shot."

"I—I'm all right. Is this your wife?"

"Yes. Lana. Please help her."

Brielle ripped off her blazer and staunched the blood pouring from the woman's stomach. "Lana, listen to me. Help is on the way. Do you hear the sirens?"

Lana coughed up blood. "Yyes!"

"Just hang on..." Brielle heard Finnigan calling her name as if she were under water before she lost consciousness.

* * *

Justice was parked at the Four Corners, keeping an eye on the teens gathered there after school just let out for the summer when Hutch hailed him over the radio.

"Chief, get to the beach ASAP. A copter is en route to take you to Cedars-Sinai Hospital. Brielle was shot during a bank robbery thirty minutes ago."

Justice's gut tightened in soul-searing fear. He turned on his lights and siren and punched the gas pedal. Keeping the fear at bay, he concentrated on getting to the beach as fast as possible. He breezed through the traffic, traveling close to a hundred miles per hour and prayed that he didn't hit anyone. Less than five minutes later he tore up the sand skidding to a stop just as an LAPD helicopter landed in front of him. He leapt from the Explorer and sprinted toward it. In twenty seconds they were airborne. Justice questioned the pilot about what happened, but he didn't have any more information.

They touched down on the helipad on the roof of the hospital, and Justice jumped to the ground.

Finnigan met him and shouted above the noise of the helicopter as it lifted off again, "Brielle's in surgery. I'll take you to the waiting room."

The number of cops spilling out of the waiting room and into the corridor scared Justice and sent his blood racing through his veins. He assumed they were from Brielle's precinct. His gaze swept the area and touched on Brielle's SWAT brothers and their commander, all of whom he met last weekend at Vinny's.

Turning to Finnigan, he demanded, "Tell me what happened to Brielle."

"We'd been tracking a trio of armed bank robbers hitting the Royal Business Banks. We knew they were striking the Sunset branch next so Brielle and I staked it out while the rest of the team surveilled us in a van. Everything happened pretty quickly. The perps started shooting, and Brielle and I identified ourselves and demanded they drop their weapons. When they had me in their sights, Brielle threw herself in the line of fire and killed one of the gunmen. She got hit twice. One bullet traveled through her left arm and…lodged near her heart. And the other struck her left leg above the knee cap."

Finnigan paused and shook his head. "She saved my ass. And ignoring her own wounds—seriously, I don't know how she managed it—she also saved two victims."

All the color drained from Justice's face, and he swayed unsteadily on his feet.

"Hey, Chief, are you okay?" Finnigan asked.

Justice gaped at him as fear and disbelief ripped through him. "No, man, I am *not* okay! The woman I love is in surgery fighting for her life because she's brave and selfless. And you!

She saved your sorry ass after the way you treated her! So, no, I'm not okay!" he shouted.

The officers had been murmuring among themselves, but now silence fell as they turned to look at Justice. Into that vacuum of sound, he added, "Has anyone contacted Brielle's family?"

Commander Mattox detached himself from the SWAT officers and approached Justice. He shook his hand and clasped his shoulder. "I called Mr. and Mrs. McAdams. Brielle's brother-in-law, Nick Stone, is letting them use Stone Enterprises' private jet." He checked his watch. "They'll be wheels up in just about ten minutes. Perhaps you should sit down, Chief McQuaid."

Justice shrugged away from him. "No, I don't need to sit down. Please excuse me."

Alone in the corridor and out of sight of anyone, Justice called Franklin. "Dad..." his voice broke.

"Justice, what is it? Are you okay?"

"No, no, Dad. It's Brielle. She's been shot. Badly. Please...I need you."

"I'm on my way."

He didn't have to call his team. Hutch, Tawny, River, Martini, and Dooley showed up on their own to offer their support.

Hours passed. Someone brought everyone cups of coffee from Starbucks. The longer Justice waited without any news the more worried and anxious he became. Officers came and went except Commander Mattox and SWAT and Justice's faithful five. His father sent him a text to let him know he'd caught a flight a couple of hours ago and would arrive in LA in about six more hours.

Tired of sitting, Justice started pacing outside the waiting room. Just as he thought about ramming his fist into the wall, a deep voice addressed him.

"Chief Justice McQuaid, I presume?"

He spun around and looked into a face that bore a striking resemblance to Brielle's, and his heart slammed into his rib cage. His eyes moved from that countenance to the petite woman at his side. Definitely Brielle's mother. Tears stung his eyes.

"I—I love your peach cobbler!" he blurted for lack of anything better to say. These were his woman's parents, and he sounded like a blithering idiot!

Brianna McAdams let out a half cry, half laugh. She held out her arms to offer an embrace. "She's going to be all right, Justice. Our daughter is a fighter. Just like her brothers Trey and Ben."

When he stepped out of Brianna's arms, Justice appraised Cameron. Tall. Imposing. Fierce. His amber eyes burned with love and concern for Brielle. Cameron held out his hand and Justice shook it with a strong grip.

"Sir, it's an honor to finally meet you. Brielle…speaks… fondly of you. Of both of you."

"You, too, Justice. We're so happy that a good man like you is in our daughter's life." Cameron paused. "Has there been any news?"

Before Justice could respond, the surgeon who operated on Brielle approached them.

"Mr. and Mrs. McAdams? I'm Dr. Nunag. Shall we speak privately?"

Cameron shook his head. "There's a whole room full of cops waiting to hear news about Brielle's condition. And this is her boyfriend, Chief Justice McQuaid."

Dr. Nunag nodded. He followed them into the waiting room. Everyone gazed expectantly at him.

"First, let me say that Sergeant McAdams is out of danger. We successfully extracted the bullet that came within a half inch of her heart. The bullet that hit her leg damaged nerves and muscles, but I'm confident she'll fully recover with physical therapy."

An audible sigh and murmurs of gratitude echoed among the officers. Relief swept through Justice. He turned away from the others so they wouldn't see the tears burning in his eyes. He couldn't deny it any longer. Didn't even want to try. Brielle held his heart in the palm of her hand, and now he ached to tell her that he was in love with her. He wasn't sure if she felt the same way about him but staying silent wasn't an option anymore. Life was too damned short not to risk laying it all on the line.

Scrubbing his face with his hands, he addressed the surgeon. "May we see Brielle?"

"I'm keeping her in ICU for the next twelve hours. Right now, she's sleeping, but you can visit her in small groups of two or three for a few minutes at a time."

Cameron and Brianna and Justice shook hands with Dr. Nunag and thanked him.

Addressing Justice, Cameron ordered, "Go on, son."

"No, sir. I can wait. I've been waiting for your daughter my entire life."

Cameron and Brianna glanced meaningfully at each other before they joined hands and went to see their daughter.

When they returned fifteen minutes later, they confirmed Dr. Nunag's observations, and kept Justice company while members of Brielle's squad and SWAT and LBPD visited her.

After seeing Brielle, Tawny marched up to Finnigan and chastised him. "You're an asshole. You treated Brielle like a piece of garbage. She told us everything you said. Something to the effect of not wanting her on your team. And now look at her. She's lying in ICU because she saved your ass, Asshole." To Dooley, she added, "Let's go, Stud."

She hugged and kissed Justice and Cameron and Brianna

and said she'd be back the next day. Dooley followed her, along with Hutch, River, and Martini.

"Close your mouth, Finny," Justice murmured. "Tawny is off limits. Besides, she thinks you're an asshole."

"I love a challenge." He smirked.

Justice ignored him. He wasn't in the mood for jokes as he waited his turn to see Brielle.

With the waiting room finally empty except for Cameron and Brianna, Justice made his way to ICU. He thought he was prepared for the sight that met his eyes, but he wasn't. He recoiled in shock as his breath hitched in his throat. Brielle lay pale and still, hardly breathing. Leaning down, he brushed her bloodless lips with his.

"I'm here, sweetheart," he whispered. "I know you're just sleeping, but I really need you to wake up so I can look into your gorgeous eyes when I tell you that I'm in love with you."

Justice sat in a chair next to her bed and brought her cold hand up to his lips. He stayed like that, caressing her hand and talking to her, until a nurse shooed him out of the cubicle. Reluctantly, he rose to his feet, unable to tear his gaze away from Brielle. He promised he wouldn't leave her alone and rejoined Cameron and Brianna, who sat speaking quietly with Franklin, who'd just arrived at the hospital.

"Dad." Anguish filled Justice's voice.

Franklin hugged him. "I'm so sorry, son. How is Brielle?"

"Sleeping. But I wish she'd wake up." Weariness colored his tone.

"Justice, you're worn out, and you must be hungry. Let's all go get something to eat," Brianna suggested.

"No, ma'am. I'm staying."

"Honey, let's check into our hotel. We can bring sandwiches back with us," Cameron interjected.

"That's a good idea," Franklin agreed.

When they were alone, Franklin pinned Justice with his eyes. "So, you love this woman, huh?"

Justice sank into a chair and stretched out his long legs. Leaning back, he closed his eyes. "Yeah. And I'm not in the mood for one of your lectures about it."

# CHAPTER 17

"Not this time. This time you hit the jackpot. Mr. and Mrs. McAdams are of the opinion that their daughter is absolutely crazy about you. Apparently, I have, and I quote, 'raised a fine young man.'" Franklin snickered. "They haven't figured out yet that you're a real smartass sometimes."

Justice chuckled and opened his eyes. "Aw, come on, Dad. I learned from the best."

"Yeah, your mother taught you well," Franklin joked. At the stunned expression on Justice's face, he laughed outright. "What? Your mother had quite a mouth on her. In more ways than one," he added just to make his son even more uncomfortable.

"Again with the sex talk, Dad? What are you? Sixteen?"

"What are you? Five?" Franklin shot back.

They stared at each other a moment before bursting into laughter.

"Wanna come with me to see Brielle, Dad?"

"I'll wait until she's awake. Go ahead. Mr. and Mrs. McAdams will be back soon with food. I'm famished."

"Have I thanked you for flying all the way out here to be with me?"

"No. You've been too busy scolding me for talking dirty."

"Well, thanks. I appreciate it. Now, go talk dirty to Adrienne."

At the mention of Adrienne's name, the levity between them ended abruptly.

"I don't think she wants to see me or talk to me," Franklin remarked.

"You won't know until you try," Justice said as he left the waiting room.

* * *

Justice refused to leave Brielle alone and sweet talked the night shift nurse into letting him stay with her in ICU. The chair wasn't comfortable, but he'd been able to change out of his uniform when Franklin brought him a pair of jeans and a T-shirt.

Cameron and Brianna, realizing their daughter was in good hands, stayed until midnight. They'd texted back and forth with their five other children, assuring them that their little sister was in stable condition.

Justice texted Faith, introducing himself and sharing what happened to Brielle. She'd texted him back, sending her love and thankfulness that Brielle would be all right.

He wondered about that as he begged Brielle to open her eyes. "Please, baby. Wake up. You've been asleep for a really long time. And I need to tell you something important."

Justice dozed off and on during the long night. At one point he jerked awake from a dream, believing he'd heard Brielle crying out for him. Glancing toward the bed, he sucked in his breath. She lay staring at him, her amber eyes dull from her ordeal.

"Justice." She croaked his name.

"I'm here, baby." He reached for the pitcher of water on a rolling bedside tray, poured a cup, and held it to her dry lips.

She took a few sips and lay back upon the pillow. "The two victims. Did they make it? The husband and wife?"

Justice's heart exploded with love for her. She'd nearly lost her life, yet her main concern was for the other shooting victims. He gripped her hand and kissed it. "Yes, they made it. How do you feel, sweetheart?"

Brielle grimaced. "In pain." She tried to shift her position. "My leg. It feels like lead."

"You have nerve and muscle damage, but the surgeon assured us you'll make a full recovery. You're going to need physical therapy," he explained. "By the way, your parents are here."

"At the hospital?"

"At a hotel at the moment. So's my dad. He's at the house."

She gazed at him and squeezed his hand. "You were that scared?"

"Yes. Petrified I would lose you."

Her eyes grew soft. "Never."

It was either now or never. He cleared his throat. "Bri, I've been praying for you to wake up because I need to tell you something. I—" He gulped. "I—I'm in love with you. Head over heels, actually. It's crazy, I know, but I almost lost my mind today when I thought you might not make it. I—I don't know how you feel about me, but all I ask is the chance to prove to you how much I love you."

"You really don't know, Beach Boy?" she gently teased him. "You stole my heart the first day we met. And when you offered to help me make SWAT, well, that just sealed the deal." She paused as she caressed his hand. Eyes lit now with a warm amber glow, she declared, "I absolutely adore you. You're the kind of man I've always wanted in my life. I—I'm in love with you, too, Justice McQuaid, and honestly, I never knew what that meant until I met you."

It wasn't that dramatic moment you read about in romance novels or watch in movies; it didn't need to be. Just a simple declaration. To Justice it was perfect. Sincere. His heart took flight and soared. He felt giddy like he'd drunk a few cans of beer. He pressed his mouth against hers.

"I really want to make love to you."

She smiled. "You'll have to wait a bit."

Noticing her smile faded into a grimace of pain, Justice said, "I'll get the nurse for you. I'm sure there's an order for pain meds."

"Yes, please!" Brielle gasped. "It really hurts."

After a nurse administered a dose of pain medication through her IV, Brielle grew sleepy again.

"Justice, you look tired. Please go home. I'm fine. You don't have to worry about me."

"No. I'm staying with you, at least until you're out of ICU."

She closed her eyes. "You're stubborn."

"As a mule. Get used to it."

* * *

Early the following afternoon, Dr. Nunag transferred Brielle to a private room. Cameron, Brianna, and Franklin finally convinced Justice to leave the hospital long enough to take a nap and shower and shave.

As Franklin drove him to Laguna Beach, Justice asked, "So, what do you think about Brielle now that you've met her?"

He glanced sideways at him. "Honestly? She's perfect for you. It's obvious she loves you, Justice."

"Yes, but do you like her, Dad?"

Franklin smiled. "You want my stamp of approval?"

"It's important to me," Justice admitted. Franklin had warned him about Clara; he just wished he'd listened to him.

"All right. I really like her. She's brave. Heroic, even. She's intelligent, sweet, and kind. Values family. And all of that is great, of course, but what matters the most to me is how Brielle treats you. How she looks at you. How she speaks to you and about you. Given what I've seen so far there's no doubt in my mind she's in love with you. You're a lucky man, Justice."

The tension left his body, and he relaxed. He wanted the two people who meant the most to him to love each other as much as he loved them.

At home he tumbled into bed and slept undisturbed until five o'clock. He rose, fully refreshed, took a shower, shaved, and dressed. Downstairs he found the house empty. Checking his cell phone for messages as he devoured a peanut butter sandwich and an apple, he read one from Franklin.

Dad: Gone to make amends with Adrienne. Wish me luck. I'll see you at the hospital later. I may need a doctor.

Justice chuckled and tossed the apple core into the trash can.

Before heading to Cedars-Sinai, he stopped at the station to check in with the department. After Tawny brought him up to date, she told him that she and Dooley had gone to visit Brielle, and she'd had another run-in with Finnigan.

"Can you believe he had the audacity to ask me out?" She rolled her eyes.

"Did you shoot him down?" Justice inquired with a smile. He hadn't been too concerned with Finnigan checking Tawny out since his focus had been on Brielle at the time.

"Down dead."

He laughed.

With Tawny keeping the department running smoothly, he didn't have to worry about leaving it to spend time with Brielle. Not to mention his captains ran a tight ship and worked well with him. All in all, he couldn't complain. He enjoyed his job. He'd formed bonds and friendships with the cops. And most importantly, he loved a good woman. Just a few months ago he never imagined life could be so sweet.

* * *

Dr. Nunag released Brielle from the hospital a week later. Because she was young, strong, and healthy, she healed quickly, and with physical therapy every day, she didn't need a walker or a cane when she was discharged. She still wasn't cleared to return to work, though. She had to undergo a mandatory psychological exam after what happened to her, and until her leg was one hundred percent again, she wouldn't be able to return to field duty.

Cameron, Brianna, and Franklin were planning to fly out that evening, so they gathered for a fabulous dinner on Brielle's deck. Brianna outdid herself preparing their meal, and even baked her famous peach cobbler just for Justice.

Franklin had invited Adrienne, much to Justice's surprise, and she shocked him further when she announced she was taking a vacation and accompanying his father back to Connecticut. Justice shot Franklin an inquisitive look, which the older man returned with a grin and a shrug.

After they finished dessert, Cameron suggested that he and Justice go for a stroll on the beach. Justice suspected he was in for "the talk."

"So, you told Brielle you're in love with her," Cameron began in a conversational tone of voice.

"Yes, sir."

"You barely know each other."

"I know what I feel when I'm with her. The rest will come in time."

Cameron glanced sideways at him. "Is that right?"

"Yes, sir."

"And I suppose you want to marry her."

"Yes, sir. And I'd like your blessing."

"Convince me that I should give it."

"Because I can't take a breath without Brielle. She is my heart. And I will spend the rest of my life proving how vital she is to me and how much I love her. I won't ever forsake her." Justice's tone rang with condemnation.

Cameron frowned. "Like I forsook Brianna."

"Yes, sir. I heard the story. Brielle told me how you and Brianna almost died when you were attacked by the Morales drug cartel and then you…"

"I had my reasons for doing what I did," Cameron cut him off.

"And they were good ones. But…"

Cameron held up his hand. "But it's water under the bridge now, except my past nearly cost Trey and Ben their lives, too." He paused. "Brielle is in love with you. She's just like her mother. Loyal and incredibly brave. Promise to treasure her and you'll have my blessing."

"I do. I will. All the days of my life."

Cameron slapped Justice on the back. "Glad we had this chat, son."

Justice let out his breath. "Yes, sir."

When they returned to the deck, Justice caught Brielle's anxious gaze and winked. All good. She flashed a radiant smile at him, setting his heart, and his body, ablaze for her.

Alone an hour later, Justice wrapped his arms gently around her and kissed her soft lips.

"I hope my dad wasn't too hard on you," Brielle stated as she leaned into him.

Her scent, a scintillating combination of flowers and sunshine, caused his head to spin. He caressed her bare arms. "No, not at all. He was just looking out for you. What about mine?" He'd seen Franklin corner Brielle in the kitchen on the pretext of helping with dessert.

She laughed lightly. "He gave me his stamp of approval, as he put it. Seems like you wanted it. Your dad was very sweet, by the way."

"Huh. I would never use that word to describe him."

Brielle smiled. "So…it's official then. We've been parent-approved."

Justice's eyes turned dark with longing. "Not yet." He cupped her face and molded his mouth to hers, holding back the full force of his passion by not using his tongue. Pressing her against him, he murmured, "Now, we're official. I've missed making love to you, but tonight I just want to hold you in my arms. Nothing more."

"What if I want more?" she asked, challenging him.

It killed him to deny her. "Not tonight. You just got out of the hospital, and right now you're looking pale." He scooped her with care into his arms and carried her into the master bedroom.

"I'm not an invalid," Brielle complained.

"No. I just love having you in my arms like this."

While he stripped down to his boxers, Brielle slipped into a sheer lavender nightgown with a lacy bodice and spaghetti straps. When Justice saw her in it, he groaned as his body reacted with a will of its own, making it difficult for him to keep his hands off her.

"Damn, woman. You're killing me. I've never seen you in that piece of sexy lingerie before."

Brielle smiled as she rubbed her hands and arms with moisturizer. "That's because I'm always naked when we're in bed."

"Point taken. But imagining what's underneath your nightgown is driving me crazy." He bent and kissed her, teasing her nipples with his thumbs through the lacy bodice of the nightgown.

She broke the kiss and playfully chided him. "Justice, need I remind you that you said no sex tonight?"

He groaned again. "Dumb."

Brielle chuckled as she pulled back the bed linens, slipped between the sheets and lay on her right side to avoid putting pressure on her left arm and leg. Justice crawled on the bed and wrapped his arms protectively around her.

He pushed aside her hair and whispered in her ear, "I really love you, Bri. You're the most incredible woman I've ever met."

She shivered in his arms as his breath caressed her neck. Turning her head, her mouth met his in a warm, searing kiss. Her tongue slid between his lips, causing him to moan low in his throat.

"I love it when you kiss me like that, Tiger Eyes."

Brielle shifted a little more toward him so she could look into his eyes. "I love you, Justice. Without question."

He kissed her deeply for long moments, savoring the taste of her lips beneath his, his heart full of love, his soul at peace.

* * *

Brielle recuperated quickly under Justice's tender loving care. Every morning he cooked breakfast for her after working out with Dooley on the beach. While he was on duty, he sent his officers to her house to check on her. Sometimes they brought her lunch, stayed for a cup of coffee and a piece of cake, and even ran errands for her. By the time she was cleared to return to the job two weeks later she swore she had met every cop on the Laguna Beach police force!

At night members of both her and Justice's teams stopped by with dinner and to hang out with them. They played cards and board games and watched the Oakland A's on ESPN. Sometimes they went down to the beach where they built a fire, made s'mores, and sang songs as River strummed his guitar.

One evening when Finnigan and Tawny happened to be at Brielle's house at the same time, which she suspected one or the other deliberately maneuvered, sparks flew.

"So, Red, what'd you bring for dinner tonight?" Finnigan asked. She uncovered a casserole dish filled with chicken and yellow rice and...peas. He made a face. "I can't stand peas."

"Well, Finnicky Finny, you can just pick them out if you don't want to eat them," Tawny suggested as she shot daggers at him.

Throughout dinner and the card game afterward, Tawny's constant insults thrown at Finnigan took their toll on him. When he could no longer bear them, he muttered, "You know, I can think of a better way for you to use that tongue, Red."

That shut her up. But she glared at him the rest of the night. Even so, he asked her for a date.

"Wanna go out with me, Red? Practice using your tongue on me?" he tossed, a smirk on his face.

"Drop dead, Finnicky Finny."

"I might, if you keep cutting me down."

Brielle just shook her head as she and Justice exchanged a look.

On the last Saturday before Brielle returned to duty, Finnigan, Macklin, two other members of SWAT, and Justice's team from the LBPD gathered at her house for a barbecue. Justice grilled a slab of ribs and everyone else brought side dishes and desserts. After gorging themselves on the delicious food, the guys removed their T-shirts and headed down to the beach for a game of football while Brielle and Tawny lounged on the deck and sipped frosty glasses of lemonade.

When she noticed Tawny watching Finnigan as he played football, Brielle remarked, "Just go out with him."

Tawny gaped at her. "Are you serious? I can't stand Finnigan. He irks me to no end."

"I couldn't tolerate him, either, in the beginning. But I'm glad now he didn't make things easy for me. And we worked out our differences. Yes, he's an arrogant jerk sometimes, but maybe you should give him a chance."

Tawny's gaze returned to the beach. "What's with Finny's tattoo?" Tongues of fire ran down the left side of his bare chest and across his heart. "He probably thinks he's pretty damn hot. A real lady-killer. Flaming Hot Finnigan."

Brielle raised her eyebrows. "His dad was a firefighter with the LAFD and died last year when all those wildfires broke out."

Tawny's eyes grew wide. "Oh no! So...Flame is Marcus Finnigan, *Junior*. I thought his name sounded familiar." She turned to stare at him again. "Maybe I *have* been too hard on him."

"Ya think?" Brielle teased.

It was almost ten o'clock when the group started to leave Brielle's house. As Finnigan passed by Tawny on his way out the front door, she stopped him.

"I'm free tomorrow if you want to go out...Finn."

His deep brown eyes raked her figure with a cold intensity. "Nah. I'm not that...hard...up yet."

Justice guffawed at the double entendre which earned him a sharp jab in the ribs from Brielle. Color shot into Tawny's face as she rushed past them and jumped into her car.

"Now why did you have to do that?" Brielle demanded.

"Because it's time for phase two," Finnigan declared, a triumphant grin on his face.

"Phase two?" Justice repeated.

"Yeah. Pretend she doesn't exist, and then when I've driven her crazy, reel her in like a prized catch."

Brielle shook her head. "Good luck, Flame. You're certainly going to need it."

"A long rod might, um, help," Justice joked with a wicked sense of humor.

They burst into laughter. Brielle just rolled her eyes.

* * *

Brielle eased back into her duties the following week, dealing with a couple of drug busts at first. Commander Mattox wanted to make sure she could handle being back in the field after being shot. He needn't have worried about her. She was on top of her game. As always.

The busy week took its toll on her, though, and by the time she arrived home on Friday, she just wanted to spend a quiet evening with Justice. During dinner he complained that they weren't making any progress on their case, and what's more, they'd lost track of Gage's yacht. To ease his frustration, Brielle suggested they watch a movie after dinner.

As they watched a mindless comedy on Netflix, someone pounded on Brielle's front door.

"Brielle! It's Tex! Open up!"

Justice and Brielle looked at each other in confusion as they rose to their feet and hurried toward the door. "What in the world…" Brielle muttered.

She yanked open the door, and Tex brushed past her, looking wildly around the vast, open living room.

"Is she here?" he demanded, his voice resonating with fear

and concern. "Faith. Is she here? Please tell me you've seen her."

Brielle's stomach flipflopped. "Tex, no. What makes you think Faith is here?"

Tex reached into his pocket and thrust out his hand. In his palm lay the delicate gold bracelet Faith wore that concealed a tracker in it. Broken.

Brielle stared at it in shock. Her face turned pale, and she grabbed Justice's arm. "Oh, my God, Tex. Where did you find her bracelet?"

"At LAX. In a bathroom. Believe me, I've scoured the security footage, and there's no sign of her. Faith didn't tell you, did she, that she was flying out here?"

"No, no. I haven't heard from Faith since she texted Justice after I got shot. Dear God in heaven, Tex! What do you think has happened to her?"

He gritted his teeth. "She's been taken."

# CHAPTER 18

*Taken.* The word echoed in Brielle's mind as she unlocked the door to Faith's apartment in Chicago a mere six hours after Tex delivered the bad news. Terrifying images of what Faith might be enduring, or worse, lying dead somewhere, danced in her mind. Guilt overwhelmed her.

*Why didn't I listen to my gut? I knew something was wrong! I should have gotten on a plane and flown out here to confront her weeks ago!*

As she, Tex, and Justice stepped into the apartment, Brielle sucked in her breath, assailed by memories. She stared at the faux leather sofa facing a 55-inch TV screen. How often had she and Faith sat there stuffing themselves with popcorn and watching *Sleepless in Seattle* for the umpteenth time? She swallowed the fear rising from her gut and looked away. She couldn't afford to lose it now. She had to be strong for Faith and use her well-trained senses to help her.

They scoped out the living area and the kitchen, but nothing appeared out of place or out of the ordinary. On a notepad in the kitchen they found the date and time of her flight to LA, and given the fact that she left clothes strewn all over bed, they guessed Faith left her apartment in a hurry.

Brielle verified that a carry-on was missing from her closet and asked, "Tex, did you find it at the airport?"

"No. Whoever kidnapped Faith is skilled and organized. He knew enough to hack into the LAX security system to prevent us from tracking the footage. But I think Faith deliberately broke her bracelet and left it behind so I'd find it. No one except our inner circle knows how I keep tabs on them."

After they thoroughly checked the master suite and the guest bedroom, they entered her office…and stopped dead in their tracks, staring agog at the sight in front of them.

The wall. Opposite Faith's desk. Covered with photos, tabs, and colored string tying it all together. Every piece of the puzzle Brielle and Justice needed to solve the mystery of the arms coming ashore on Laguna Beach and who was orchestrating it was here.

As the whole picture formed in their minds, Tex muttered, "Shit. Why didn't we know about this?"

"Fuck," Justice cursed. "Fuck. *This* is what Madam Secretary sent me to investigate. Oh, fuck me!"

"Oh. My. God," Brielle murmured. "Oh, my God. Why in the world did Faith keep something of this magnitude to herself?"

While Tex and Justice took pictures of the wall and discussed its implications, Brielle rummaged through Faith's desk and found a slew of handwritten pages of the article she intended to publish.

Based on the information Faith had uncovered about Axel Anderson, he'd decided to act on his anti-America sentiments. He'd gone off the grid with his entire family, and with other likeminded individuals had formed a group bent on staging a revolution right here in America.

Faith had discovered how and when the arms were

coming onshore in Laguna Beach but didn't know exactly who was selling them to Anderson. Anderson's group was well financed and connected, and Faith had learned the names of the major players. Gage. Ferguson. And Nash Carson.

In her notes Faith mentioned she'd met face to face with a former member who had very little to say and refused to get her into the compound or reveal its location. Then he'd vanished. She didn't know whether he was alive or dead. There wasn't much to her story after that final comment.

"Faith knew everything except the location of the compound and who is selling the arms to Anderson," Brielle said in a quiet voice, amazed and proud of Faith's investigative skills, which may or may not have gotten her killed. "Somehow Anderson learned about her investigation and kidnapped her." As a sudden thought occurred to her, she slapped her forehead. "I'm such an idiot. The *bank robbers*. We never did find out what they were all about. What if they were tied to Anderson? Gold and diamonds would have brought him a small fortune on the black market."

Justice agreed with her. "You might be onto something, Bri."

"We're going to find her," Tex affirmed. "Alive. I see it like this. Faith is the niece of a retired FBI commander. If Anderson can turn her, she becomes an asset. A valuable one."

"You're talking about brainwashing. Like a cult," Justice commented.

"Something like that."

Reading the fear and guilt in Brielle's eyes, Justice wrapped his arms around her and tried to offer comfort and support.

"It's not your fault, baby. Faith lied to protect you. I agree with Tex. Anderson is going to keep her alive. And when we find her, he's going to wish he hadn't messed with us, or with our country."

Tears blinded her for a moment, and she buried her face in Justice's hard chest, choking back her sobs. "I pray you're right," she murmured.

The trio left Faith's apartment after they finished taking pictures of what they'd discovered and headed to O'Hare.

Turning to hug Brielle, Tex said, "I'm concerned we haven't been able to reach the Stokers, but I don't want you to worry. We're gonna get this done. Trust me."

Justice and Tex shook hands. They parted, then, heading toward separate gates when their flights were announced over a loudspeaker. As Justice and Brielle's plane headed west, they discussed what to do next. Both she and Justice decided to tell their teams about the kidnapping in order to solicit aid from them. It was all they could do at the moment.

* * *

A week later Brielle and Justice scoured maps of California and Oregon, trying to pinpoint possible locations of Anderson's compound. Military drones had flown over the Redwood National Forest but didn't detect any unusual activity. Now, they were looking at a wider range of territory.

After sunset, a thunderstorm raged outside. White-capped waves crashed against the shore as jagged lightning flashed in the dark night skies and thunder boomed, rattling the windows in Justice's home.

Brielle had just handed Justice a cup of hot coffee when his cell phone vibrated with an incoming call.

"Chief McQuaid." He listened for a moment, then said, his voice brisk, "I'm on my way."

He grabbed two LBPD rain jackets from a closet and

tossed one to Brielle. "Come on. We've got to go. A semi bearing a heavy load of redwood logs jackknifed, causing a major pileup on the coastal highway. With fatalities."

They hurried toward his Explorer. Justice turned on his lights and siren and pulled onto the highway. A little more than a mile later they ran into stalled traffic. Moving onto the shoulder of the road, he bypassed the other cars. Up ahead chaos claimed the highway. Emergency vehicles and patrol cars blocked traffic in both directions as EMTs and police officers handled the gruesome scene.

Justice and Brielle climbed out of the Explorer. He handed her a flashlight and yelled above the noise caused by the wind and rain, "I'm going to help the victims! See if you can get some of this traffic re-routed!"

She nodded. "Be careful, Chief!"

"You, too, Sergeant!"

No vehicle was getting past the accident scene anytime soon. Brielle used her flashlight to direct drivers to either make a U-turn or pull off to the side to wait until at least one lane was unblocked. Most of the drivers expressed their concern and even offered to help, but Brielle instructed them to stay in their vehicles.

A dark blue metallic Ford F-250 traveled north on the shoulder of the highway. Brielle stepped in front of it and motioned the driver to stop. Through the heavy rain she noticed a tarp covering the cargo area. She aimed her flashlight at it, lifted one corner, and glimpsed wooden crates. Through the planks she discerned the dark shape of assault rifles. Her eyes widened with surprise, and her pulse leapt in her veins as her instincts kicked into high gear. She reached for her gun and cautiously approached the front of the truck on the driver's side.

She yelled, "Roll down your window! Now! Let me see your hands!"

"Is there a problem, Sergeant?" Officer Nash Carson asked from behind her.

Before she could react, he jabbed a needle in her neck.

* * *

Several hours later, after the horrific accident scene had been cleared, Justice searched for Brielle. All of the emergency vehicles had left some time ago, along with California Highway patrol officers and Justice's own squad. River and Dooley were still on the scene, waiting to see if he needed them. When he couldn't find Brielle, his blood started to run cold and his stomach clenched.

"Hey, River!" Justice called. "Have you seen Brielle?"

"No, Chief!" River addressed Dooley. "Have you?"

"Nope. Not for a while now."

Justice called Brielle's cell phone, but it went straight to voicemail. "Dammit, she's not picking up!"

"She's got to be around here somewhere," River offered. "Let's look further up the highway."

Justice continued to call her cell phone as River and Dooley shouted her name. Rain still fell in heavy sheets as they canvassed the area. All three grew worried when they couldn't find her anywhere. Desperate, Justice pressed her number again. Lightning flashed.

River grabbed Justice's arm and pointed. "Over there!"

Brielle's cell phone lay smashed on the shoulder of the road.

Pure, unadulterated fear coiled in Justice's gut as he reached for the cell phone. In that paralyzing moment, when it mattered the most for him to make sense of what happened, images and sounds of the events of that night played in his mind's eye. *Trucks.* Had he heard trucks? Yes. Focus on the sound. How many? He didn't know. But now he made the connection. Faith learned when the guns were being moved, and she'd been taken. And Brielle must have seen one or more trucks carrying the arms during the chaos of the accident, and she'd disappeared, too.

"Fuck! That son-of-a-bitch grabbed Brielle!" he screamed as he sprinted toward his Explorer, followed by Dooley and River.

"Who?" Dooley yelled.

"Nash Carson!" Justice remembered him directing traffic a few hours ago.

Dooley and River jumped into their cruisers, and they and Justice turned on their lights and sirens.

Justice shouted into his radio, "I need an APB on Officer Nash Carson! Sergeant Brielle McAdams is missing! And a BOLO on every single goddamned truck in the area! I want roadblocks set up north and south of Laguna Beach! Officer Nash Carson is armed and dangerous!"

"Copy that, Chief McQuaid," dispatch replied. "Notifying CHP and other agencies now."

Five minutes later Justice, Dooley, and River screeched to a halt in front of Carson's simple, one-story home. Through curtains of rain it stood dark and silent. They drew their guns and approached the porch with caution.

"Cover me," Justice commanded. He kicked open the front door, and they rushed past him.

"LBPD!" Dooley called. "Show yourself, Carson!"

They swept the rooms, flipping on lights and shouting, "Clear!"

"The place is clean," River noted. "Sterile."

"Staged," Justice added, his voice grim.

A search of the entire house left no doubt in their minds that it was just a façade. It didn't contain any personal possessions. Not a single piece of paper—junk mail or otherwise. No receipts. No girly magazines. No family pictures.

No books or DVDs or CDs. There wasn't even a toothbrush or a comb in the bathroom they could test for DNA. A size ten pair of shoes in the closet confirmed they might be the same size as the military boot print they already had on file.

"I'm sorry, Chief, but this place has been scrubbed down," River remarked. "No need to waste any more time here."

Justice gripped the butt of his gun. "I'm going to kill him," he vowed. "If he touches a hair on Brielle's head, I'm going to kill him."

He ordered Dooley and River to head south to the police blockade while he headed north. They kept the roadblocks in place until long after the sun rose that morning, stopping and questioning every single driver of a truck, no matter the make and model.

Eventually, Captain Locke approached Justice and placed a hand on his shoulder. "It's done, Chief. There's no point in continuing the roadblock. CHP has already called it quits. Whoever took Sergeant McAdams had too good of a head start."

Justice glared at him through blazing eyes. "Nash Carson took her. There's no sign of him. He's a damn ghost, too. I've been investigating him. Carson appeared in Laguna Beach out of nowhere, and now he's disappeared. This isn't a coincidence, Captain. Now, get your officers organized and help me find my girlfriend!"

* * *

Within forty-eight hours of Brielle's disappearance, a massive manhunt coordinated by several law enforcement agencies was underway.

Justice hadn't slept in seventy-two hours. His eyes were bloodshot, his face was covered in scruff, and his clothes and hair were disheveled. He kept blaming himself for putting

Brielle in danger. If only she hadn't gone with him to help that night. If only he'd insisted that she stay at home. *If only.* Now the *what ifs* plagued him. What if Anderson killed her? Or worse, what if he tortured her? Violated her? He shook his head to clear the cobwebs from a lack of sleep and food. No. He couldn't allow his thoughts to go to that dark place. He needed to stay focused. Strong. For Brielle. Because she was counting on him.

At the moment he faced the group gathered at Brielle's house which had become the command center for the search for her and Faith, too. Cameron and Brianna, along with Brielle's four brothers, had arrived yesterday. Tex sat across from them, discussing strategy as Cynthia and Adrienne served sandwiches, chips, and offered bottles of water. Justice saw it all as if he were standing outside of himself. Dread clutched his heart.

Franklin stood nearby, keeping a close eye on him. He could tell his dad thought he might keel over any second now. But he drew upon a deep well of strength and grit fueled by his great love for Brielle. He had a mission to complete.

"My team is unavailable, but we can call on Delta. Team two is on stand-by, just waiting for instructions," Tex said.

"No," Justice interjected. He stood with his feet planted apart on the floor, his arms crossed uncompromisingly. "We're not using Delta. Brielle is my woman. The woman I love with my entire heart and soul. It's my responsibility to rescue her, and Faith Stoker. This is my mission, and I'm running it my way."

His eyes dared Tex to argue with him. Tex merely inclined his head, understanding full well how Justice felt. "All right, McQuaid. Tell us what you need done."

Justice's arm swept across the group. "My team is in place, and so is Brielle's. We've got all the force we need right here in this room. First, we have to find Anderson's compound. It has to be in the largely uninhabited forests of Oregon or northern California. Hutch, you and Tex focus on Oregon. The rest of us will concentrate on northern California. Mr. McAdams and Trey will coordinate resources and check with the other agencies. We're putting all of our time and energy into finding Brielle and Faith. Is that clear?"

Everyone nodded.

As soon as their meeting broke up, Justice, Tawny, Macklin, and Finnigan headed toward the Sierra Nevada Mountains in a rugged jeep. Behind them the McAdams brothers followed in a Mountaineer. When they reached the foothills, they jumped out of their vehicles, and Justice removed a set of maps from his backpack. He spread them out on the hood of the jeep.

"Okay, so Tawny, Finnigan, Macklin, and I will take this section northeast of our current location."

Trey studied the second map. "We'll head straight north. We're looking for a compound that has to be underground. The drones we've sent haven't picked up a damn thing. Watch where you're going, too. Look sharp. You don't want to trigger any kind of explosive device. Mark where you've been. We don't want to cover the same ground twice."

"And stay with your partner," Justice added. "No wandering off by yourself. Keep hydrated. We've got a long day ahead of us." He tossed Trey a radio. "There's no cell service up here so we'll communicate using our radios."

"And if we do find the compound, no heroics," Trey warned them, looking straight at Justice. "We call for backup. Is that understood?"

Justice bristled. This was his rescue mission, and part of him resented Trey giving him orders. But he was Brielle's eldest brother, so he bit back a sharp retort and merely inclined his head.

Tawny answered for him. "Understood Special Agent McAdams."

"Good. Let's head out."

Armed with semi-automatic rifles slung over their shoulders and concealed handguns and Kevlar vests worn over their clothing, Justice, Tawny, Finnigan, and Macklin spread out in a line but kept within sight of each other. They moved methodically through the dense forest, marking the territory they covered, looking for evidence of beaten paths that a truck might make, and mounds of any kind, other structures, and listening for the sound of generators.

The temperature grew cooler the higher they hiked. Golden sunlight slanted through the tops of the giant trees, reminding Justice vividly of Brielle's eyes. They haunted him. He imagined them filled with pain. Agony. Condemnation. Death. Grief gripped his heart. No. He couldn't torture himself with those images. He needed to envision them shining with vitality. Hope. Love. Most importantly, *love*.

Justice clung to his love for Brielle as they tramped through the foothills and the hours waned without discovering Anderson's compound. Every hour that passed increased his anxiety, causing his heart to pound as the blood raced through his veins. Trying to get his mind off his fear, he concentrated on watching his feet and his team as they scoured the area with the same intensity as his.

In spite of his own situation, Justice noticed subtle changes in the way Finnigan and Tawny treated each other. Ever since he refused her offer of a date, Finnigan had kept his distance, showing Tawny a polite deference whenever circumstances threw them together. Justice and Brielle had laughed at his plan to reel Tawny in, but it seemed to be working. The more Finnigan ignored her the more determined Tawny became to get his attention. But now with

Brielle missing, both dropped their guard and their coyness in order to aid Justice in his search for her.

At one point Tawny tripped over exposed roots and fell heavily to the ground. Finnigan rushed to help her. Unable to place her full weight on her right ankle she cried out in pain. Finnigan lowered her onto a fallen log and removed her boot and sock. He ran his hands with expertise over her ankle, quickly at first and then more slowly, caressing her tender flesh. Heat rose in her cheeks, and she bit her lower lip.

"It's not broken or sprained," Finnigan commented, his voice soft. His deep brown eyes regarded her with intensity. "You probably twisted it a little." He continued to massage her ankle. "Does it feel better?"

She nodded, her eyes never leaving his. "Yes. Thank you."

"You're welcome." Finnigan helped put on her sock and boot and held out his hand. "Let's see if you can put your weight on it now."

Tawny gingerly took a step. "I'm good."

"Are you sure?" Justice demanded. "I don't want you to end up with a damaged ankle. We still have a lot of ground to cover."

"I'm sure, Chief."

"Okay, but let me know if it bothers you," he ordered.

"Ten-four."

Justice turned away, then, as Finnigan stayed close to Tawny. He couldn't bear to watch their budding romance at the same time he might have lost the love of his life.

*God*, he prayed. *I'll do anything. Please just let me find Brielle alive.*

Long after sunset, the two groups met back at their starting point. They'd covered fifty square miles of virgin territory without finding anything. Discouraged, the McAdams brothers headed to their sister's house, and Justice returned to his.

Alone in his master suite, he turned on the water in the shower and stripped. He stood, leaning forward, head down, arms braced against the cold tile, letting the warm spray sluice down his tired, sore body. Tears fell unheeded and mingled with the water.

*Hang on, baby. I'm coming for you.*

Stepping out of the shower stall, Justice wrapped a towel around his waist. Overcome by a sudden weakness, he collapsed on the edge of his bed. His hands began to shake. Then his legs. A moment later his entire body convulsed. He knew he wasn't having a seizure, but he couldn't control the tremors.

"Dad!" he cried. "I need you!"

# CHAPTER 19

Franklin burst into Justice's bedroom and saw him shaking uncontrollably. He perched next to him and wrapped his arms around his son's trembling body.

Justice choked on the searing emotion rising in his throat. Great sobs wracked him. "I can't lose her, Dad! I can't lose her! Not now when I've just found her! She's—she's my whole world. I can't lose someone else I love. First Mom, then my team, my career. I don't think I can survive this. *Not this.*"

Franklin held Justice until his physical and emotional crisis passed. "Pull yourself together, son. You have a mission to complete. Everyone is counting on you, especially Brielle. She's incredibly strong and clever, and you taught her how to survive like a SEAL. Don't forget she has years of experience on the force, and now she's SWAT. I know in my gut she's alive, and she'll figure out a way to make it until you rescue her. What would Brielle say or do if she saw you like this?"

"She'd kick my ass." He met his father's concerned eyes. "But, Dad, I didn't have time to teach her everything I know. Especially what to do in a situation like this."

"Trust me. She knows." He patted Justice on the back and rose to his feet. "Get some rest. You've got long days ahead of you."

Justice tried to sleep but tossed and turned, unconsciously reaching for Brielle only to find the empty space next to him.

Within a week of Brielle's kidnapping, the task force dwindled down to just a few personnel. Commander Mattox returned to SWAT headquarters, promising to aid in the search in any way he could, and gave permission for Finnigan and Macklin to stay behind on personal leave. Brielle's brother Ben had to return to Rutherford, Maine, to check on his wife Callie and their children and to appear in court to argue a case he was handling.

"I'll be back as soon as I can," he swore as he shook Justice's hand and hugged his parents.

After Ben left, their frustration mounted. Even Tex, working every connection he had and trolling the dark net with Hutch, made little headway in the search for Brielle and Faith. As the days passed, Justice caught Tex cursing and pounding his computer keyboard. Trying to build the trust of faceless contacts he'd made using the dark net was taking too much time.

At the end of a tough day tramping through the mountains, Justice lost his temper. Focusing his anger on Brendan, he grabbed him by the shirt and threw him against a wall.

"This is all your fault! You knew what was happening out here, and you deliberately kept Brielle in the dark. *You* put her in danger. If anything happens to her, I swear to God, I'll kill you!"

Trey and Bryant pulled Justice off their brother, and he twisted out of their grasp.

Brendan coughed as he caught his breath. "Justice, I swear, we didn't know. Homeland Security…"

"Bullshit. Fuckin' bullshit!" Justice spat.

"We didn't know everything." Brendan gazed at his parents. "Secretary of State Washburn wanted to use Brielle, and I wouldn't let her. That's when she decided to send Justice out here."

"Why? Why me? And don't bullshit me."

"All right, you want the truth? Madam Secretary didn't want you to know you led your team into an ambush."

Justice reeled. His heart slammed into his chest. "What the fuck do you mean?"

"You were led to believe you were taking medical supplies to a village filled with sick women and children, but that was a lie planted by insurgents to lead you into a trap. You weren't supposed to know you'd been given false intel. Why do you think the Navy retired you? Madam Secretary arranged it. In fact, she insisted upon it."

Pain tore through Justice's gut. He emitted a roar of rage and lunged at Brendan, intending to rip him from limb to limb. He landed a single upper cut to the jaw that knocked Brendan off his feet before Cameron and Franklin intervened.

"Justice, stop!" his father commanded.

Cameron hauled Brendan up, and held Justice at arm's length when he tried to hit Brendan again. Franklin grabbed Justice's arm and yanked him away from Cameron and Brendan.

"You're not helping the situation," Franklin admonished.

"Oh, yeah? Decking that bureaucratic asshole felt pretty good to me."

Brendan tested his sore jaw. "For the record, McQuaid, I urged Madam Secretary to tell you the truth."

"Yeah? Tell that to my team's families. I'm the one who has to live with this. Knowing my team died because someone passed along bad intel. And even though that's true, in the end *I* was responsible. *I* was their leader. Their lieutenant commander. The buck stopped with me." His voice rose in fury. "They're dead! And it's my fault!"

Justice tore out of Brielle's house and fled down to the beach. He ran fast, his arms and legs pumping rhythmically, his heart keeping time. Memories of that day flashed through his mind. Eating breakfast in the mess tent. Talking smack. Making plans to play football when they got back from their mission. Only they didn't make it back. Because he'd led them into a trap.

He screamed.

He cursed.

He stumbled and dropped to the sand.

He failed the mission. Failed to protect and keep his men safe.

He drew his knees up to his chest. His head pounded, and he felt nauseous. He leaned over and vomited. Reeling from the truth, he dragged the back of his hand across his mouth. He and his team had been betrayed, but he couldn't allow that to defeat him. Not now. Not now when Brielle's life depended on him. He took a deep, cleansing breath. He'd deal with what happened in Afghanistan later. Time to step up and be the leader, no, *the man*, Brielle needed him to be.

Justice gazed up at the sky, heavily laden with stars. "Time to get my shit together. Get my focus back. Deal with what's in front of me."

He took his time returning to Brielle's house. Justice still wanted to pound Brendan into the ground, but he apologized, bid Cameron and Brianna good night, and went home to try to get some sleep. He had another long, fruitless day planned. And another. And another.

\* \* \*

Three weeks. Twenty-one days. Five hundred and four hours. Thirty thousand two hundred and forty minutes. One million eight hundred and fourteen thousand and four hundred seconds. That's how long Brielle had been missing. Her brothers didn't want to give up, but they had put their lives, families, and careers on hold to search for their sister. Only Finnigan, Macklin, Tawny, Hutch, River, Dooley, and Martini remained to help Justice. Cameron and Brianna and Tex, of course, refused to give up or stop looking for Brielle.

After deciding to focus on Oregon in their search for Brielle, Justice grew tired of feeling like a hamster spinning on a wheel. Dressed in his uniform in order to intimidate his quarry, he stepped briskly into City Hall and rode an elevator to the second floor.

Ignoring Mayor Gage's watchdog who sat at a desk outside his office, Justice burst through the double oak doors.

"Chief, you can't go in there!"

"What the hell do you think you're doing?" Gage demanded in an irritable voice. He glared at his uninvited guest. "I'm busy."

"I'll bet you are. I'm through playing games, Mr. Mayor. Time to lay our cards on the table. Brielle McAdams and her friend Faith Stoker have been missing for more than three weeks now, and you know exactly where they are."

Gage crossed his arms over his chest and snorted with disdain. "You're delusional. After barging in here and making such a ridiculous accusation, you're finished as chief of police."

"You think so?" Justice braced himself against the mayor's mahogany desk and leaned forward. "I know you're carrying arms from Nicaragua on your yacht and bringing them ashore right here in Laguna Beach. That night Brielle and I were guests? Not an accident. Brielle finagled an invite. And guess what she found? Proof."

Mayor Gage didn't blink. "You're crazy. You've completely lost your mind, McQuaid."

Justice pulled up the pictures Brielle had sent to him on his phone and tossed it onto Gage's desk. "Take a look."

Gage barely glanced at the pictures of the wooden crates inside the rectangular containers on his yacht. "Not only are you crazy, you're just plain stupid. These pictures don't prove a damn thing."

Justice shoved his cell phone back into its case clipped to his waist. "You're committing the worst kind of treason there is. Nothing would make me happier than to lock you up for the rest of your pathetic life. However, I'm willing to offer you a deal. Full immunity in exchange for the location of Axel Anderson's compound. You have thirty seconds to make your decision."

"Get out of my office. I'm done talking to you."

"Suit yourself. Enjoy sitting in that chair while you still can, *Mayor*. The next time I see you, I'll have a warrant for your arrest. And you can kiss this," he waved his arm around the office, "goodbye, along with your family. Have a nice day."

Outside City Hall Justice spoke into his shoulder mic. "Anything?"

While leaning against Gage's desk, he'd planted a bug, sanctioned by Madam Secretary. She happily accommodated him after Brendan had confessed he'd blurted the truth about what happened in Afghanistan. Justice planned to confront her as soon as Brielle and Faith were safe and secure. He wanted the person or persons responsible for feeding him bad intel punished. Part of him wondered if his commander knew the truth. God, he hoped not. If he knew and kept quiet, that would be the ultimate betrayal.

Hutch spoke in his ear. "Not yet."

"Keep me posted."

"You got it, Chief. You're covering the beach tomorrow for the Fourth of July, right?"

"Yeah. I'll be out all day. Stop by Brielle's house when you can, Hutch. Her mom is cooking a feast for the department."

"I will. When are you going off duty?"

"In about an hour."

"Copy that."

Bright blue cloudless skies heralded the Fourth of July. By nine o'clock in the morning, hordes of people congregated on the beach. The majority of the LBPD patrolled the streets, and extra officers helped Justice cruise the beach. He kept busy checking in with the lifeguards and the food truck vendors, and maintaining order. Aside from a few minor skirmishes, everyone cooperated and enjoyed themselves. He'd become easily recognizable as the face of the LBPD, especially after Brielle disappeared, and many beach-goers spoke to him, offering their sympathy and encouragement.

His sagging spirit lifted somewhat when he caught sight of Rosie tossing a beach ball with a group of other little girls. He waved to her, and much to his relief, she smiled and waved back at him. The small gesture filled him with hope. Hope that she would trust him again.

While riding up and down the beach on his UTV, Justice kept an ear to his radio. He half expected Axel Anderson to launch his coup today for its historical significance. Staging a revolution on the most important date in American history.

He wondered what Brielle might be facing at the moment. How she endured every day. How she feared not being rescued. Had she given up? Stopped hoping? Did she hate him? He could handle her hatred as long as she was alive.

*Dear God, let her be alive.*

With so much to do, Justice skipped eating. At seven he took a break and parked his UTV at the base of the steps leading to Brielle's deck. Several cops, their spouses or significant others, and their families sat on lounge chairs or hung out in the spacious living room. They held cans of beer or soda or bottles of water as they consumed plates of barbecued chicken and ribs and various side dishes and desserts prepared by Brianna.

After greeting everyone, Justice filled a plate with ribs, baked beans, and potato salad and sat in an empty place on the deck. He took a couple of bites of his meat and felt nauseous.

He pushed his plate away and muttered, "I can't eat."

Brianna dropped into the vacant chair next to him. She reached out and touched his arm. "Justice, you've been on duty all day. The officers said you haven't eaten or taken a break. Please eat something. You don't look well."

The gentleness of her tone reminded him so much of Brielle it ripped his heart into jagged pieces. "It's too...difficult, Mrs. McAdams." He wasn't referring to eating.

"Yes, I know. But if Brielle thought for one second I wasn't taking care of the man she loves, she'd be disappointed. She'd give me a piece of her mind. So, please, eat!"

A ghost of smile crossed his face. "Yes, ma'am." He lifted a forkful of potato salad to his mouth.

Brianna patted his arm. "Stay strong, Justice. Have faith."

"Yes, ma'am."

*Have faith.* Rage simmered anew in him as he watched Gage's super yacht sail past Brielle's house during the fireworks display after sunset. He vowed to see the mayor incarcerated.

*I'm coming for you. Your days are numbered.*

Three days later Justice figured he didn't have anything to lose by confronting Linda Ferguson. He considered the possibility that she'd been drawn into Anderson's conspiracy by either accident or by coercion. Just in case he'd be met with the same lack of cooperation as the mayor, he'd secured permission to bug her house. He'd have to be clever about planting it, too, for Linda was sharper than Gage.

When he knocked on her front door, Linda didn't seem surprised to see him.

"Coffee, Justice? You look like you need it."

"Yeah, sure." He followed her into the sunny kitchen.

As she handed him a coffee mug, she remarked, "I know why you're here. Elliott told me about the visit you paid to him a few days ago."

Justice sipped his coffee. "Linda, please, I'm begging you. Help me stop Axel Anderson. Help me find Brielle and Faith Stoker."

Linda gripped her coffee mug, and she avoided his direct gaze. "I can't. I don't know anything."

"You were once a good cop. Decorated. Respected. What changed? Is it money? I've looked into your finances, Linda. There isn't any evidence of large transactions, unless you're hiding the cash really well. So, what is it? Are Gage and Anderson holding something over your head? Tell me. I can help you."

Her hands started to shake. "I'm clean."

"Until two years ago, I believe you were. Now you're dirty. And what's more you're betraying the oath you took when you became an officer." Justice set down his mug. "You've left me no choice, Linda. Cooperate and I'll make sure you get full immunity. If not, I'll be back to arrest you."

When she remained silent, he sighed. "All right. Have it your way."

She would probably find the bug he'd attached underneath the kitchen table, but at least he'd tried.

He'd just reached the door when she called, "Justice, wait!"

"What?"

Unbridled fear shone in her eyes. "Anderson has my son."

* * *

Brielle fought against the darkness enveloping her and regained consciousness. She blinked at the harsh florescent lighting above her. Her tongue felt thick and heavy in her mouth, and she ran it over her dry lips. A terrible thirst consumed her. She pushed a woolen blanket off her and tried to sit up, but a wave of dizziness caused her to fall back against the pillow. As the fogginess in her head subsided, she noted her surroundings.

She lay on a mattress and box spring in an underground cell with smooth cavernous walls. A solid steel door blocked escape from her prison. Brielle heard the low thrum of generators which provided electricity to the compound. Without her watch or a clock, she didn't have any idea what time of day or night it was or how long she'd been unconscious. Hours? Days?

Her gaze moved around the cell. Next to the bed stood a sink and a toilet. They reminded Brielle that she was thirsty and also needed to relieve herself. At that moment she realized she was stark naked beneath a plain gray linen dress. Panic rose in her as she examined herself for signs of sexual assault. Thankfully, there weren't any. She assumed Anderson didn't need to use sex to control or humiliate her. He planned to break her in other ways. She shivered.

Rising on shaky legs, she stumbled toward the sink and splashed cold water on her face. Cupping her hands, she drank deeply before she used the toilet. Afterward, she approached the nearest wall and ran her hands with trained expertise over it, looking for any evidence of weakness or cracks. The methodical process took more than an hour, but she had to be certain she was trapped. No way out other than through the steel door. She checked the hinges. Maybe if she could get her hands on a tool of some kind, she could pop them out. Perhaps the bed frame could be of use to her.

The physical exertion caused her knees to buckle. She drank more water, and this time it hit her empty stomach like a rock. It roiled and rebelled and she gagged. Falling back upon the bed, she curled into a fetal position and breathed through the intense pain.

When she felt better, Brielle lifted her eyes and gasped. In an upper corner of her cell blinked a red dot.

She swore aloud and tore the sheets off the bed and checked every inch of it until she found a tiny microphone.

Staring straight into the camera, she said in a raspy voice, "Okay, I'm awake, you son-of- a-bitch. Let's talk."

Fifteen minutes later someone unlocked the steel door and it slid open. Brielle leapt to her feet and emitted a short laugh.

"Officer Carson."

He trained a gun on her. "After you."

Outside the cell she declared, "You know I could easily disarm you."

Carson rolled his eyes. "Yeah, I know all about your training with Chief McQuaid. But you're smart enough not to try anything. You have no idea how to get out of this place and wouldn't get very far until you were caught."

Brielle digested that information as Carson led her through a maze of short and long underground corridors. She memorized the turns they took and noted any sounds she heard coming from behind row after row of steel doors.

If these were the living quarters of Anderson's regime, they were little better than prisoners themselves.

"You're a traitor," she commented after they'd descended a set of concrete steps. The coldness stung her bare feet.

Carson halted and stared hard at her. "To what? To a government that abandoned and betrayed its people several generations ago? To a government that turned its back on the weak and the poor in favor of the elite?"

His answer revealed a significant piece of information. "Do you really believe that? Or are you just repeating Anderson's sick, twisted philosophy? Have you forgotten he's a one percenter?"

"I haven't forgotten anything. Anderson is using his money to finance change."

"Really?" she scoffed. "It seems to me he's using his money to stage a revolution that will result in the deaths of hundreds, if not thousands, of innocent people. If he wanted to effect real change, why didn't he run for office? Why hasn't he used his millions to build job training and education centers for the poor and displaced? Do you know how many starving and homeless people he could feed and shelter with his money?"

Carson shoved his gun into her belly. "Shut up."

"You're a disgrace to the badge."

"I was never the badge." He waved the gun. "Move."

*Never the badge.* What did that mean?

# CHAPTER 20

From the closed expression on Carson's face, Brielle decided not to press him about what he meant. She needed him to view her as non-threatening and impotent. Besides, their destination lay immediately to their right—a massive set of double steel doors. Apparently, they'd arrived at the center of the hive.

Anderson was smarter than she'd thought. He'd set up a retinal scanner that allowed Carson access to his inner sanctum. She wondered how many others had such a high level of trust and security clearance. The doors swooshed, and they stepped across the threshold.

The inviting space replicated a homey atmosphere at odds with reality. This might have been Anderson's living room in his home on the surface. Rows of books lined the walls. Around a fake fireplace, leather recliners and a sofa sat in a U. Soft lighting illuminated the area and jazz music played at a low volume in the background. Beyond this, Brielle noticed a kitchen with a wooden dining table large enough to seat eight people. She wasn't sure if Anderson and his family slept in this confine or somewhere else.

Her tall, slender host smiled at her and dismissed Carson with a wave of his hand. Anderson possessed classic good looks—rugged facial features, dark eyes, and short-cropped salt and pepper hair. A neatly trimmed beard covered the lower portion of his cheeks, jawline, and chin.

He offered his hand. "We finally meet, Miss McAdams."

His rough, workworn hand and his cultured voice and politeness belied his true nature. She dropped his hand, and he gestured toward the sofa.

"Please, sit down." He made himself comfortable in a recliner and perused her.

"Where's Faith Stoker?" Brielle demanded.

Anderson smiled again, revealing perfect, even white teeth. "You don't disappoint. True to your nature, your first concern is for your friend, not yourself."

"She's here, then. Alive?"

"Of course. She has the most amazing brain. I've enjoyed rewiring it."

Cold fear crawled up Brielle's spine and across her scalp. Sweat beaded on her forehead and started to run down her face. "May I see her?"

"Not yet. I don't want to interrupt her training."

At least he didn't flat out refuse her request. "You mean her re-education."

"Yes. Faith Stoker is one of my valuable assets."

"Is that what I am?"

Anderson's eyes narrowed as he leaned forward. "The *most* valuable. Provided you cooperate."

"And if I don't?"

"I'll toss your cold carcass to the wolves."

Brielle forced herself to grin. "I like your directness. Will you answer another question?"

"Go ahead."

"Where are we?"

"Deep underground in Oregon."

"That's what we thought. How long did it take you to complete your lair?"

Anderson quirked an eyebrow. "An odd choice of a word, but to answer your question, it took five years."

"Just out of curiosity, how do Mayor Gage and former police chief Linda Ferguson fit into this?"

"You tell me, Miss McAdams."

She noticed he didn't address her as "sergeant." A telling point. "Well, I know you're using the mayor's yacht to transport arms, but honestly, I can think of more expedient methods. I don't understand Ferguson's involvement. Care to enlighten me?"

"Filial bonds are a powerful motivator, Miss McAdams." Anderson rose to his feet. "Our interview is over."

Pondering what he meant by *filial bonds*, Brielle followed his lead. "What's next?"

"You begin your re-education."

"I won't betray my country or my conscience."

"Oh, but you will, Miss McAdams. I promise in the end you'll betray both."

The steel doors opened and Anderson addressed Carson. "Take Miss McAdams back to her quarters and bring her a decent meal." To Brielle, he added, "You'll have to earn your next one."

"And how do I do that?"

"Do as you're told. Cooperate." He grinned. "I'm going to enjoy scrambling your brain, Miss McAdams. You'll be my greatest challenge to date. I've decided you'll be the face of my revolution. That will be my revenge for killing three of my allies. And that poor lackey Dewitt."

"You mean the bank robbers? I knew it," she cooed, her eyes glowing with triumph. "But Artie Dewitt? I don't even want to know how he managed to hook up with you. That was a stupid mistake on your part."

Anderson glowered at her. "Enjoy your victory, Miss McAdams. The next one will be mine. Good night."

As Carson escorted her back to her cell, without a gun pointed at her this time, she asked questions about the layout of the compound, but he ignored her.

"Can you at least tell me what time it is, Carson?" she demanded, exasperated.

"It's a little past seven PM."

"How long was I unconscious?"

"About thirty-six hours."

She nodded and they didn't speak again until they reached her cell.

"I'll be back with your dinner."

"Um, can you include a pair of panties and a box of feminine products, please?" Brielle sounded appropriately pitiful.

"Uh, sure."

Carson said he'd be back in an hour, so Brielle used the time to rid herself of the lingering effects of the drug she'd been given. She drank cold tap water and started to jog around the perimeter of her cell. At least she had plenty of room. Pushing all thoughts of her family and Justice, *oh, God, Justice,* out of her mind, she focused on exercising, pumping blood and oxygen through her veins and up to her brain. She'd need to use every ounce of her training, skill set, and her intelligence to outwit Anderson.

When Carson returned with her dinner on a rolling cart, Brielle's mouth watered and her stomach growled. Tantalizing aromas wafting from a thick grilled steak, a baked potato, and seasoned green beans teased her senses. A warm yeast roll and strawberry shortcake completed her meal. On the bottom of the cart she spotted a pair of granny panties and the box of feminine products she'd requested. A towel, wash cloth, a bar of soap, toothpaste, and a toothbrush had also been provided.

"I'll leave you alone for a little while to eat and refresh yourself. Take advantage of the luxury of a sponge bath while you can," Carson advised.

Brielle pointed at the camera. "Can I have some privacy?"

Carson scowled. "This isn't the Ritz."

"All I need is five minutes."

"You're a rich, entitled, spoiled princess," he complained, "and I can't wait to see you broken and humiliated. You've got your precious five minutes."

Brielle forced herself to eat slowly, not knowing if she'd be allowed another meal as good as this one. She kept an eye on the camera, and when the red light disappeared, she tore into the box of tampons, removed the absorbent material and dropped it into the pocket of her dress. She planned to stuff it into the door jamb when an opportunity arose and prayed it would prevent the lock from fully engaging. Within the allotted time she completed her toilette and felt better after she brushed her teeth.

Carson appeared a few minutes later and took everything away from her except the toothpaste, toothbrush, and tampons.

"So, you're policing me, huh? Ironic, considering you said you were never the badge."

Confusion crossed his face. "What? Never the badge…" he muttered. "But I'm a…" Blankness replaced his confusion. His eyes focused on a spot on the far wall. His body shuddered, and he shook himself free of whatever held him in its grasp.

Carson's nostrils flared, and his gaze turned dark with anger. "I'm a lieutenant in Axel's army."

"You screwed up, though. You left an HK416 and a box of ammo for us to find."

He grew wrathful. "No! I didn't!"

"Yes, you did. We found your prints on the HK416, and your shoe print on the ammo. You took a beating for it. Axel punished you, didn't he?"

Carson balled his fist. "Stop trying to manipulate me, Sergeant, or I'll devise your punishment myself!"

"I'm sorry, Carson." She followed him into the doorway.

He pulled his gun. "Back up. Now!"

"Look, I'm not going anywhere, as you said. Do you really have to threaten me with violence?"

"You're far too clever for your own good." Without warning, Carson grabbed her and threw her against the stone wall. One hand closed around her throat and squeezed. He leaned into her as her eyes grew wide, and she prepared to defend herself. "Hide it," he whispered. "For God's sake, hide it."

He stepped back. Brielle gagged and coughed.

"Don't mess with me again," he warned her.

"Sorry!" she gasped. "Sorry!"

"The lights operate on a timer," Carson went on, as if nothing out of the ordinary had happened. As if he hadn't just tried to choke her. "Off at nine, on at five."

The steel door closed behind him and locked automatically. Brielle let out her breath and sank onto the mattress. She touched her sore neck and faced away from the camera so whoever watched her wouldn't be able to read her thoughts. With a shudder, she recalled Winston's torture in Room 101 in Orwell's novel *1984*. She feared something far worse than rats awaited her.

As far as Carson was concerned, Brielle detected cracks in his conditioning. Tex still hadn't been able to find out anything about him which led her to suspect he might be either CIA or an FBI agent deep undercover. Nothing about

Carson made any sense at the moment, especially what he'd whispered.

*Hide it.*

Just what she planned to do.

*God, give me strength.*

The overhead light flickered off. Alone in the dark, Brielle allowed herself to think about her family. They must be worried sick about her and frantically searching for her. She knew her father and Trey and Tex would use every resource at their disposal to find her. *And Justice.* Her heart flipped in her chest, and she dragged the scratchy blanket over her head. Stifling a sob, she whispered his name. Again and again.

"Find me," she begged him. "Oh, God, find me."

She couldn't bear the thought of what he was going through right now. What he must be imagining. What he knew she would endure to stay alive. Yes, she would stay alive. For him. Because he'd captured her heart and soul the first time he'd smiled at her on their beach. Because she wanted her own happily ever after, like the heroines in her mother's historical romance novels. And because she didn't want Justice ever to have to face life alone again.

"I promise I'll do whatever it takes to stay alive, Justice," she whispered. "Just don't give up on me. I love you so much."

She finally fell asleep with an image of Justice's rugged face floating in her mind.

The following morning Brielle awoke as soon as light flooded her cell. Grateful she hadn't experienced any lingering side effects from the drug Carson used to knock her out, she splashed her face with cold water, dried it with the hem of her dress, and brushed her teeth. While she jogged around her cell, a synthetic voice spoke soothingly over a loudspeaker.

"Good morning. This is a new day. Rejoice in it. Embrace it and your place in our New America."

Brielle laughed aloud. She imagined she'd been transported into a bad version of *Brave New World* or a poorly written episode of *Twilight Zone*. Her laughter died, though, as the stark reality of her situation hit her hard in the gut as if she'd been punched. This moment might be her last to laugh as herself. She knew techniques to resist brainwashing, but would they be enough to keep her mind intact? When she emerged from the program, would she be broken, a mere shell of her former self?

She worried about Faith, too, who didn't share her background or training or survival skills. What had Anderson done to her?

*Please, God, let Faith be okay.*

Brielle had been awake for almost an hour, she guessed, when the steel door slid open, and Carson joined her. He handed her a pair of black sweatpants, an old T-shirt, clean panties and a bra, and tennis shoes.

"Follow me," he ordered, his voice curt.

"What no cheerful 'good morning'?" When he shot her a dirty look, she smiled. "Where to?"

"The communal showers."

Brielle quirked an eyebrow and couldn't resist a snarky reply. "Communal showers? Is this a revolutionary group or a hippie commune?"

"You have a smart mouth."

"If you're a lieutenant in Anderson's army, why have you been assigned my watchdog?"

"I do what I'm told."

"Uh-huh. So, if I told you to throw yourself off the nearest cliff, would you?" she baited him.

"If it meant I wouldn't have to listen to you anymore, yeah, I would."

"Wow! An original thought. Who knew?" Brielle teased him. "Where are you from, Carson?"

She threw the question at him so quickly he didn't stop to think about it. "Texas. I'm from Texas..." Carson's voice trailed away, and he stiffened beside her. "What the hell are you trying to do?"

"Just making friendly conversation," she replied.

By this time they'd reached an open area near the surface. To say it hummed with activity like a beehive would be a paradox. The men passing them, dressed in business suits and other casual attire, and heading toward a bank of elevators that rose out of the compound, were mute. None of them spoke to each other or to Carson and Brielle. Only their eyes communicated suspicion and blatant dislike. She could understand why they might feel that way about her, but why Carson?

"Where are those men going?" Brielle inquired.

"To their jobs on the outside."

"Like yours."

"Like mine. But I can't go back now."

"Does it matter? You said you were never the badge, remember?"

"No, I... No, guess not." Carson frowned at her.

"Well, they don't like you, or me, either," she commented.

"They're jealous. I moved up the hierarchy pretty quickly. And you're a newbie so that's understandable. You're also a cop. Makes you a target. So does your last name," he informed her.

As they continued toward the communal showers, Brielle noticed modestly dressed women herding childrenall equally as silent as the men.

"Carson, what are the women doing?"

"Preparing for their day. They cook all the meals, do the

laundry, clean, and take care of the children too young to attend school and educate the older ones."

"Those are their roles?" Brielle flung a scathing look at him. "Anderson just set women back a hundred years."

"What do you think you're going to be doing?" Carson tossed. "Peeling potatoes and working in the laundry room."

They arrived at the communal showers which had two entrances. The one to the right led to the women's stalls. Fortunately, they were empty at the moment, but Brielle didn't care one way or the other. She'd lost her modesty years ago and didn't mind taking a shower in front of other people. There wasn't much water pressure, but she reveled in being able to thoroughly cleanse herself and wash her hair.

After she dressed, she asked Carson if she could have a blow-dryer, but he rolled his eyes and replied that they didn't have any, and besides, it was a self-indulgent luxury.

"Where to now, Agent Carson from Texas?" Brielle threw at him on a hunch.

Carson's eyes glazed over, and he stood frozen in shock. "Wh—what did you call me?"

"Agent Carson."

He grabbed her arms, his gaze becoming fierce and locking onto hers. "Don't ever call me that again, do you understand, Sergeant? Are you trying to get us both killed?"

"Are you an FBI agent?" she whispered.

Carson released her. "I—I don't know what I am, except a lieutenant in Axel's army." Stepping away from her, he added, "Come on. Axel is expecting you."

He didn't speak to her again as he led her to Anderson's living quarters.

Outside the entrance, Brielle said just one word. "Fight."

It's what she intended to do with every breath she took.

Carson remained silent, but she knew she'd rattled him by the paleness of his countenance.

The doors opened with a hiss, and Anderson drew Brielle forward. "Good morning." He propelled her into the kitchen. "I'd like you to meet my wife, Lola."

A stunning brunette dressed in navy slacks and a white blouse smiled at her. "Good morning, Miss McAdams. Axel told me about you. It's an honor to meet the face of our glorious revolution. The face of our New America."

Anderson pulled out a chair for her. "Sit down."

Brielle complied and Lola set a huge chunk of bread and a bottle of water in front of her. She considered her meager breakfast. To remain physically fit and mentally alert she required protein, not useless carbs.

Her trial had begun.

Lola patted Brielle on the shoulder. "I'll leave you two alone. I've got business to oversee." She leaned down and shared a long, romantic kiss with her husband. "She's got defiance in her," she murmured in Axel's ear.

He chuckled. "She won't have it for long, Lola."

"Assign her to the laundry room when you're finished with her. She needs to be taught her proper place."

"Of course, my love. As you wish."

Brielle's face remained impassive, but inside she simmered with anger. Lola may be far more dangerous than her husband.

Ripping off a piece of bread, she began, "If I'm going to be the face of...our New America, I need to know your plans. For instance, what other weapons do you have aside from assault rifles?"

"Hand grenades. Rocket launchers. Dynamite and plastic explosives. We also have chemical and biological weapons."

The bread lodged in her throat. She took a long swallow of her water to hide her horror and fear. "Anthrax, I assume?"

"Tons of it, and I do mean that literally. Tear gas. We have chemicals to poison the water, the air, and our food supply.

And," Anderson paused as he caught her gaze, "we have vials of smallpox."

"So, you're wiping out the population." Brielle kept her voice even, though she quaked with terror.

"Culling the herd," he corrected her.

"What happens first?"

"I'll create mass hysteria and chaos. Everyone associated with the government will fall, Miss McAdams. Make no mistake about that."

"And after that?"

"The bombing of corporate America, beginning with Stone Enterprises and Collins Industries." He stared at her, waiting for her reaction.

Brielle swallowed the bile rising in her throat. "You know my brothers-in-law, Nick and Matt Stone, run them respectively."

"Exactly. They'll be sacrificed. So will all social media and news outlets. We'll bomb Wall Street. We'll hit the New York Stock Exchange and the major banks. People will panic trying to withdraw their money. Anarchy is our ally."

"And the military?"

"The Pentagon will be destroyed first. Then the military bases. Without any clear leadership, the military will be powerless."

Brielle shook her head. "You'll be leaving America vulnerable to attack by our enemies, crippling us with civil war. Trade will come to a standstill. Our economy will fail. Our infrastructure will be ruined. China holds most of our national debt. What if she decides to invade? We'll lose the support of our allies, and without a military to defend us, we can't possibly defeat such a massive army. This won't be the New America. It will be the New China."

# CHAPTER 21

Anderson's eyes darkened with anger, though he merely shrugged. "So be it."

*So be it? What kind of a crazy response is that?*

Brielle couldn't hide her disdain, even if it meant she would suffer for it. "You're delusional, Axel. Your master plan won't survive your first attempt to poison us."

"It would be a mistake to underestimate me, Miss McAdams." He jumped to his feet and yanked her out of her chair.

Anderson hustled her through a maze of corridors, his body taut with fury, until they reached an area marked *Research and Re-Education.* A pair of glass doors slid open, and he shoved her forward into a lab.

A towheaded man wearing a white lab coat and gold-rimmed glasses lifted his gaze from his computer screen when they interrupted him.

"Level five, Dr. Schow," Anderson ordered.

"But…" Dr. Schow began to protest.

"Do as I say!" Anderson snapped. "I'll be watching."

Dr. Schow led Brielle into a room that resembled an

IMAX theatre with screens three hundred and sixty degrees. He instructed her to step onto a round pad and hooked her up to electrodes that would send signals to a monitor gauging her heart rate and pulse.

After he placed a virtual reality helmet on her head, Dr. Schow said, "It's just like playing a video game. If at any time you want to stop, just shout 'End program!' Understand?"

She nodded.

"Good. I'll be monitoring your vitals the whole time."

The program began. Brielle entered a home and noticed a bomb counting down to zero on the floor in front of her. She didn't have time to react before it exploded and knocked her backward through the living room window. Pain wracked her body as she rolled over onto her back.

Breathing heavily, she gasped, "What the hell? I'm not supposed to *feel* anything!"

She struggled to her feet and felt blood running down her face and arms and legs. Just as the thought occurred to her that she needed to stop the bleeding, she noticed four men armed with semi-automatic assault rifles advancing on her. She dove for cover in the rubble of the house. A barrage of bullets barely missed her. Scrambling through the wreckage of cement and plaster and broken glass and splintered wood, Brielle made her way to the back of the house. Bullets pinged and ricocheted next to her. Without a weapon of her own, she needed to outsmart her attackers.

She noticed she was standing in the kitchen left relatively intact from the blast. A gas stove. Perfect. She switched on the gas and hunted for either matches or a lighter. Her pursuers drew closer as she yanked open drawers and cabinets.

"Come on! Come on! There's got to be matches around here somewhere!"

Bullets flew. Her eager hand finally clutched a box of

matches. Before the house blew up a second time, she checked her escape route, a gaping hole behind her. She waited until the gunmen were in range and then tossed a lit match onto the stove. A moment later the explosion shook the earth beneath her as she fled the fiery scene.

Brielle didn't have time to catch her breath before she found herself behind the wheel of a car as it plunged into icy black water. The interior filled rapidly. She pressed the window button, all four, to no avail. Water covered her head. She began to shiver from its freezing temperature. Bracing herself, she kicked at the windshield and the window on the driver's side, but neither cracked. Her lungs burned. She ached to take a breath.

If she died in this bizarre virtual reality world, would she die in real life, too?

She wasn't about to give up. Spotting the keys in the ignition, she yanked them out. Good. No electronic key fob. She held her panic at bay as she kicked out the backseat and managed to swim into the trunk. Inspecting the contents, she discovered a lug wrench and hit the safety latch. The trunk popped open. If that hadn't worked, she would have broken the taillights and tried to unlock the trunk from the outside.

Brielle broke the surface of the water and inhaled air into her lungs, choking and gasping.

The program continued with three more terrifying trials: finding her way out of a burning building blocked at every turn, fighting three assailants while blinded, and finally solving a puzzle which opened an escape hatch in a vault filling with dangerous fumes.

Exhausted, Brielle dropped to the floor. She pulled the leads off her chest and tossed away the virtual reality helmet. Just as her heart rate returned to normal, Anderson's voice ordered through a loudspeaker, "Get up. You're not done yet."

Dr. Schow approached her and reattached the leads, in addition to new ones he placed on her temples.

"What are they for?" she asked in a raspy voice.

He didn't answer her question. "For what it's worth you're the only one who has ever faced level five and…beaten each challenge." Admiration shone in his eyes. "Good luck, Miss McAdams."

*You're going to need it.* She read his mind.

The program began again in the same house with the same bomb, only this time it was strapped to…her mother who was tied to a chair.

"Brielle! Help me! Please don't let me die!" Brianna screamed.

Brielle rushed forward, crying, "Mom! Don't move!"

As soon as she started grabbing at the duct tape holding the bomb in place, strong electric currents coursed through her body, incapacitating her. Her body jerked and she yelled, "No!"

The bomb exploded just like before, and Brielle found herself lying on the street amongst shattered glass and other debris.

She knew what came next—a hail of bullets. When her hearing returned, she scrambled to her feet, preparing to sprint toward the back of the house, and…stopped dead in her tracks. The four gunmen approaching were her brothers! And this time an assault rifle suddenly appeared in her hands.

"Oh, God, no!" She threw the rifle down. "I'm not killing my brothers!"

An electric jolt shocked her. Her brother Bryant lifted his assault rifle and fired. The bullet struck her in the shoulder. Excruciating pain shot through her. Ben fired next and another bullet hit her thigh. She fell to the ground.

"No, dammit! No!" Brielle gritted her teeth as more electricity traveled along her central nervous system.

Still, she refused to pick up her weapon.

A higher voltage of electricity caused her entire body to spasm.

She bit her tongue and the coppery taste of blood filled her mouth.

Brendan fired a round of bullets; two pierced her left leg.

The electrical shocks continued, and her heart fluttered in her chest. Trey lifted his gun, took aim, and fired. The bullets tore into her abdomen.

Tears streamed down her face. Blood pooled beneath her body. And then she heard Trey's gentle voice in her head.

"Don't be afraid, Bri. This is just a computer program. None of it's real. You can kill us. You've *got* to kill us. You don't have a choice if you want to live."

"Not real," she muttered. "Not real."

Summoning her strength, she reached for her gun. Her brothers fired at once. She returned fire, putting a bullet dead center in their foreheads. Seeing those round holes blossoming with blood as her brothers dropped dead caused her stomach to roll, and she gagged.

"I can't do this!" Brielle sobbed. "Please don't make me do this!"

In the next scenario Cameron was trapped in the car with her, too, as it sank beneath the freezing dark water. As soon as Brielle tried to free him from the seat belt, she was electrocuted. Fighting through the pain, she yanked and pulled but could not release it. Quickly, she kicked out the backseat, found the lug wrench and again attacked the seat belt buckle while bolts of electricity caused unbelievable agony in her body. It was no use. She couldn't free her father.

Tears blurred her vision. Helplessly, she gazed into Cameron's beloved face filled with sorrow and love. He

pointed toward the surface of the murky water. She shook
her head and tried again to save him. Only when she realized
he'd drowned, did she pop the trunk and escape, nearly
drowning herself.

Wracked with pain and guilt, Brielle suffered even more
when she was forced to abandon her sister Brooke in the
burning building and then kill her three Stone brothers-in-
lawNick, and twins Michael and Matthew.

But the worst part of her ordeal wasn't over yet. When
she saw Justice trapped in the vault with her, she screamed,
"No! No! This isn't happening!"

They both started to choke on the white cloud of gas
pouring through a vent.

Justice grabbed her arm. "Solve the puzzle, Bri!"

It was far more difficult this time. Brielle couldn't think.
Her hands shook. When she begged Justice to help her,
another round of electrical currents stunned her. She felt her
heart stop a moment before it resumed beating.

"Bri…hurry!" Justice urged.

His voice sounded faint.

It took three more minutes of precious time to solve the
puzzle, but by that time Justice had passed out.

"Justice!"

In spite of the punishment she would incur for saving
Justice, she refused to leave him to die in that gas-saturated
vault.

"Wake up!" she screamed. "Wake up! We have to get out of
here!"

Justice roused and stumbled to his feet. Brielle wrapped
her arm around his waist and led him to the escape hatch.
They both made it out as incredible bursts of pain tore cries
from Brielle's raw throat. She'd succeeded! She'd succeeded
in saving the one person who mattered the most to her.

Just as he leaned down to embrace her, Justice disappeared. Darkness descended.

She fell to the floor. She seized. Froth formed at her mouth, and she vomited.

Dr. Schow joined her and turned her on her side so she wouldn't choke on her vomit before she lost consciousness.

* * *

Horrified by what he'd just witnessed, by the sight of Brielle seizing and vomiting, Carson rushed into the virtual reality room.

"Jesus, Axel!" he exclaimed. "What the hell did you do to her?"

"My wife was right. She needed to be put in her proper place," Anderson answered, his voice cold and hard.

Dr. Schow studied the heart monitor. "Her pulse is fast, and her heart is racing at one hundred and seventy beats per minute."

"She needs to go to the infirmary," Carson declared.

"No. Take her back to her cell," Anderson commanded.

A protective instinct buried deep in Carson's psyche rose within him. Tenderly, he lifted Brielle into his arms and carried her through the maze of corridors to her cell. He bathed her face with cool water, frowning when he noticed burn spots on her temples. They needed to be treated with salve.

*Barbarians!*

Rising from the bed, he went to fetch a bottle of water. When he returned a few minutes later, Brielle had regained consciousness. Lifting her head, he held the bottle to her dry, cracked lips.

"My...family...okay?" Brielle asked in a hoarse voice.

"Yeah, they're okay." Carson pressed the wet rag against her forehead.

"J-J-Justice?" she stammered. Fear and longing shone in the amber depths of her eyes.

"He's okay, too. They're looking for you. And causing Anderson a lot of grief in the process."

Her mouth parted in a tiny smile before she grabbed his hand and placed it on her chest.

"Heart…arrhythmia."

He felt her heart stop, then start, then stop, then start beating again in an irregular rhythm. She could easily have a heart attack or a stroke.

Scooping her into his arms, he muttered, "Screw Anderson!"

Carson sprinted all the way to the infirmary located near the communal showers, much to the amazement of those who witnessed his mad dash with a now unconscious Brielle in his arms.

He burst through a pair of glass doors as they slid open automatically and yelled, "Dr. Sherman!"

A middle-aged woman hurried toward him. "Lay her on the bed. What's wrong?" she demanded as she held a stethoscope to Brielle's chest.

"Heart arrhythmia. Level five…and six."

Dr. Sherman's head shot up. "Levels five and six?" She attached leads to a heart monitor and inserted an IV needle into Brielle's hand. "But no one has ever made it through five…alive."

"She did."

"Who is she?" Dr. Sherman wanted to know as she injected medication into the IV intended to stabilize Brielle's heart rate.

"Sergeant Brielle McAdams, LAPD and SWAT. Is she

going to be okay? I mean…I can't believe the amount of electricity she withstood. Will there be any side effects?"

Dr. Sherman gently rubbed a soothing aloe gel onto the burns on Brielle's temples. "Yes. Her central nervous system suffered major trauma. And her heart may weaken over time. The fact that she survived at all is a miracle. But she's young, healthy and obviously strong. That's good news, provided she's not subjected to further trauma."

The words barely left her mouth when Anderson strode into the cubicle. Without a word he threw a hard right and knocked Carson off his feet. He kicked him in the ribs a couple of times and hauled him up.

Squeezing Carson's throat, Anderson hissed, "I thought I told you to take Miss McAdams back to her cell."

Another primal instinct overwhelmed Carson. The instinct to fight back. He yanked Anderson's hands away from his throat. "I did!" he replied, gasping for breath. Pain shot through his mid-section. "You damn near killed McAdams. Her heart rhythm is unstable. Dead, she's worth nothing to you. Whatever she said to piss you off, get over it. And for God's sake, let her see her friend Faith Stoker. She'll be far more likely to cooperate if she's allowed to speak to Faith. You've worked miracles with her."

*Flatter him.*

The thought just popped into his head.

Anderson's eyes burned for a moment with an insane light. "Don't disobey me again, Nash. Or I may have to put you through the program a second time."

"Yes, sir." He hesitated. "One more thing. Will you consider moving McAdams to more comfortable quarters? She needs to be rewarded for her performance today in her trial."

"All right, all right," Anderson answered with an impatient wave of his hand. Addressing Dr. Sherman, he added, "Keep her alive. We need her."

"Of course. She's already improving with the medication I administered."

When Anderson left the infirmary, Carson relaxed and sank into a chair next to Brielle's bed. He lifted his shirt and saw his bruised ribs. Not broken, thank goodness. He felt strange. Like two halves of himself were melding together. Liberated, almost, though he consciously understood his imprisonment. What was happening to him? Something inside him screamed for its freedom and clawed at his gut.

He leaned back, stretched out his long legs, and closed his eyes. It was quiet in the infirmary except for the humming of the heart monitor and the soft sound of Brielle's breathing. Within a few minutes his mind took him to a safe place. To the memory of a sweet, hometown girl. Her golden hair shone in the sun and her dark blue eyes sparkled like sapphires. Her angelic face warmed his heart. She jumped into his arms, welcoming him home as he stepped off a cargo plane. He wore military fatigues.

In his sleep he frowned. Fatigues? He didn't remember. Was he in the military?

His heart started to pound. Another memory surfaced. His girl begging him not to go, not to leave her.

"No, please, Nash. No, don't do this. It's too dangerous."

"I've got to, baby. It's my duty. My responsibility."

She pulled a ring off her finger. "I'm sorry. I can't wait for you to put me first…"

Carson clenched his fist around an invisible ring as the memory faded into a thick mist. After that his mind went blank.

\* \* \*

Brielle awoke a few hours later after her heart had stabilized and a bag of fluids had emptied into her veins. She felt better physically but drained and lost. What Anderson planned to do to her next couldn't be any worse than the terrifying scenarios she'd just experienced. And what was the point? To teach her to be selfish? If Anderson hoped that pain would be a deterrent, he would be sorely disappointed. She would take the pain, even if it killed her.

*Justice, I promised you I would stay alive, and I'll do my best, but I may not survive. Please know that I'll fight. Until my last breath. I love you.*

"You're brave." Carson's quiet voice cut into her thoughts. "Probably the bravest woman I've ever met. No wonder Chief fell in love with you."

Brielle's eyes swung to meet his. "Thanks, Carson, for helping me today. I owe you my life."

He waved his hand. "Don't mention it. Dr. Sherman is keeping you overnight. I've gotten permission to take you to the living quarters for single women. You'll have a private bathroom with a shower. Clothes and personal items, too. You can't eat with the others yet, but I'll bring your meals to you."

She nodded. It was more than she expected.

# CHAPTER 22

The next morning both Carson and Dr. Sherman insisted that Brielle be allowed to eat a hearty breakfast before she released her. Anderson didn't like it, but he agreed. He also didn't like the fact that Dr. Sherman recommended a day of recuperation before Brielle resumed her program.

"Coddling this one is a mistake," Anderson grumbled.

"You're not coddling her," Carson soothed him. "You're turning her into your champion, your ally. You've seen her loyalty for yourself. You want her to be loyal to *you,* Axel."

"All right, Carson. You and Dr. Sherman win. Give her a day and then tomorrow her programming begins in earnest."

When they were alone, Carson bent over Brielle and murmured, "You heard every word, didn't you?"

"Yes." Brielle opened her eyes. "Again, thanks for looking out for me."

"Don't get used to it. The sooner Axel turns you into an ally the better for both of us."

"Ally?"

"We're called Axel's Allies."

"Original."

"You still have a smart mouth."

"Much to my dad's dismay."

"Word of advice? Don't mention your family in here. Forget about them. When the rebellion starts, Anderson will make sure they're eliminated right away. Especially *your* family."

Brielle rolled her head away from him. "Please leave me alone."

"Fine. I'll go get your breakfast."

Carson must not have been in the mood to talk to her, for he dropped off her breakfast and left the infirmary. Brielle didn't care. She needed time to think. To figure out her next move.

She ate slowly, mapping the layout of the compound in her mind, though her head ached. Escape lay near the surface where she'd seen the elevators. If she could convince Anderson that he'd successfully begun to brainwash her, she might have a chance to free herself. She needed more information about their location, but questioning Carson would prove tricky. It had to be done subtly to avoid arousing his suspicion. Although the better part of his nature was still intact and desired to help her, she couldn't count on it.

After she ate, Sherman suggested Brielle get out of bed so the doctor could check her heart rate. Brielle's legs felt like Jell-O, but she forced herself to take tentative steps until she grew stronger. She traversed the length of the corridor, and except for a tiny flutter in her heart, she didn't experience any other symptoms.

"You're doing really well," Dr. Sherman commented when they returned to the infirmary. "Just don't do anything else to warrant more punishment."

"I'm not afraid of pain."

Dr. Sherman studied her. "You should be, Miss McAdams.

You don't know what's in store for you if you fail to perform to Anderson's expectations."

"Have you treated Faith Stoker?" Brielle inquired, redirecting their conversation.

"No."

"Do you know where she is?"

"Living in the communal section with other unmarried women and working in the kitchen from what I've heard."

"Is she...you know...?"

"Stop asking me questions!" Dr. Sherman snapped. "Time for you to be taken to your new living quarters. You're fine."

Carson strolled into the infirmary with a half-smile on his face. "You pissed off Dr. Sherman. She can't wait to get rid of you."

"You seem in a better mood," Brielle remarked as she followed him through the sliding glass doors.

"You bug me like an annoying little sister."

"Do you have a sister?"

He stopped and scowled at her. "I don't know. Jesus, Brielle, leave it alone."

"Isn't there anyone you miss on the outside?" she pressed.

His scowl deepened. "No. No one. You need a muzzle."

"So I'm often told. Let's talk about something else." She pointed toward a corridor on their right. "What's down there?"

On their way to the special living quarters for single women who'd successfully completed the program, Carson explained how the organization operated. Along with weapons, they'd been stockpiling food and water and bringing in people with various skills and knowledge Anderson claimed they would need after the revolution. They had a greenhouse, too, in order to grow fruits and vegetables and herbs. Every person knew his or her role and place in the organization and accepted it without question.

No one possessed more than his neighbor. Wealth and material comforts were shared equally.

Socialism and brainwashing worked hand in glove, Brielle mused to herself.

She appreciated her new living quarters, thankful they were central to everything and close to the elevators. It contained a full-size bed, a recliner, and a floor lamp. A mini-fridge and microwave sat next to a counter with a sink and cabinets. She even had her own Keurig. An armoire held clothes in her size. A row of books lined a shelf. Beyond this area lay her private bathroom. She couldn't wait to take a long, hot shower.

"Take advantage of the reprieve you've been granted," Carson advised. "Rest. You'll need all of your strength for the next phase of your program." He paused. "By the way, you have the freedom to come and go as you please. The door opens automatically from the inside when you trigger a sensor. However, visitors have to be buzzed in. You can see them through this camera." Carson pointed at it. "Understand?"

"Yes."

"I'll bring you lunch and dinner."

"Thank you."

"Trust no one."

"Not even you, Carson?"

He blinked. "No."

Brielle luxuriated in the shower until the hot water ran out. Smelling vomit in her hair, she washed it again, and felt the tension in her muscles leave her body. After she dried herself, she found a cotton nightgown in the armoire and slipped it over her head. Her eyes swept the ceiling, noting the security camera, but it wasn't recording her movements. She wondered if Carson turned it off, or if the camera operated on a timer, too.

Curious about the content in the books, she removed one off the shelf entitled *A Legacy of Crime Against Humanity*. Brielle read a few pages and tossed it aside. Nothing but propaganda designed to paint America in the worst possible light. Yawning, she eyed the bed. The hot shower sapped her strength. She sank onto the mattress and fell into a deep sleep.

She slept all day, though disturbing dreams plagued her. When she felt someone shaking her, she finally roused and rubbed her eyes.

"I thought you said visitors had to be buzzed in," Brielle muttered in an irritable voice.

"You obviously woke up on the wrong side of the bed," Carson replied. "Sit up. It's time for dinner. You slept through lunch."

Dinner consisted of a roasted chicken breast, mashed potatoes and gravy, sweet buttered corn, a roll, and brownies for dessert.

"Anderson's allies certainly eat well," she remarked after taking a few bites of the chicken.

"Yeah. Healthy body, healthy...mind, and all that," Carson said, throwing himself into the recliner.

"Healthy mind? Right," Brielle drawled, sarcasm dripping from her voice.

"Just shut up and eat, McAdams."

Brielle finished her meal and gulped the rest of a bottle of water. Her mini-fridge was stocked with plenty of water and juice, too, if she wanted it.

Carson watched her. "What are you thinking?" she asked.

"That being around someone like you is dangerous."

"Why?"

"Because you make me question...myself." His gaze held hers. "You asked if I have a sister. I honestly don't remember. That's the truth."

"How long have you been an ally?"

Carson frowned and rubbed his forehead. "More than two years I think."

"How did you meet Anderson?"

"Don't remember." His leg twitched. "I have a favor to ask. When your family and Chief McQuaid rescue you, I want you to kill me, Sergeant. Please. I don't want to live like this."

"Carson, no. I can't do that."

"Please. I'm begging you," he pleaded. "Please. If you don't resist the program, you'll end up like me. Split. Broken."

She nodded. "All right. But you have to do something for me in return."

"What?"

"Get a message to Faith for me."

\* \* \*

She didn't see Carson again until the next morning. He handed her a breakfast tray and uttered, "Love."

Brielle's heart rejoiced. That was Faith's response to her code word: hope. They'd arranged the code words when they were in college to let the other know she was all right. If Faith's memories had been completely wiped out, she wouldn't have understood how to reply. She wanted to press Carson for details, but he'd already taken a huge risk for her. Not to mention her own trial commencing as soon as she finished eating. She had to focus on resisting the brain-washing techniques Schow would use on her today.

Carson spoke to her with quiet urgency as they headed toward the Research and Re-Education lab. "Fake it, McAdams. You can't handle any more shocks to your system. Don't let them put you in the sensory deprivation tank. It will drive you insane. Fake it. Please fake it."

"I will."

When they reached the lab, Anderson peered at them. The blank expression on Brielle's face mirrored Carson's.

"You put up quite a fight yesterday, Miss McAdams. I trust you've learned your lesson."

If she suddenly turned meek, she'd arouse his suspicion. "Is that all you've got?" she flung. The challenge hung in the air between them.

Anderson clenched his fist, and Carson straightened his body, staring at her as if she'd lost her damn mind.

"I've never hit a woman, but I'll gladly make an exception in your case," Anderson threatened.

"I wouldn't if I were you," Carson interjected, feigning a mild interest in the conversation. "McAdams knows a bunch of kung fu shit. She'll knock you on your ass before you're able to strike her."

An angry muscle leapt along Anderson's jawline. "Just get on with it!" he ordered Dr. Schow.

Brielle glanced back at Carson as she followed Dr. Schow into the virtual reality room, but he ignored her.

This time she was instructed to sit in an uncomfortable armchair as he hooked her up to more electrodes. A shiver ran down her spine.

Noting her reaction, Dr. Schow said, "Just watch the screen. That's all you have to do to avoid punishment."

She didn't respond. *Fake it. Fake it. Fake it.*

A kaleidoscope of images appeared on all the screens around her. Narration accompanied each set of images, designed to perpetuate the propaganda Anderson wanted everyone to accept as truth. Brielle listened and watched for a while and grew disgusted by the blatant distortions of reality. Aware of subliminal messages affecting her brain, she closed her eyes, but a tiny shock caused her to open them.

Time to use techniques Trey taught her.

Her eyes focused on a spot above the screen. Then she

allowed her mind to take her away from this time and place and back to her childhood spent in both Rutherford, Maine, and Boulder, Colorado. Blocking out the hate speech, she heard only the soulful sound of the Atlantic as it rushed to shore while she rode her pony on the beach. Shrieks of laughter filled her ears as she tussled with her brothers in the great room of their parents' Victorian overlooking the beach. She smiled as her prissy sister refused to get down and dirty and wrestle with the boys.

Flashforward to the Triple B. At fifteen she sat at the kitchen table, her hands propping up her head as she discussed boys with Brianna and watched her mother bake one of her famous peach cobblers.

"What was it like falling in love with Dad?" she wanted to know.

"Like freefalling over a cliff," Brianna responded with a smile.

"Was it really that easy?"

"No. You know your father was hiding from the Morales cartel."

"If he had told you the truth, what would you have done?"

"Stayed with him in spite of the danger."

"And Brendan Stewart might still be alive."

Brianna winced. "Yes."

"Brendan hates his name. He thinks you named him after the other Brendan out of guilt."

"No, Brielle, I didn't. I named him after Brendan out of love. I wanted to honor his memory."

"Because he was there for you when Dad couldn't be."

"That's true." Brianna placed the cobbler in the oven.

"Mom, can I please, *pretty please*, start reading your novels? I'm fifteen, and all my friends have read them already!"

Brianna offered an indulgent smile. "All right, sweetheart. Go get *Emerald Fury.*"

Brielle jumped up and hugged her mother. "Thanks! I'll let you know what I think!"

"I'm sure you will."

Hours dragged on. Brielle mentally recited her favorite scenes from her mother's novels. She wrote sequels in her mind. Swashbuckling heroes met and clashed with landed gentry. Sometimes they became bitter enemies, sometimes best friends. Their women always liked each other and often tried to broker peace. When one gentleman's wife got kidnapped, it was up to the swashbuckler to help him rescue her. The scenes played with vivid clarity in Brielle's mind until her first session came to an end.

Dr. Schow unhooked the leads and helped her rise to her feet. She'd grown stiff and sore from sitting in one position for so many hours.

"I must say, Miss McAdams, that went really well. Your brain was actively engaged the entire time."

"Huh?" she replied, a vague expression on her face.

He chuckled. "Axel will be pleased. *Very* pleased with today's results. Go to your room now, and I'll have Carson bring you something to eat."

"Room. Oh, okay."

Brielle pretended to stumble a little as she recalled the way to her quarters. She deliberately ignored the camera, not sure if it was on or not, and drank an entire bottle of water before collapsing onto her bed. She closed her eyes. The strain of maintaining her focus on her memories and writing scenes in her head took its toll on her. But it worked because she couldn't recall much of what she was exposed to today.

\* \* \*

*Fake it.*

As the days flowed together into weeks, Brielle became an expert at faking her re-education. She adopted the blank expression she often saw on Carson's face, and as she became integrated into the community, she mimicked the mannerisms and speech of the other single women. She noted the sexes weren't allowed to socialize if they were single. Carson explained that Anderson arranged marriages so couples could engage in carnal activity. None of the brainwashed allies could understand how Anderson had stripped them of their individual rights and freedoms and personalities.

By the end of the third week of her captivity, Anderson finally gave permission for her and Faith to be reunited. Brielle didn't know if Faith's mind survived the brainwashing or not after all this time. Even she found it difficult to keep up the façade, and with each day that passed she began to fear her family and Justice would never find her until it was too late. Too late to stop the apocalypse Anderson planned to unleash. And then it wouldn't matter anymore because everyone she loved would be dead.

They met in the cafeteria. Tentative at first, Brielle and Faith studied each other. Both had lost weight. Faith appeared not only gaunt, but haunted, too. Her eyes flitted back and forth, much to Brielle's dismay.

She took Faith's hand in hers and signed the code word *hope* against her cold palm. The friends had taken American sign language in college, inspired by Tex's wife Melody.

"My sister and Ally," Brielle invoked the required greeting while waiting with bated breath for Faith to respond by signing the correct code word into her palm.

"My sister and Ally," Faith replied automatically, even as her fingers signed *love*.

Faces appropriately blank, they sank into chairs next to each other.

"Life is better here," Faith began in a monotone.

"We have everything we need," Brielle agreed.

"No rat race, trying to get ahead."

"No. I work in the laundry room. You?"

"The kitchen. But sometimes I'm assigned to pick herbs in the greenhouse." Faith smothered a girlish giggle. "I miss sex."

"So do I. If you want it, Axel will arrange a good marriage for you."

"Maybe he'll have better luck than I did finding me a good husband." Faith paused. "I heard rumors about someone surviving levels five and six. Was it you?"

"I'm not sure." Brielle drew her brows together in a frown, as if she were trying hard to remember.

"It doesn't matter. A great change is coming, sister. A great change is coming."

"A great change is coming. We'll be the mothers of children born into a New America."

*I can't believe I'm spouting this crap.*

Brielle kept her face expressionless.

Beneath the table Faith grabbed Brielle's hand and signed *courage*. "I think you should ask Axel to let you marry Carson. He seems nice. He's going to do great things in our New America."

*Courage*, she signed in return. She considered adding *rescue* but didn't want to raise Faith's hope. Brielle shrugged and let go of Faith's hand. "Maybe."

At that moment the subject of their conversation joined them. "Time's up, sisters," Carson announced.

Faith feigned another girlish giggle. "'Carson and Brielle sitting in a tree, k-i-s-s-i-n-g,'" she trilled.

Carson's eyebrows shot up. "What the hell?"

Brielle offered a blank look. "Huh?"

Faith fluttered her hands. "Oh, don't be so silly!" She

hugged Brielle and whispered, "I'm okay. Love you."

"Love you, too," Brielle returned fiercely, though she carefully controlled her facial expression.

"What was that all about?" Carson wondered as he and Brielle ambled toward the communal center.

"How do you feel about an arranged marriage?" she deadpanned.

"Oh, fuck me!"

# CHAPTER 23

Justice stared at Linda in astonishment. "Did I hear you correctly? Officer Nash Carson is your *son*?"

"Yes."

"That's fucking unbelievable! He worked under your command for two *fucking* years! What kind of bullshit are you feeding me?"

"Sit down, Justice, and shut up. It's been almost four weeks. What do you think has happened to Brielle? Imagine what that sociopath has done to my son in *two and a half years*!"

He dropped into a chair. "Okay. I'm listening."

"I'll make this quick. My maiden name is Barrington. Special Agent Jackson Barrington is my cousin. Nash idolized him and followed in his footsteps. Went into the Marines. Served six years. Earned his degree in criminal psychology while in the military and joined the FBI after he was discharged. And then he was recruited to look into Axel Anderson's disappearance. Don't ask me how he found him. He was so deep undercover no one knew about it."

Linda started to pace and wring her hands. "I almost had

heart failure when my son, my eldest, showed up in my department as Officer Nash Carson and didn't recognize me. I tried to jog his memory, but he just gave me those blank looks you mentioned. He's gone, Justice. Whatever he was before he went undercover is gone. He's so far gone the FBI gave up on him. Anderson turned my boy against the country he swore to defend."

"So, that's what Anderson's been holding over your head."

"Yes. I didn't have a choice. I had to protect my son."

"Now you do. Where's the compound, Linda? I'm not leaving Brielle to suffer the same fate as your son. Tell me everything you know."

"Promise me you won't let anything happen to Nash. That you'll get him out of there alive."

"Linda, you have my solemn word I'll do my best to bring your son home alive."

She expelled her breath. "Here's what you need to know."

* * *

Two hours later Justice met with Commander Mattox, Tex, SWAT, his team of five, and SAC Wilder from the FBI's LA field office. Together they planned their rescue mission to be executed at 0200 hours with help from law enforcement agencies in Oregon. That gave Brielle's brothers time to fly to California to be there when he brought her home. Cameron and Brianna met their sons at LAX, who flew in together from Denver. Ben, Bryant, and Brendan were expert shots like Trey and Brielle and wanted to take part in the rescue mission, as Justice assumed they would.

Because Justice didn't trust Linda, he'd quietly brought her down to the LAPD with him. He didn't want her to inform Elliott Gage or send a message to Anderson to warn him that she'd given up the location of the compound. She hadn't complained. Justice knew she was more concerned about Nash than any consequences she might be facing.

At eight PM, the rescue team boarded two Blackhawks that would transport them to Oregon. Tex stayed behind at the LAPD headquarters doing what he did best—commanding the operation from the SWAT center.

By twelve AM, the team landed in Eugene, Oregon. Oregon state troopers, local police departments, and the FBI coordinated with them to plan the final details of their assault on the compound.

"Special Agent Nash Carson is not to be harmed," Justice reminded everyone involved in the mission as they rolled out in armored vehicles.

"Copy that, Chief McQuaid," came the response.

Justice's heart pounded in his chest. He had no idea in what kind of shape he would find Brielle, or if she was even still alive.

Cameron read the expression of grief and fear on Justice's face and sought to reassure him. "She's alive, son. I'd feel it in my gut if she weren't."

"I pray you're right, sir. I wasted so much time. Why the hell didn't I go straight to Linda in the first place?"

"You weren't thinking clearly. It happens when you're struck with fear for someone you love. Don't worry about that right now. Focus on what we have to do to get Brielle, and Faith, back."

Justice nodded. "Yes, sir."

An hour later when they were in position, Tex spoke into their earbuds. "It's a go." Typing a few commands into his computer, he shut down the compound's outside security system. "You've only got a few minutes before they figure out something is wrong," he warned the team.

Moving stealthily through the dense Deschutes National

Forest, Justice and the rest of his force approached a barn that housed the elevators leading underground.

In groups of four and five the force rode the elevators to the hub and rushed forward into the dim area when the doors slid open. Semi-automatic rifles flashed in an exchange of gunfire as Justice's men faced Anderson's allies guarding the entrance to the compound.

He yelled, "Take 'em down!"

\* \* \*

A shrill alarm awoke Brielle in the middle of the night, and she knew, without a doubt, that Justice had finally found her. She dressed hastily and cursed the fact that she didn't have a weapon as she left her quarters and sprinted down the corridor. Her first thought was to find Carson and Faith.

She rounded a corner and nearly collided with Carson. He tossed her a semi-automatic rifle.

"You're going to need to protect yourself," he told her in a grim tone of voice. "Anderson will come after you first. Come on. I'll make sure you get to the surface."

"Not without Faith!" Brielle exclaimed.

Carson cursed. "Damn, Sergeant! Your loyalty to the people you care about is bound to get you killed."

"Let's go, Carson!"

Dodging people in a panic running in every direction, Carson and Brielle hurried toward the communal women's quarters. Just as they reached the communal showers, Lola Anderson stepped into their path and raised her assault rifle. Brielle didn't hesitate. She fired. Several bullets hit Lola midchest. Blood stained her blouse. She fell to the ground, stark dead.

"Faith!" Brielle yelled. "Faith! Where are you?"

Carson grabbed her arm. "There she is!"

"Faith! Over here!" Brielle called. "I'm here!"

Faith heard her name and darted toward Brielle and Carson. The women embraced as Carson declared impatiently, "We've got to get out of here. Anderson is just crazy enough to kill us all."

No one knew what to do. Some screamed Anderson's name, crying and begging him to help them, to lead them as he'd promised. Others had the same idea as Carson, Brielle, and Faith and were fleeing toward the hub. Not knowing Anderson's whereabouts bothered Brielle. She held her assault rifle in front of her, ready to defend them, if necessary.

Chaos ensued when she heard the rapid exchange of gunfire as they approached the hub.

"Stay behind us, Faith," Brielle ordered.

They reached the open space of the hub. Members of the commune scrambled around dead bodies to get into the elevators, helped by law enforcement wearing Kevlar vests and other protective gear and weapons.

Brielle scanned the crowd, searching for Justice.

And then she heard his voice.

Shouting her name.

"Brielle! Look out!"

From the corner of her eye she saw Anderson lift his assault rifle and fire at her. Reacting instinctively, she avoided the shots and fired back. Bullets hit him center mass, and he dropped dead.

And then Carson grabbed her and held his gun to her head. "I'll kill her!" he screamed.

Justice took aim.

"Justice, no!" Brielle cried.

He fired.

Carson howled in pain as he dropped his weapon and fell to the floor. Blood gushed from a wound in his shoulder.

Faith knelt next to him, ripped off the sleeve of his shirt and used it to staunch the flow of the blood.

Justice and Brielle rushed toward each other. He held her head between his hands and kissed her hard, again and again. Their tears mingled as they ran unchecked down their cheeks. Justice leaned his forehead against hers.

Wiping away her tears, he murmured, "Are you...okay? Baby, please tell me, are you...*you?*"

She gripped his arms. "Yes! Yes, I'm okay!"

He pulled her closer to him. "Oh, God, I was so afraid! Afraid you wouldn't make it! Afraid you'd hate me for taking so long to find you."

"I never gave up hope. I knew you'd move heaven and earth to find me. I..."

"You promised!" Carson moaned. "You promised you'd kill me! Why didn't you kill me?"

"That's a good question. Why didn't you kill him, Justice?" Brielle asked.

Before he answered, he spoke into his mic. "We need medical down here by the elevators. Special Agent Nash Carson is down. Anderson is dead. I repeat, Anderson is dead."

"EMTs are on their way, Chief McQuaid."

"Special Agent? What the hell are you talking about?" Carson groaned as he struggled to rise.

Faith pushed him back down. "Stay still."

Justice led Brielle farther away. "He's a Barrington cousin, Bri. His mother is Linda."

Her eyes grew wide. "Oh, my God! How...?"

"There's a lot to explain, but he's an FBI agent, and a former Marine. He..."

At that moment they were interrupted by Brielle's parents and brothers. Only because Trey was FBI and Cameron a former member of the Department of Justice were any of them allowed to get near Brielle after the worst of the gunfight ended.

She found herself practically suffocated as they pulled her into a tight bear hug. The brothers shed tears, kissing Brielle on the cheek and checking to make sure she hadn't been hurt in the raid.

Her tears flowed anew when Cameron and Brianna wrapped their arms around her. "Mom! Dad!" she sobbed. "Oh, God, it...it was terrible! I...I had to watch you die!"

"It's over," Cameron comforted her. "It's over, sweetheart."

EMTs strapped Carson to a flat board and rolled him toward the elevators. Brielle grabbed his hand.

"Thank you, Carson, for everything you did for me. You're going to be okay. My brother Trey will help you."

Carson coughed. "My fucking chief shot me!"

"You asked for it," Brielle reminded him.

He glanced at Brielle's brothers who listened to their exchange with amusement on their identical faces. "You have an annoying little sister! Please keep her away from me. She never shuts up."

The McAdams brothers grinned at him. "Yeah, we know!" Trey answered for them.

Justice wrapped an arm around Brielle's shoulders and tucked her against him. "Let's go home, baby."

\* \* \*

Two weeks later Brielle sat in Justice's lap at her kitchen table as they read aloud part one of Faith's five-part series on Axel Anderson.

When the article ended, Brielle commented, "If Faith doesn't win a Pulitzer for this series, I'm going to be upset."

"Her writing is captivating," he murmured as he nuzzled her neck.

"Do you know what else is captivating?" she asked. Her breath caught in her throat.

"What?"

"This." She wiggled her bottom against his erection.

"Oh, *that*." He swept off her blouse and unhooked her bra. His mouth captured first one hard nipple, then the other, swirling his tongue around them. She held his head against her breasts and closed her eyes, reveling in the sensations he created in her.

His mouth claimed hers in a long, erotic kiss. Tongues met and clashed. Justice lifted her and carried her to the master suite. He laid her on the bed. His sensual lips followed his hands as they caressed her breasts and her torso, and still lower. When his skillful tongue found her center, Brielle sighed with pleasure and arched her back to give him more access to her core. As her body spasmed with her sexual release, she cried his name.

He loved the way his name sounded on her lips during her orgasm. His mouth moved up her body and settled on hers as he teased her with the tip of his manhood before thrusting fully into her. She moaned in the back of her throat. His body moved against hers in a timeless rhythm, and she met every thrust with one of her own until they climaxed together.

Long after Brielle fell asleep snuggled against him, Justice lay staring at the ceiling. Her homecoming had not been as sweet as he'd hoped. For days afterward he'd held her in his arms during crying jags, and at night he'd comforted her as she screamed in terror from nightmares.

She'd only recently been able to share with him what she'd endured in the virtual reality room. He'd had to rein in his own feeling of helplessness in order to support her, but now he allowed his anger to flow through him. He imagined torturing Anderson the way he'd tortured Brielle and Nash, who was now undergoing intense deprogramming under Trey's supervision.

Linda had flown to Virginia to be with her son. She'd been granted full immunity against prosecution as Justice had promised. Elliott Gage, though, awaited trial in a federal prison. Slapping a pair of handcuffs on the arrogant son-of-a-bitch filled Justice with immense satisfaction.

Brielle moaned in her sleep, deep in the throes of another bad dream. Justice molded her body closer to his and whispered, "Shh. You're safe now. I've got you, and I'm never letting go."

She slept late that Sunday morning. Justice prepared a sumptuous breakfast of French toast with warm strawberry compote, eggs, bacon, coffee, and orange juice and served it in bed. They savored the meal and kissed the sweetness of the strawberries from each other's lips.

Justice ordered Brielle to stay in bed while he took the tray to the kitchen. When he returned to the bedroom, he held a fluffy white kitten in his arms. It meowed. Loudly.

He grinned. "So, I, uh, did a thing. I thought it was time we adopted a kitten."

Brielle smiled in delight as he handed the ball of fur to her. It purred as she held it. It had the most amazing pair of blue eyes. "Oh, it's adorable! Is it male or female?"

"Female. And she needs a name."

"A name. What..." Brielle stared at an object dangling from the kitten's collar. "What? Is that...is that what I think it is?"

Justice chuckled. "A diamond engagement ring?" He slipped it off the collar. "You're right." Growing serious, he held her hand in his. "Brielle, I'm crazy about you. I was only half alive until I met you. You are my sun, my moon, my heaven. I'm a better man because of you. I want to raise this kitten with you and a whole houseful of kids. I want to grow old with you. I promise I'll cherish and protect you all the days of our lives. Miss McAdams, will you marry me?"

As soon as he'd started to propose, tears brimmed in her eyes and rolled down her cheeks. Pure joy exploded in her soul. "Yes! Yes! I'll marry you! I'm crazy about you, too, Beach Boy."

He laughed as he slid the ring onto her finger. It sparkled in the sunlight shining through the windows. Justice pulled Brielle into his arms and kissed her with sweet abandonment that led to a playful bout of lovemaking, unmindful of the kitten curled into a tight ball at the foot of the bed. When they noticed it much later, they laughed.

"Diamond," Brielle declared, her amber eyes sparkling with mirth. "Her name is Diamond."

"Perfect," Justice agreed. "I love it."

"I love you," she responded as she rolled on top of him. "More than words can say."

"I love you, too, baby," he murmured before he took her mouth with his.

* * *

A week later Justice and Brielle waited in an anteroom for Secretary of State Washburn to see them. Justice needed answers about Afghanistan before he could finally make peace with the loss of his team. Brielle held his hand in a tight grip as Brendan announced that Madam Secretary was ready to meet with them. They sat on a comfortable sofa facing her massive desk.

"Why didn't you tell me the truth?" Justice demanded, foregoing pleasantries.

"It was a mistake," she admitted.

"Damn straight it was."

"Look, Justice, I…we…needed you in Laguna Beach. We'd

already lost Special Agent Nash Carson, Ferguson, rather, and when he showed up in Laguna Beach out of the blue..."

"Wait. What?" he interrupted her. "You knew about Nash?"

"Of course. We sent him undercover."

"And turned him into a ghost. You're a real piece of work," Justice flung in a scathing tone of voice. "So, to cover up another mistake you sent me to Laguna Beach. A man barely recovered from a brain injury."

"Yes. We wanted, *hoped*, you'd be able to help Special Agent Ferguson and find out what he knew about Anderson's plans."

"Well, now you know. We stopped a madman from launching a domestic terrorist attack." He squeezed Brielle's hand.

"Do you intend to stay on as Chief of Police? If not, I could..."

"Hell, yes, I'm staying in Laguna Beach. Those are my men and women. I'm not abandoning them. There's only one thing I want from you, Madam Secretary. The truth about what happened in Afghanistan."

Secretary Washburn sighed. "We were betrayed. Deceived. By someone on the inside who's been court martialed and will spend the rest of his life in a federal prison. He provided the intel that caused you to lead your men into a trap."

"And my commander? Did he know the truth?"

"No. As soon as we told him, he retired his commission."

"What about my team's families?"

"They were sent letters explaining what happened. Their widows and children will receive death benefits for the rest of their lives."

"And what about me? You stole my career from me. How can you compensate me for that?"

Secretary Washburn shook her head. "I'm sorry, Justice. I can't."

He and Brielle rose to their feet.

"Thank you for your time, Madam Secretary. Honestly, I hope I never lay eyes on you again." Justice offered his hand.

She took his hand in hers. "When I'm in the Oval Office as the first woman president, I want you on my security team, Chief McQuaid."

He tilted his head. "We'll see."

At sunset two months later, Justice and Brielle exchanged marriage vows on Laguna Beach. She wore a simple, strapless, white wedding dress with a lacy bodice and flowing silk skirt. Her dark hair was arranged in a classic French twist with curly tendrils framing her face, and baby's breath adorned it. In her hands she carried a bouquet of fresh, multi-colored roses. They'd decided to keep the wedding party small and intimate with only Faith and Franklin serving as their maid of honor and best man.

When Justice caught his first glimpse of Brielle as she approached a flowered arch, his heart leapt into his throat. He thought she was the most beautiful bride he'd ever seen. His jaw dropped and Franklin clasped his shoulder.

"Close your mouth, son," he whispered, smiling.

After Cameron placed Brielle's hand in his, Justice murmured, "I'm in awe. You're so beautiful."

Brielle smiled, her eyes shining with love. "And you take my breath away in that tux."

They faced the minister and repeated the traditional vows they wanted to make to each other. After they were pronounced man and wife and Justice pulled his bride into his arms for a hot kiss, the festivities began.

Brianna and Adrienne had planned the reception, a luau on the beach. A wooden platform had been erected for dancing to music provided by a steel drum band. Tables laden with food, including a roasted pig, sat around the platform. Tiki torches created a soft ambiance.

After Justice and Brielle shared their first dance, he handed his bride over to her father and stood off to the side, watching them.

"I'm really happy for you, son," Franklin murmured next to him. "You've married an extraordinary woman. I know your mother would approve."

Justice's gaze left his wife and settled on his new stepmother. As soon as Brielle had recovered from her ordeal, they had traveled to Las Vegas with Franklin and Adrienne to witness their wedding.

"I'm happy for you, too. I'm so glad you're not alone anymore. I love Adrienne."

"Child approved," Franklin responded with a smile. "Not that I needed your approval, of course."

"Of course not," Justice mocked him. "We're lucky men, Dad. Now, go dance with your wife while I dance with mine again."

During a moment when Justice and Brielle sat at their table enjoying a little privacy, Cynthia brought Rosie to say hello to them. As soon as Justice smiled at her, Rosie burst into tears.

"Chief, I...I..." she sniffed, unable to speak.

"It's okay, Rosie," he said, patting her shoulder. "It's okay."

"I...I'm glad you and Brielle got married."

Brielle leaned forward and hugged her. "Thank you, Rosie. Hey, you know the Chief and I have a kitten. Come by and see her whenever you want."

"Sure. That'd be nice." Rosie offered a small smile before

she scampered off, followed by Cynthia, who offered her congratulations.

"It's a start," Brielle commented.

"Yeah, I know. I still want to adopt her." He lifted his wife's hand to his mouth. "Happy, my love?"

"Delirious. You?"

"Over the moon. I can't wait to get that dress off you later."

"Mmm." Brielle pressed her mouth against his. "Just wait, Chief McQuaid, until you see what's underneath it."

"I can only imagine, Sergeant McQuaid."

"I love the sound of my married name."

"I'm glad you decided to use it."

"I'm old-fashioned that way."

Justice grinned. "Shall we dance, Beach Girl? I'm old-fashioned that way."

"Shall I lead?" she teased.

"By all means."

Brielle's body melted against his, and she caught her mother's eye.

Brianna smiled. "And they lived happily ever after," she murmured.

# EPILOGUE

Four months later Dooley strolled into the meeting Justice called that morning. He listened as Chief McQuaid ran through the team's cases, old and new. All of them had been blown away by the discovery that Rosie's brother had been caught up in Anderson's plot to stage a terrorist attack, even more so that the drug-addled boy passed muster with the leader.

After thirty minutes, Justice stared straight at Dooley and declared, "We have a lead. We believe we've found your sister's murderer."

Dooley's heart slammed into his chest. Was Chief right? Had they found the man who killed his sister after all these years? "Where is he?"

"Right here in Laguna Beach."

## THE END

# NOTE FROM THE AUTHOR

I hope you enjoyed *Fighting for Brielle*, the first book in my new Laguna Beach Cops Series. I plan to write stories for Dooley, Tawny, Martini, River, and Hutch. Book Two will feature Dooley and his struggle to put his sister's murderer behind bars. It will be released sometime in 2021. My Waiting Game series continues with a new release in November, Waiting for Addie. I'd like to thank Susan Stoker for allowing me the opportunity to write in her world by including Wolf and Tex, and, of course, mentioning Patrick and Susan Stoker and giving them a niece in my novel. She has developed an amazing cast of characters! If you liked Justice and Brielle, don't worry. They will appear again as their love story continues.

# ACKNOWLEDGMENTS

First and foremost, I would like to thank my wonderful, loving husband Stan for allowing me to write to my heart's content without complaining. You are truly my best friend.

Nicholas, my talented and funny son, you have always been my pride and joy. Maybe one day we can write that children's book about the red panda and the hamster.

Mom, Bobby, Mary, Chris, Kelley, Joey, and Cristina, family means everything.

Betsy, Carla and Sherri, thanks for being the best friends I ever could have wished for. We are more than just friends; we are sisters in the truest sense of the word.

Wanda, my dear, dear friend and former colleague, you epitomize grace and charm. Thanks for being such an inspiration to me through the years!

I would like to thank MJ Nightingale who has been a dear friend and colleague for more than twenty years. You are the first person I ever allowed to read my manuscripts, and I appreciate your wisdom and experience.

Thanks, Debbie G., for your honest critique!

Drue Hoffman, thank you from the bottom of my heart!

Readers, you inspire authors to keep writing, so thank you!

# ABOUT THE AUTHOR

Dee Stewart has spent more than three decades teaching high school English. Although she enjoys being a teacher and shares her love of literature with her students, her passion is writing. She started writing at age thirteen after being inspired by Nancy Drew and Trixie Belden mysteries. In high school she was introduced to her first historical romance and fell in love with the genre. She wrote her first romance during her senior year of high school. Since then she has spent the majority of her adult life working on her craft with *Logan's Choice* being her first published novel. She is looking forward to hearing from her readers. Currently, she lives in Florida with her husband and her incredibly hairy cat, Leo.

Email me here: authordeestewart@gmail.com

Please like me or friend request me on Facebook to see exclusive teasers for upcoming books. Follow me on Instagram and Twitter. You can also find me on BookBub.

facebook.com/dee.stewart.75033

twitter.com/deestewartbooks

instagram.com/deestewartbooks

bookbub.com/profile/370812207

ALSO BY DEE STEWART

**Special Forces: Operation Alpha**

Conner

Fighting for Brielle

**Choice Series**

Logan's Choice Book One Choice Series

Christian's Choice Book Two Choice Series

Ben's Choice Book Three Choice Series

Stone's Choice Book Four Choice Series

Killer's Choice Book Five Choice Series

Link to series page

**The Waiting Game Series Books 1-2**

Waiting for Brianna

Waiting for Jaime

Link to series page

**November 2020**

Waiting for Addie

*There are many more books in this fan fiction world than listed here, for an up-to-date list go to www.AcesPress.com*

*You can also visit our Amazon page at:*
*http://www.amazon.com/author/operationalpha*

### *Special Forces: Operation Alpha World*
Christie Adams: Charity's Heart
Denise Agnew: Dangerous to Hold
Shauna Allen: Awakening Aubrey
Brynne Asher: Blackburn
Linzi Baxter: Unlocking Dreams
Jennifer Becker: Hiding Catherine
Alice Bello: Shadowing Milly
Heather Blair: Rescue Me
Anna Blakely: Rescuing Gracelynn
Julia Bright: Saving Lorelei
Victoria Bright: Surviving Savage
Cara Carnes: Protecting Mari
Kendra Mei Chailyn: Beast
Melissa Kay Clarke: Rescuing Annabeth
Samantha A. Cole: Handling Haven
Sue Coletta: Hacked
Melissa Combs: Gallant
Anne Conley: Redemption for Misty
KaLyn Cooper: Rescuing Melina
Liz Crowe: Marking Mariah
Sarah Curtis: Securing the Odds
Jordan Dane: Redemption for Avery
Tarina Deaton: Found in the Lost
Aspen Drake, Intense
KL Donn: Unraveling Love
Riley Edwards: Protecting Olivia

PJ Fiala: Defending Sophie
Nicole Flockton: Protecting Maria
Michele Gwynn: Rescuing Emma
Casey Hagen: Shielding Nebraska
Desiree Holt: Protecting Maddie
Kathy Ivan: Saving Sarah
Kris Jacen, Be With Me
Jesse Jacobson: Protecting Honor
Silver James: Rescue Moon
Becca Jameson: Saving Sofia
Kate Kinsley: Protecting Ava
Heather Long: Securing Arizona
Gennita Low: No Protection
Kirsten Lynn: Joining Forces for Jesse
Margaret Madigan: Bang for the Buck
Kimberly McGath: The Predecessor
Rachel McNeely: The SEAL's Surprise Baby
KD Michaels: Saving Laura
Lynn Michaels, Rescuing Kyle
Wren Michaels: The Fox & The Hound
Kat Mizera: Protecting Bobbi
Keira Montclair, Wolf and the Wild Scots
Mary B Moore: Force Protection
LeTeisha Newton: Protecting Butterfly
Angela Nicole: Protecting the Donna
MJ Nightingale: Protecting Beauty
Sarah O'Rourke: Saving Liberty
Victoria Paige: Reclaiming Izabel
Anne L. Parks: Mason
Debra Parmley: Protecting Pippa
Lainey Reese: Protecting New York
TL Reeve and Michele Ryan: Extracting Mateo
Elena M. Reyes: Keeping Ava
Angela Rush: Charlotte

Rose Smith: Saving Satin
Jenika Snow: Protecting Lily
Lynne St. James: SEAL's Spitfire
Dee Stewart: Conner
Harley Stone: Rescuing Mercy
Jen Talty: Burning Desire
Reina Torres, Rescuing Hi'ilani
Megan Vernon: Protecting Us

### *Police and Fire: Operation Alpha World*

Freya Barker: Burning for Autumn
Julia Bright, Justice for Amber
Anna Brooks, Guarding Georgia
KaLyn Cooper: Justice for Gwen
Aspen Drake: Sheltering Emma
Deanndra Hall: Shelter for Sharla
Barb Han: Kace
EM Hayes: Gambling for Ashleigh
CM Steele: Guarding Hope
Reina Torres: Justice for Sloane
Aubree Valentine, Justice for Danielle
Stacey Wilk: Stage Fright

### **Tarpley VFD Series**

Silver James, Fighting for Elena
Deanndra Hall, Fighting for Carly
Haven Rose, Fighting for Calliope
MJ Nightingale, Fighting for Jemma
TL Reeve, Fighting for Brittney
Nicole Flockton, Fighting for Nadia

*As you know, this book included at least one character from*
*Susan Stoker's books. To check out more, see below.*

## SEAL of Protection: Legacy Series
*Securing Caite*
*Securing Brenae (novella)*
*Securing Sidney*
*Securing Piper*
*Securing Zoey*
*Securing Avery*
*Securing Kalee (Sept 2020)*
*Securing Jane (novella) (Feb 2021)*

## SEAL Team Hawaii Series
*Finding Elodie (Apr 2021)*
*Finding Lexie (Aug 2021)*
*Finding Kenna (Oct 2021)*
*Finding Monica (TBA)*
*Finding Carly (TBA)*
*Finding Ashlyn (TBA)*

## Delta Team Two Series
*Shielding Gillian*
*Shielding Kinley (Aug 2020)*
*Shielding Aspen (Oct 2020)*
*Shielding Riley (Jan 2021)*
*Shielding Devyn (May 2021)*
*Shielding Ember (Sep 2021)*
*Shielding Sierra (TBA)*

## Delta Force Heroes Series
*Rescuing Rayne (FREE!)*
*Rescuing Aimee (novella)*

*Rescuing Emily*
*Rescuing Harley*
*Marrying Emily (novella)*
*Rescuing Kassie*
*Rescuing Bryn*
*Rescuing Casey*
*Rescuing Sadie (novella)*
*Rescuing Wendy*
*Rescuing Mary*
*Rescuing Macie (Novella)*

## Badge of Honor: Texas Heroes Series

*Justice for Mackenzie (FREE!)*
*Justice for Mickie*
*Justice for Corrie*
*Justice for Laine (novella)*
*Shelter for Elizabeth*
*Justice for Boone*
*Shelter for Adeline*
*Shelter for Sophie*
*Justice for Erin*
*Justice for Milena*
*Shelter for Blythe*
*Justice for Hope*
*Shelter for Quinn*
*Shelter for Koren*
*Shelter for Penelope*

## SEAL of Protection Series

*Protecting Caroline (FREE!)*
*Protecting Alabama*
*Protecting Fiona*
*Marrying Caroline (novella)*
*Protecting Summer*

*Protecting Cheyenne*
*Protecting Jessyka*
*Protecting Julie (novella)*
*Protecting Melody*
*Protecting the Future*
*Protecting Kiera (novella)*
*Protecting Alabama's Kids (novella)*
*Protecting Dakota*

*New York Times, USA Today* and *Wall Street Journal* Bestselling Author Susan Stoker has a heart as big as the state of Tennessee where she lives, but this all American girl has also spent the last fourteen years living in Missouri, California, Colorado, Indiana, and Texas. She's married to a retired Army man who now gets to follow *her* around the country.

www.stokeraces.com
www.AcesPress.com
susan@stokeraces.com

Made in United States
Orlando, FL
10 July 2025

62841512R00175